TIDAL FALLS

#1 Wounded Hearts

JACQUIE BIGGAR

ISBN: 978-0-9938814-2-8

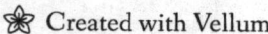 Created with Vellum

I have so many people I'd like to thank in the making of this, my first novel. First, and foremost my husband, Robert John. Without you I wouldn't have had the courage to pursue my dreams.
Thank you, baby.
My mom, who always told me I could be whatever I wanted to be, I just had to try. You were right, as always.
To my critique buddies, you know who you are. Without you pushing me to better myself, this book might not have ever happened.
And to Kim Killion and Jennifer Jakes, for the beautiful cover I'm so proud of, and the services you provided to save this newbie from pulling her hair out. Thank you.

Love isn't something you find. Love is something that finds you.

Loretta Young

WHAT READERS ARE SAYING

The highlight of the book is without a doubt the characterization. The characters shine and make the book worthwhile.
InD'Tale Magazine-Feb/15

Jacquie Biggar has a wonderful gift for writing hot and extremely likable military men! I couldn't decide who was my favorite: Nick, Frank, Jared or Adam. Luckily this novel is the start of a series so the good news is that I'll be seeing a lot of these men again in future books by Ms. Biggar. Hooyah!
J. Reed

WHAT READERS ARE SAYING

INTRODUCTION

"How did you find me?" Sara fell back as Tom pushed his way inside, followed closely by Sam, and then she caught sight of Fiona being led in by two other men. Her friend was cuffed, her arms pulled taut behind her back. Her mouth, covered by a bright red handkerchief tied so tight it cut into her whitened cheeks, highlighted an obscene bruise. Her eyes, one of them black and blue, filled with tears, begging Sara to forgive her.

"GPS, my dear, you've heard of that I presume? I traced you from your own phone. That wasn't very smart of you. So, this is where you've been hiding."

He waved the others into the room, locking the door behind them. "What, no kiss for your Husband? You do recall you have one of those, don't you?"

He looked the same, so tall and handsome standing there in his perfectly pressed suit and tie, not a hair out of place. A wolf in sheep's clothing.

PROLOGUE

Sara Sheridan tapped her toes with nervous anticipation, and when her husband turned away to network with the senator and his wife, she made her move. Excusing herself from her half-hearted discussion on the state of the economy with old Judge Perkins, she edged out of the dining room and hurried down the dimly lit hallway, ignoring the condescending stares from Tom's ancestors lining the walls in their expensive frames.

Knees quaking now she'd in fact committed to her plan, Sara slid the key *borrowed* from his nightstand into the lock, entered his office and pulled the heavy oak door closed. She Flipped on the lights and froze as his mahogany desk loomed out of the darkness. The pungent scent of his tobacco violated her nostrils, but she forced her stiff limbs to move across the room. She wanted nothing more than to run, fast and far. But couldn't, not yet. Rolling his heavy leather chair out of the way, she slid her fingers across the keypad to wake his computer.

Password protected, she'd expected that. Pulling a list from her pocket, she started at the top, working her way down.

Nothing. Please, please, plea...

The screen changed, signaling success.

Yes.

Her eyes slid shut in a brief moment of gratitude. Then, knowing she had to hurry, Sara grasped the thumb drive Fiona had smuggled to her and plugged it in. A quick search brought no results.

Now what?

Frustrated, she entered random words from the password list.

Nothing. Nothing. Nothing.

Crap.

Covert stuff wasn't her forte. Her hand sweaty on the mouse, and her ragged breathing loud in the otherwise silent room, she keyed in one last word.

Phoenix.

The screen switched and a list of names, dates and times appeared. She'd done it. Excitement skittered up her spine. The download took the longest minute of her life. When it was done she shut everything down, replaced his chair and turned to leave.

A muffled thud out in the hall just about stopped her heart. She wasted precious seconds staring at the closed door wishing herself invisible, before frantically searching for a place to hide. There were heavy velvet drapes covering the windows, they'd have to do.

Praying her dust allergies wouldn't give her away, she hid

between the folds, clenching the edges of the fabric in her hands and kicking herself seven ways to Sunday for leaving the key in the outer lock.

Sara held her breath when the door opened, praying it wasn't Tom.

It wasn't.

Belinda, Jessica's nanny, entered and sauntered across to the leather sofa along the opposite wall.

What was she doing?

After an extensive search among the pillows the nanny smiled in triumph, pulling a pink bit of nothing from between the plump cushions. She was just pushing the material into the cleavage of her skin-tight dress when Sara's worst nightmare came true.

Tom snarled from the open doorway. "What are you doing in here? I told you to go upstairs and find my wife. Our guests are preparing to leave."

He strode across the room and snatched Belinda up by the arm, jerking her against his chest. "What are you hiding?" Pushing her hand away he shoved his fingers down the front of her dress and withdrew the scrap of cloth still peeking from between her breasts.

"Tom, please. I only wanted to find those before the staff or your wife found them. Let me go. You need to get back to the party. Everyone will be looking for you." Though her voice betrayed her nervousness, she still flirted with him through her lashes.

He crushed the silk, giving a sneering laugh as he bunched his hand into her blonde hair. "Do you really think I give a shit

3

if anyone finds some thong? I've told you before not to come in here without me. I won't tell you again." His voice was a dark omen in the twilit room.

He dropped his head to hers in a punishing kiss that swiftly changed to passion when Belinda's arms and legs wrapped around him as though she were riding a stripper pole.

After long minutes that seemed to last forever to Sara, she broke away with a sultry laugh and backed through the open door, her finger crooking a follow-me message.

Tom hesitated, his gaze scouring the room before he slowly followed, closing the door behind him.

Sara remained hidden; her heart pounding. Even though her husband's actions had long ago managed to erase any of the tender feelings they'd ever shared, it hadn't made this scene any less repugnant.

Finally deeming it safe she inched her way back to the door, pressing her ear against the smooth wood.

Silence.

She turned the brass knob, grateful it slid open and hurried to her room, her mind already filled with the next step of her crazy plan.

Escape.

CHAPTER ONE

Tom Sheridan rubbed his aching temple, lifted the cup to his lips and grimaced at the disgusting taste of cold coffee. He glanced at the Cartier on his wrist and frowned. Eleven. He'd been working his way through the backlog of cases on his desk for hours.

His hand jerked at a sharp rap on the door, causing coffee to spill on the papers. He sighed, and barked an order to enter, swiping ineffectively at the stain.

Sam Willets, his head of security, stepped into the room.

"Well, do you have some news?"

"No, sir. We almost had 'em in Chicago, but they slipped away. Since then she's gotten smarter, must be using cash. No worries though, she'll turn up."

"Close the fucking door."

Tom surged to his feet, his heavy chair toppling backward with a crash in the quiet room. "That bitch is going to cost me everything."

Sam's eyes flickered. He shifted back a step. "We'll get her. It's only been a couple of months, Boss. How do you want me to handle it when we do?"

"You just worry about finding them. I'll *take care* my wife."

He stalked past the idiot and moved to his liquor cabinet, pouring a healthy glass of Glenlivet scotch. It slid down the back of his throat in a single hot shot. He hissed and sucked in a searing breath before pouring himself another.

"Go now, and make sure you keep me updated. Take a couple more men with you. The more eyes looking, the better."

Nodding, Sam left the room while Tom cradled his drink and brooded over the large painting filling the wall behind his desk. His wife's work. It depicted an old grey rustic cabin set against a backdrop of Glacier Mountains. A brook flowed through waving green grass. The colors were so vibrant he felt as if he were looking through a window at the water bubbling past. Could almost smell the wildflowers climbing the cabin walls.

How dare she think she could walk away from him?

Nobody walked away from him.

Ever.

HER COVERS A TWISTED MESS, Sara awoke and gazed through the partially open window of her small bedroom. The dreams always left her unsettled—a kaleidoscope of love, laughter, screaming, blood and death.

The sun cresting from the bosom of the Cascade Mountains

caught her attention. She couldn't believe almost a year had already passed since their arrival in Tidal Falls.

The pinks and oranges lighting the distant sky highlighted the yard's lone fifteen-foot cherry tree. Filled with shiny red new leaves and delicate pink blossoms, it soothed her tired mind. Fresh cut lawns blended with the tang of lemony-scented roses, and the heady sweetness of night stock and lavender. An already warm breeze blowing through the screen stroked her cool skin and made the white eyelet curtains flutter.

Her eyes slid closed and she was just relaxing back to sleep when a sudden hammering at her front door startled her out of bed.

Her pulse pounding, she hurried to throw on her chenille bathrobe, and make her way through the still dim house. Grateful for the steel door, she peered through the little viewer. Tess Garrett, their next-door neighbor, landlady, and good friend, stood on the other side.

"Tess, is there something wrong?" she called, releasing the deadbolt lock.

Concern for her friend had her hurrying to open the door, and that's when she noticed the stranger crouched behind Tess rubbing the broad back of a Shepherd. The man came to his feet, and she saw he towered several inches over her own head. She took a quick step back, a hand going to her uncombed hair and the other into the lapels of her robe, drawing them together.

"Sorry to worry you, Sara dear. This is Nick, one of my tenants. He seems to believe his dog might have been in your new flower garden. I've already told him I didn't think so, but he insisted on talking to you himself." Tess's acerbic tone relayed what she thought of him not taking her word on the subject.

"I'm sorry to bother you, ma'am. Jake here came home pretty mucked up this morning. I followed the tracks and they led me here." His voice rumbled through her chest, causing goose bumps Sara put down to being chilled.

"Mommy, who's here?" Jess stumbled out of her room, rubbing sleep from her eyes.

"Everything's fine, honey," she soothed. The hound, hearing Jessica's voice, whined.

Turning her attention back to the door, she tried not to stare, but holy cow, the man could have graced a magazine cover. The eyes looking down at her were the deepest cobalt blue she'd ever seen; with long dark lashes any woman would envy. His face was all angles and planes of perfection, except for an angry looking scar she could see peeking out from under the coffee brown hair at his temple.

She started, realizing he was waiting for an answer. "No, I don't think that could be possible. Our yard is fenced."

"You might want to take a look around. I can't have him roaming the neighborhood destroying people's property," he said. His penetrating gaze made her nervous, causing her to shift her bare feet, which he immediately picked up on, one eyebrow lifting in humor.

A long dark nose poked through the gap.

"Oh Mom, look at him." Jessica moved to pet the animal before Sara could reach out to stop her.

"Jessica Anne Marie! That dog could be dangerous, get back."

"He's not mean Mom, look," she giggled. "Please, can I pet him?"

"Jake loves attention." That raspy voice again.

The big brute wedged his face further into the opening, trying his level best to lick Jessica's shining face as she gazed up at her Mom, and like an under-done cake, Sara caved. Catching Tess's smiling nod, she opened the door a little wider. Grimacing a little at the wet dog smell, she let the animal into the house.

"I wanted to apologize for any destruction Jake's done, and offer to pay for damages." He held his hand out. "Nick Kelley. I've just moved in across the road."

Self-conscious, she lowered the hand trying to tame her bedhead hair, but ignored his outstretched one in favor of tightening the belt on her robe.

"Look at young Jessica." Startled out of her preoccupation with the disconcerting man, Sara turned at Tess's words to see her daughter's arms wound tight around the dog, face buried in his damp fur. "You need one, Sara. It'd be good for both of you."

As she lconsidered Jess's pleading eyes, she knew her friend was probably right. "Thank you for your concern, Mr. Kelley, but I'm sure our garden is just fine. And if it isn't, we'll fix it. No worries."

"Well, if you change your mind, I'm more than happy to pay for the repairs. Jake sometimes thinks he's still out in the field. We're working on that though, aren't we, buddy?" At the loving inflection in his master's tone, Jake's ears perked up and he peeled himself away from Jessica, returning to Nick's side for a pat.

"He's beautiful, mister."

Sara sighed at the envy in her daughter's tone, picturing previous conversations they'd had in the past. Jess had a way with animals, they seemed to sense how much she loved them. Too bad her father had never allowed her one of her own.

"Yes, he is. He's also very smart." Nick fondled Jake between the ears as he smiled at Jessica. "He likes little girls, too. Maybe one day if your momma says it's okay, he can play with you for a while in your yard." He turned his gaze on her and the glint in his eye had nothing to do with kids and dogs, and everything to do with getting to know her better.

"We'll see. For now, you better go get some clothes on kiddo, it's almost time for school."

"Oo...kay, bye, Jake. Bye, mister. Bye..."

"Now, young lady." Leaning over, she gave her a light swat on the butt at the same time kissing her daughter's downy cheek. "Scoot."

Jessica shrieked and the dog woofed as he stood up, ears perked forward.

Nick held his hand up in a stop motion, at the same time issuing the command, "Stay." Jake sat on his haunches, looking to Nick for his next command. "Sorry, he's trained to protect. It's instinct."

"No problem, he listens well."

"Yeah, well, we've been together for a while now. We trust each other." Nick dropped his hand and rubbed Jake's side. "I'd better get going, he needs a run. It was nice to meet you—Sara."

Heat rushed up her neck at the way he said her name. "Mr. Kelley. Welcome to the neighborhood."

Tess gave her a big wink behind the man's broad back as they turned to walk away.

"See you later, Tess." Sara scrunched her nose at her, and pushed the door closed, cringing at the Medusa image staring back at her from the hallway mirror.

Re-engaging the deadbolt, she headed for a much-needed cup of morning coffee, stopping along the way to straighten the mussed-up hall runner. If it took an overgrown moose of a dog to bring some cheer back into her daughter's world, it was well worth a little bit of chaos.

The aromatic smell of strong coffee from the preset machine greeted her as she turned into her cute little kitchen. Sara reached for her favorite mug and poured herself a large cup, leaning against the countertop to survey the changes she and Jess had made to the room.

With Tess's blessings, they'd gotten rid of the outdated wallpaper and window hangings. Now the walls were a soft butter yellow. White gingham curtains with colorful butterflies flirting along the edges dressed up the herb-lined windows. In the breakfast nook sat a white wooden table and chair set found at one of the many yard sales they'd attended since arriving in town. An assortment of spring flowers, poppies, daisies, and daffodils, all picked from their own yard finished the look.

In the time they'd been here, they'd made a home for themselves. Jessica was coming out of her shell and becoming the exuberant little seven-year-old, she should be. As far as Sara was concerned that made the strain of the past few months fade away. She wasn't sure what she'd do if Tom's goons managed to track them down, but shelved that worry for the moment. Right

11

now, she knew of a little girl that needed the tickle monster to pay her a visit.

———

CUTTING ACROSS THE QUIET, tree-lined street to his little bungalow after a strenuous five-mile run, Nick noticed Sara's neighbor, their landlady Mrs. Garrett, picking her newspaper out from the bush the paperboy had managed to hit. She gave him a little wave and turned when another neighbor, an old man, leaned over his fence to offer her a bouquet of fresh flowers.

Where was he, Mayberry?

He'd grown up in Bay Village—a rough neighborhood in Boston. You kept your eyes to yourself there or faced the consequences—about as different from this place as you could get.

Entering his kitchen through the back door, he breathed in a sigh of relief at the coolness against his overheated skin. He did a few deep bends and stretches to work out the kinks. Then, after first making sure Jake had water in his bowl, he moved down the hall, pulling off his shirt with a wince and letting it drop along the way. A shower would feel great right about now.

Back in the day, he could have managed a run like that without even breaking a sweat. Now, not so much. After the accident his therapist had warned him he needed to learn some patience. These things take time, yada, yada. At least he'd managed to get himself off the pharmaceutical train. That was something. For the first while, after he'd returned stateside, they'd kept him so full of dope, he wasn't sure which way was up. He knew it was for his own good, the scars across his back proved that, but he'd hated losing those days. Again. Everything from just before it happened, to his weeks of recovery—all of it a blur.

Fingering the jagged scar at his left temple he decided maybe that was a good thing. Turning away from the dissatisfied guy staring at him in the mirror, Nick dropped his sweats and climbed into the tub. Turning the water as hot as he could stand it, he let it pour down his head and back, groaning as it relieved stressed muscles.

Soaping up, he ran his hands through his hair, then over his chest and stomach. Thinking about his prickly new neighbor, Sara, he smiled. She'd been surprised to see him standing there with Mrs. Garrett this morning. He grinned, remembering her obvious discomfort. Her hair all mussed up, dressed in an old pink robe, her cheeks a matching color. He'd been trying to figure out a way to meet her ever since he'd moved in.

Good dog.

She reminded him of a spitting kitten with those flashing gold eyes and mussed-up sandy colored hair. That robe of hers had done nothing to hide her generous curves. The belt cinched tight under her breasts had highlighted their fullness, along with rounded hips and long slim legs he'd caught glimpses of as she fidgeted. Her voice, husky from sleep, had been a siren's call, making him think of her soft and tumbled in a bed.

His soaped hands slid lower, cradling the hardened length of him. It been too long since he'd been with a female. That's all this was, his body's natural needs. He didn't do family. Not anymore. A rough sound escaped as his body re-heated. He threw his head back under the streaming water, and his hand began to move faster and faster, searching for release. His mind's eye brought her into the shower with him.

Wet.

Soapy.

Sexy.

And that's all it took. His shoulders shook with the force of his release, his free hand grabbing onto the wet wall just as his knees loosened.

She was going to be trouble.

CHAPTER TWO

Nick crouched painting the bottom slats along Mrs. Garrett's split board fence, grateful for the slight breeze. Jake whined and he lifted his head over the top rail to see what the problem was. Jessica was tying the ribbons of a floppy pink hat she'd placed on the dog's furry head. Nick smiled as Jake sighed in resignation, dropping his head on his paws while she fiddled a little more, and then sat back to admire her handiwork.

Her voice floated over the fence. "Hold still, Jake, I've almost got it. You're going to be the prettiest dog in the whole wide world."

When he'd arrived this morning, she'd been sitting outside looking bored, playing with a doll. Thinking maybe Jake could keep her company while he painted, he'd asked her to run and see if it would be all right with her mom, and she'd agreed. Nick had seen her and her daughter around town a few times in the past couple of weeks. The little girl always gave him a shy little wave, while Sara shared a cautious smile, as if not sure whether seeing him was a good thing or not. He could relate.

His sneaky landlady had somehow managed to ferret out the fact that he was taking therapy twice a week with a clinic downtown, and asked him if he would mind doing a bit of handyman stuff on her rentals while he was recuperating, offering him a discount on his house and silence about his career. He didn't care about the first, the second however, was another story.

Smart woman.

He was pretty sure she was trying to set him up with his sexy neighbor. He could have told her not to bother, neither party was interested, but something stopped him.

His progress slowed when he heard the child confiding to the dog.

"I wish Mommy would cheer up, Jake. She thinks I miss home, but I don't. Daddy was always mad at us."

She dropped her head, and swiped at her eyes and nose, her focus on the grass between her sneakers. "Him and mommy got into fights, *all the time.*" Sadness radiated from her small frame.

Nick frowned.

She rubbed long strokes down the dog's broad back. "I'm glad we left. I like it here, this place is pretty cool. Grace is my mommy's friend. She has the diner downtown. And there's Ms. Campbell at the craft store, and her kid Chris. He's ok—for a boy. And you know Mrs. Garrett, she lives next door. She makes the best cookies." Jake's tail swished in the tall grass. "Hey, wanna go and see her? We can show her your new hat." His pink tongue snaked out and licked her cheek as she leaned over to give him a hug. "I love you too, boy."

Nick let his brush drop into the tray. He stood and rested his arms on top the fence, stretching tight muscles. Startled, Jake took notice, and barked as if a hundred cats were racing past.

"Settle down, it's just me, goofball."

Jake jumped up, racing over to rest his paws on the fence, his tongue lolling out. "Watch the wet paint, you're going to make a mess."

"He's been real good," Jessica said in a timid voice, keeping a worried eye on the dog.

"Yeah, he's a pretty smart boy. Sometimes he just forgets to pay attention, that's all. You'll have to help me teach him to be careful not to go out on the road, or he might get hurt."

She inched a couple of steps away, patting her leg to get Jake's attention, "Yes sir, I will. Is it okay if we go to Aunty Tess's for cookies?"

"I don't see why not. You'd better..." Too late, they were already off and running. Jake loping down the sidewalk alongside the little girl, pink hat bouncing off the side of his head.

Nick stared after them, rubbing an unexpected tug in his chest. The conversation he'd overheard between child and dog had disturbed him. He knew all about the pain and bewilderment of a parent's betrayal—had lived through it himself—and hated the thought of such a sweet little girl going through that kind of a hell.

Guess he'd better have another chat with Sara. He didn't want her concerned where her child had disappeared to. Jessica was chattering like a magpie through the open kitchen window

17

next-door. The spicy scent of cinnamon and ginger tickled his taste buds to life, making him wish he'd followed them over.

The front steps groaned under his weight. He'd just lifted his hand to knock on the door when it flew open. Seeing his raised hand, Sara let out a strangled little cry and flung herself backwards, smacking her head against the heavy steel with an audible whump.

Disconcerted, he lowered his arm and stepped forward to help. When she cowered, he backed away to give her some space. "Hey, take it easy. I wasn't trying to scare you. I just thought I'd stop by and let you know Jessica is next door and properly introduce myself, since we got off on the wrong foot the other day."

Yeah, like today is going so much better, you dummy.

Sara's posture slumped in relief as they heard her daughter's laughter floating along the breeze-ruffled leaves. "Oh...okay then. Normally she's so responsible about asking if she can go out of the yard, I worried when I couldn't see her anymore."

Attempting a smile, which came out looking more like an over-stretched elastic band, she thrust out her hand. "I'm Sara, Sara Reed. I think I forgot to introduce myself the other day. I guess I've overreacted, huh? It's a mother thing."

Nick took her dainty hand into his calloused one. Awareness shot heat through his veins. She had what his mother used to call piano hands, with long delicate fingers and fine bones. He didn't want to let it go.

"I thought I should stop by and let you know she'd gone over there. She did ask. I didn't see any harm," he said, disappointed when she pulled her hand away.

"No, that's fine. She goes over to Tess's all the time. She just should have cleared it with me first. Could I offer you a cup of coffee, Mr. Kelley? I've just made a fresh pot."

He hesitated, not wanting to get involved, but something about her tugged at him. Shadows lurked at the back of her eyes, hinting of secrets he itched to uncover. "I'd love some, thank you. And it's, Nick." Now if he could just get his mind off watching those cute hips and amazing ass, he'd be fine.

"Well, Nick, have a seat." She gestured towards a set of white wicker furniture tucked into a corner of the deck before going inside for the refreshments.

Okay, keep it simple stupid. She needs a friend.

"Have you and your daughter lived in Tidal Falls very long?" he asked, when she came back through the doorway carrying steaming mugs of black coffee. He noted the slight hesitation in her step, and how her lips tightened before she smoothed them out and continued towards him. She set a large, chipped cup in front of him before taking a chair on the opposite side of the little table. By the rich, bold fragrance, he knew it'd be strong enough to stand a spoon up. Just the way he liked it.

"No, not too long. And yourself, Mr. Kelley? You don't seem the type to spend your days lolling around. What is it you do for a living, besides frightening the neighbors that is?" A teasing smile lit up her face, causing a cute dimple to appear in her cheek. He liked that dimple.

He didn't want to talk about his own story. "I'm just taking a little breather. Picked a spot on the map, and here I am. It's a big change from city life." The little town appealed to him, he liked the slow easy pace compared to the craziness of Boston.

"What city are you from? Jess and I took a trip to Seattle a couple of weeks ago. We went to the Woodland Parks Zoo for Mother's Day."

"Every kid loves the zoo," he replied, a little gruffness in his tone. He pictured mother and daughter wandering around the exhibits. Nick would've loved the opportunity to do something like that with his own child. He never had.

He avoided giving her an answer, strangely loathe to bring his past into the conversation. "So tell me, is there a Mr. Reed in the picture?" He waited, his chest uncomfortably tight, feet planted hard to the floor. He had to resist the urge to lean forward to catch her answer.

"My husband is...gone." Her voice, losing its smoothness, came out a little higher pitched, and she fiddled with a loose piece of wicker on the arm of her chair as if her life depended on it/ Her eyes met his for a swift instant before sliding away.

Hmm, what's up with that?

His interest rose as he watched her almost defensive posture. Years of training kicked in. He wasn't liking the picture forming in his head.

The breeze teased shoulder length strands of honey colored hair, and she absently brushed them behind her ear. His gaze followed the path of her hand as it trailed down her neck to toy with the collar of her blouse.

He cleared his throat. "You'll be seeing a little more of me around, I'm afraid. Mrs. Garrett found out I know a little carpentry and asked if I would mind doing some work on her rentals, like those creaky stairs of yours. I'll try to keep out of your way, but if there's anything I can help you with, just let me know."

Where did that come from? He didn't need any more complications in his life. He had enough of his own to deal with.

"Thank you, Mr. Kelley, but we're fine." She smiled.

That was relief he was feeling, right? "Hey now, after sharing a cup of coffee with me you can surely break down and call me, Nick. Come on, let's hear it." He teased her.

She burst out laughing. "Nick, it is then."

He liked that husky laugh of hers. Rising, he stepped around the little table, frowning at her sudden tension as her hand tightened on the arm of her chair.

"Good, I'll drop by tomorrow, take a few measurements and start getting the supplies together, if that's okay. Do you have any problem with my coming and going out of your yard?"

"No, that's fine. I'll warn Jessica to keep out of your way."

"I like the company, it's no trouble if she wants to come out and help." He surprised himself by meaning it.

———

SARA ADMIRED HIS LONG, athletic legs encased in boot cut jeans as he strode away. Her gaze rose past his drool-worthy butt and broad back covered in a tight black t-shirt. His short dark hair glinted with auburn lights in the morning sun and left the back of his strong neck uncovered, revealing copper tanned skin.

Wonder if it's the same color all over?

Embarrassed at where her thoughts were going, she rested

her head against the wicker chair and appreciated how the sunlight turned the leaves above her into shimmering shades of burgundy. She'd missed this the last few years, gazing upon the world with an artist's eye—she'd thought Tom had all but drummed that out of her.

Picking up her cup from the resin table, she admired the furniture she and Jess had found a couple of weeks ago. They'd been walking to the market when they'd come upon the cast-offs sitting by the curb, a *for free* sign taped to the back of the settee. She was trying to figure a way to get the pieces home, when Tess's nephew Ty happened along in a shiny white pick-up.

Noticing them, he'd pulled over. With a soft whirr, the driver's window rolled down and a tanned arm rested on the sill as his friendly face leaned out, "Morning ladies, looks as if today's my lucky day."

Ty Garrett was a regular visitor at his aunt's home, and at six feet with shaggy blond hair and blue eyes, he was a very attractive man. He'd made no secret of his interest in Sara, often joining them in the mornings for a quick coffee before heading off to work. He owned a restoration business, specializing in preserving landmark buildings in the area. Right now he was rebuilding the Twilight Theatre, an old brick building at the bottom of Main Street. It was reclaiming its gracious heritage, thanks to Ty's efforts.

"Actually it must be ours." She'd smiled up at him, squinting a little in the bright light. "We were working on how to get this home when you miraculously appeared."

He'd turned off the idling truck and opened his door to hop out. Going around back, he opened the tailgate with a flourish.

"My white steed," gesturing towards the pick-up which made Jessica giggle, "and myself, are at your service, my ladies."

He bowed and then clutched at his back, which sent Jess into another peal of laughter. He'd loaded the furniture into his truck and driven them home, placing it on Sara's old porch—where it looked every bit as perfect as she'd pictured it.

Toying with a loose piece of wicker, Sara wondered what Tess was up to. If she wanted stuff done on her properties, Ty would most likely have been happy to do it for her. She was good at picking up strays. They were proof of that. Maybe Mr. Kelley—Nick—was down on his luck and she was helping him out. She liked that better than the other scenario she could come up with.

Matchmaking.

She and Grace were infamous for their matchmaking endeavors. Sara wanted nothing to do with that, no matter how nice the man looked.

Jessica came skipping up the walkway, the dog following close behind. "Hi, Mom, we were over at Aunty Tess's house. She made cookies."

Sara tried to maintain a serious face, but it was hard. Jake had one of her gardening hats flopping off the side of his head, and Jessica had chocolate streaks on the side of her mouth. "Young lady, what did I tell you about leaving the yard?"

"I know, Mommy, but it was only for a minute, and Jake's daddy said we could." Her hazel eyes pleaded. She looked so worried she'd done something wrong that Sara capitulated, holding her arms out for a hug.

As she held her baby in close to her body, she breathed in

23

the sweet smell of strawberry shampoo and green grass. All too soon, Jess pulled away and went running inside, screen door slapping shut behind her.

Jake padded over for his share of some loving, settling at her feet with a heavy groan. She bent over and rubbed his sides, frowning when she felt a raised welt along his right hip. It was under his fur, so not recent, but still. Nick had mentioned he and Jake had been through a lot. So were the injuries connected, then? What had caused them? It bothered her to think of either of them lying hurt somewhere, needing aid.

"Oh you poor boy, you need a bed for those old bones, don't you? We'll have to see what we can do. You're such a sweetheart, yes you are." His ears perked up, and his wavy tail swished the floor.

She didn't like the reaction thoughts of her new neighbor caused. Picturing him earlier, sitting across from her. Smiling at her. Her pulse fluttered. The very last thing she needed was to get mixed up in someone else's problems. She had more than enough of her own and appreciated her luck in having found this quaint town. They'd traveled across the country in search of a safe haven, as far from her estranged husband as they could get. She didn't want to even think what would happen if he managed to find them.

CHAPTER THREE

For spring, it'd been unseasonably warm the last few days. Nick pulled a cloth from his back pocket and glancing up at the bright sun, swiped his forehead. His plan was to repair the back deck on Sara's house today. He envied Jake, lying in a cool patch of shade. Oh well, it was his own fault. He'd offered to do the job, and truthfully, he was glad. It gave him less time to stew over his past.

"Can I help?"

Startled, Nick swung the hammer prematurely, almost nailing his thumb to the board. After a little creative cussing beneath his breath, he turned to see Jessica standing a few feet away. Always so solemn, a miniature replica of her momma.

"Sure kid, can you hold this tape measure for me? Shouldn't you be in school?"

Jessica gripped the measure and walked to the other end of the post where he pointed. "I'm not in school right now," she mumbled, carefully holding the tape against the wood.

He scanned her expression, and then looked away. "That's good. Yep, right there." He took the pencil from behind his ear and jotted down the measurement on a scrap of paper. "Why's that?"

"It's spring break, there is no school," she stammered, walking back to him, the tape whistling as it re-spooled into its case. "Besides, we're hiding."

His pulse picked up the pace, competing with the spiraling tape. "You're hiding? Like from the bogey man or what?"

"No silly." She giggled. "Me and my mom's playing a long game of hide and seek with my dad. She says it's an adventure." Jess's bottom lip jutted as she shuffled her sparkly pink shoes in the grass, staining the toes green.

So, there was more to the story. He'd been afraid of that. Nick had been an only child himself—thank Christ, with how messed up his home life had been. School had always been nothing more than a trial, filled with too many embarrassing questions. He knew the teachers were worried, but the carefully worded queries, "How did you fall, son?" or his personal favorite, "Would you like us to talk to your parents?" only served to widen the gulf between him and the other kids who were more than happy to pick at the scabs of anger and embarrassment he wore like a mantle. Now it sounded as if this little girl and her mother might be going through something similar. It pissed him off.

Jake ran up and stole the gloves from his back pocket and proceeded to *kill* them, growling and shaking his head, the leather dangling lifeless from between his sharp teeth. The two of them stood together smiling while they watched the goofy dog. A rare feeling of serenity slid over Nick. Most of his friends were single like himself, so he was surprised with how comfortable he felt with half-pint here.

He turned when Sara called out from the back porch, "Hey, you guys. How about taking a break for a cold glass of lemonade?"

She looked pretty, decked out in a bright yellow T-shirt that lovingly outlined her full breasts. White denim shorts hugged her hips and led the way down to a set of perfect shaped legs. His stomach clenched when he got to her bare toes painted a heart-stopping flame red.

Turning away, he said, "Sure, leave it on the step. We'll be over after we get this piece nailed together." How in the Sam hell had he gotten himself into this mess? He had a feeling Mrs. G was finding him make work projects at the Reed house. He knew what she was up to, but hadn't the heart to turn her down. He needed his head examined.

"Jess isn't getting in your way, is she?" Her warm voice coming from over his shoulder made him jump for the second time this morning. He was going to give himself a blackened thumb yet.

"Mo-om, I'm helping Nick."

"It's Mr. Kelley to you, young lady. If he doesn't mind, that's fine. I don't want you interfering with his work though."

"It's Nick, and she's not in the way. She's a good little worker." The words came out as if put through a meat grinder. Jess wasn't the problem, his attraction to her mother was.

Jessica's eyes shone at the compliment. "See Mom, I can help."

"Well, make sure you listen. I don't want you getting hurt out here."

When Sara turned to go back to the house he noticed she hadn't bothered with shoes before walking outside. He opened his mouth to warn her to watch her step just as she let out a little yelp, bouncing around on one foot. Hearing the commotion, Jake came trotting over from his game of chase the tail and circled them, jumping and barking, loving the new entertainment.

"Mommy, what happened? Are you okay?"

Nick hurried over and wrapped his arm around her slender waist to support her before the silly dog knocked her other foot out from under her. "Why in the he...ck were you out here with no shoes on?" he growled. Boosting her into his arms, he ignored her flinch and headed for the open screen door. "Hold still, before I drop you." She was squirming around like a fish on a hook.

"Put me down, you big oaf. I can walk." Then seeing the blood, she completely ruined the tough girl routine by shuddering and turning her head into his shoulder.

He tried to ignore the way she smelled of fresh air and vanilla. And how soft her skin looked, or how silky her hair was where it brushed his chin.

"Mom, mommy, are you okay?"

Jessica's agitated tones as she followed right on Nick's heels made him grimace. He hated the fright he could hear in her quivery voice. "Don't worry, kid; your mom's built tough."

"Oh, gross!" she exclaimed, spotting the bloody foot. "Now I see why you always say to put your shoes on before you go outside. Guess you should have listened to your own advice, huh?"

"All right, miss smarty pants; your Mom probably doesn't need your two cents worth right now. Can you find me a first aid kit, maybe some warm water, and clean towels? You can be my nurse."

"Cool. You sure you're okay, Mom?" At Sara's carefully neutral smile, Jessica ran down the hall for the requested items.

"You're not going to faint on me, are you?" Glancing down, he noticed she'd turned an interesting shade of green. He set her down on the kitchen counter to get a better look at the injury. Lifting her small foot into his hand, he was glad to see a clean cut, not too deep. She'd been lucky.

"Well, the good news is, you'll live. We'll get you cleaned up and you'll be good as new. I don't suppose you've had a Tetanus shot recently?" he asked, grabbing ahold of some paper towel and applying pressure to the wound, relieved it was superficial.

"*Ouch*, you could have given me a warning." She cried, her eyes flashing liquid fire at him.

"Yeah well, you're welcome. For future reference, you make a lousy damsel in distress." Exasperated, he released the foot he'd been holding, letting it thump down lightly against the cupboard. Even irritated with her, another part of him remained all too aware of her. Her long legs dangled over the edge of the old countertop. Mouth-watering breasts stretched her sunny t-shirt right at eye level. The more he saw of her, the more she fascinated him.

Tracing a slow path up her slender throat, he noticed her pulse fluttering just under her skin. Zeroing in on her plump lips, he groaned under his breath as the pink of her tongue flicked out to moisten them. A banquet for him to savor. Just a little.

"Sara—"

"Look, I'm fine, Jessica can..." She sputtered to a nervous halt as he stepped forward and nudged her legs apart with his hips.

His jeans scraped her bare skin, and he caught the awareness in her expressive eyes. At least he wasn't alone in this. Cradling her hips on the cool countertop, he leaned in, giving her ample time to back away. A few light sips, that's all he needed. His heart pounded so hard it threatened to leave his chest. The plump softness invited him to taste, to feast. His tongue flicked out teasing her, until with a soft sigh, she opened to him. Ravenous now, he sank deep, indulging in the honey and cinnamon taste of her.

Sweet, so sweet.

He forced himself to stop, and leaning back a little, cupped her jaw. His thumb rasped back and forth over her satiny skin, waiting for her beautiful eyes to slide open. And yes, there it was. The same want and confusion and mistrust plaguing him, filled the amber depths.

"Sara." Her name a sigh, he moved in just as she backed away, clunking her head against the cupboard door behind her.

"Stop, Nick—I can't do this. I'm sorry, I just can't." Her gaze avoided him, a shaky hand rubbing the sore spot on the back of her head.

Running slightly unsteady hands of his own through his mussed hair, he stepped back with a wry grimace, shifting to find some relief from the pressure behind his zipper. They had to quit meeting like this, she was going to end up with a concussion. Her arms were crossed over her chest while she contemplated the wall over his shoulder. She refused to look him in the eye, so he attempted some damage control. "Look, I'm sorry. I had no business kissing you like that."

"No, you didn't"

"Mom, which towels should I grab?" Jess yelled from down the hall, and he cursed. He'd been so caught up in Sara he'd forgotten the kid was even there.

"They're under the sink." She called out to her daughter, still not looking at him. "Maybe this isn't a good idea," she murmured. "You should go. I'm sure Tess can find someone else to finish the repairs."

He was about to let her know what he thought of that idea when Jessica came racing back into the kitchen, a towel trailing on the floor behind her.

"Mom, how could you say that? Nick's doing a great job."

After a very pregnant pause, which had him almost shuffling his feet like an errant child, she reluctantly agreed. "Yes, he is. Fine, you can stay. Unless you'd rather not?" It was more than obvious she hoped he'd turn her down.

He wanted to. Nearly as much as he wanted to go back to her vulnerable mouth and finish what they'd started. The damn woman drove him crazy.

Gritting his teeth, he turned to the little girl defending him so vehemently and forced a facsimile of a smile. "Thanks, sweetheart. Glad to hear someone appreciates my carpentry skills. I think your mom is feeling better now." A quick glance caught her dropping down from the counter. Her pert breasts bouncing under the too thin top had his inner caveman growling. He turned his back before he did something foolish. "I'll let you bandage her up while I get back to work, okay?" With that he stomped outside, slamming the screen behind him.

Moving around, cleaning up the jobsite—making sure all the damn nails were off the damn ground, he hauled himself over the coals for kissing her. Shivers of excitement still danced along his spine as he recalled the feel of her cool hands stroking his nape. Her tongue playing tag with his. The sweet, tart taste that was hers alone.

He didn't want to get mixed up in anyone else's life. His own head wasn't screwed on right. He needed to stay the hell away from her.

CHAPTER FOUR

Sara stood at the kitchen window, hands in dishwater, eyelids closed in simple pleasure, her face lifted toward the warmth of the sun's rays. She'd always loved the promise of spring with all the fresh scents. Shiny new leaves on the trees. Birds singing as they go about the business of nest building and caring for their young. It felt like anything was possible.

Voices coming through the screen had her opening her eyes to see Nick at work restoring the garden from Jake, who had managed to dig up all her tulip bulbs. Darn mutt. Jessica and the dog followed behind him pretty much step for step. It'd been almost a week and she still couldn't fathom what she'd been thinking of to let him kiss her like that.

It's not the end of the world, get over it.

He didn't seem to be suffering from any such anxiety—not showing by the slightest hint, his tongue had been halfway down her throat. It was almost like it hadn't happened, except it had.

Her pulse leapt remembering the hot look in his eyes, and those full lips lowering to hers. Jessica had been right down the hall, but for one, all too brief, exciting moment, she'd forgotten the disillusioned woman staring at her now.

Fiona, the only person Sara trusted with her whereabouts had called just yesterday with an all too grim reminder.

"Hi, babe, how are you and that gorgeous God-daughter of mine making out?" Her effervescent personality bubbling through the airwaves warmed Sara's heart.

"Fiona. We miss you so much." She wasn't sure what she would have done without her friend's help and encouragement. And now, through her gallery, Sara could provide a living for Jessica by selling her paintings under a pseudonym.

"And I miss you. Life's boring around here without you two."

There was a slight pause and Sara could feel the tension flowing down the line. "What's wrong, Fiona? Tell me."

"It's nothing, your dickhead husband showed up here a couple of days ago."

Sara sucked in a sharp lungful of air, her hands clenching the dishcloth. "Tom didn't bother you, did he?"

"The air he breathes bothers me, my dear, but that's not the reason I called. I just wanted to give you a heads-up, that's all. Don't worry about me, just take care of yourselves and I'll be happy."

"He's not going to give this up, is he? I'm so worried." Tears clogged her throat, turning her voice husky. "When he catches up to us—"

"That's not going to happen." Fiona swore, her voice full of venom. "Sooner or later he's going to screw up and then we'll have him. I spoke to a friend of mine in the DEA—don't worry, she's solid—anyway, she's looking into it, Sara. You're not alone in this. He's going to jail. And then you guys can come back home."

After a bit more conversation, they'd hung up, promising to stay in touch. Sara wished she felt half as confident as her friend. She'd read the file she'd taken when they ran and been shocked by the contents. She'd known it contained valuable information, but hadn't realized how the same man who dealt in million-dollar drug deals and weapons exchanges, could be the respected one she'd married.

The sun warmed her chilled skin as her daughter's contagious laughter floated through the partially open window. Deciding to take a trip down to the Craft Shack for a dose of Annie's cheerful optimism she phoned over to Tess, who was more than happy to watch Jessica.

Opening the kitchen window a little wider, she called, "Jess, I'm running out to do a couple of errands. You can stay with Aunty Tess, okay?"

"Mom, can't I stay with Nick? I'll be good," she yelled, shyly grasping Nick's large hand, and gazing up at him with a severe case of hero worship.

Nick's gaze speared Sara's through the glass, some complicated expression chasing across his face before he dropped down to Jessica's height. His deep tones easily carried across the small yard. "Actually, squirt, I've gotta run and pick up a couple of things myself, maybe you should go to Tess's for now."

"Aw, Nick, I wanted to stay with you," Jessica whined.

"Well, maybe if you behave yourself I might bring you back a little something, how's that sound?"

"Okay, I guess." Her bottom lip just about dragged in the dust as she moped while gathering up a couple of toys. It soon turned to delighted shrieks however when Nick lifted her into the air and helicoptered her a couple of times before setting her lightly over the fence into Tess's backyard who'd come to the door to see what the fuss was about. Waving, she ushered Jessica into the house, no doubt for another baking marathon, and round of afternoon soaps.

Nick's lower abs, exposed in the lift, had stopped Sara's breath. Then he turned and caught her staring. Blushing hotly, she backed away from the window and grabbed up her purse and keys.

Idiot.

She was acting like a teenager with her first crush for crying out loud. She'd known he had a muscular build—but—Wow.

Embarrassment had her hurrying out the front door, intent on getting to her car before Nick decided maybe they should ride together. She'd just gotten the key in the ignition when he came striding around the corner of the house.

Opening the passenger door, he asked, "Hey, can I catch a lift?" and slid into the seat, slamming the door shut behind him before she could reply.

"Cripes, you call this thing a car? There's more room in a tin can," he grumbled, jamming the seat back as far as it would go and his head still brushed the roof. With shoulders jammed against the window and his knees bent at an awkward angle, he looked like a pretzel. "How safe is this contraption anyway?"

Sara couldn't help it, she snickered at his predicament. "Beggars can't be choosers, and besides...you shouldn't cast stones on poor Mirabelle. You'll hurt her feelings."

"You named your car? Why am I not surprised?" he grunted, trying without much success to shift to a more comfortable position. "Look, my truck's in the shop and I figured since you were going anyway?"

Deciding to let him off the hook—the poor man looked like he was in enough pain—she relented. "Okay, you can come, but no more nit-picking remarks about my girl here, she's sensitive." Patting the cracked vinyl dash, she peeked at him as he fought to reach his seatbelt, when had her car become so small?

His big body crammed in this close had her nerves springing around like Mexican jumping beans. There were laws about distractions while driving, weren't there? The thought of him among all the sewing do-dads in Annie's store was enough to threaten the eruption of a mile-wide smile. "Are you sure you want to come with me? I'm going to be a while. I need to stop at the post office to check on a parcel first, and then I'm meeting my friend over at the Craft Shack, you won't like it."

A LIGHT, summery fragrance filled her little car, teasing him with the scent of her. She wore some kind of summer dress that left way too much skin showing for his peace of mind. He itched to touch her right where it ended, halfway up her mouth-watering thighs. Thin straps showed off creamy shoulders, and the front crossed and tied in a neat little bow on the side—

begging him to pull the strings. This wasn't one of his brighter ideas. He'd started out with the notion of getting to know her a little better, maybe finding out what their story was. But now, sitting beside her in the too small car, his thoughts were definitely not of the 'let's be friends' sort.

"There's no rush. But on the way home could you drop by the hardware store?" Listen to him, sounding all domesticated.

"You really want to trail behind me all day? What are you, a masochist?"

Yep, I'm starting to think so.

The smile she sent his way showed a hint of teeth, proving he got to her at least half as much as she bothered him. Good.

The geriatric car groaned to life, spitting and gurgling, happier to be spending its days sunning on the warm asphalt drive than lumbering across town. Nick was just relieved when they pulled up in front of the post office without him having to push. An obvious landmark in the little community, its rosy brick facade cast a benevolent shadow over the main street.

He followed Sara out of the rattletrap, startled to hear a voice calling out to her from across the road.

"Good morning, Sara, beautiful day, isn't it?" A buxom blonde was sweeping the sidewalk in front of a hair salon, aptly named Hair Affair.

Shading her eyes from the morning light, Sara waved and called back, "Hi, Jenny, it is a lovely day. I'll have to come see you soon for a trim, before it gets too warm out."

"Sure thing, anytime, honey. And you're more than welcome to bring *him* with you." She cast admiring eyes up and down Nick's body, and practically purred. "I'm great with men."

After another short wave, Sara sent him a look, and brushed by to climb the stairs entering the post office.

Nick gave the woman across the street a smiling shrug before turning to stare at Sara's ass as it twitched back and forth like an angry cat until it was out of sight. He trailed her into the building, not sure why her panties were in a knot. But then, he'd be the first to say he didn't understand women. He'd always enjoyed them. How they looked, how they smelled, and even how they cried at the drop of a hat, but he'd never understood their way of thinking.

He could have been crossing the street right now to cozy up to that cute little blonde, instead here he was, trailing after Sara like a sad-eyed puppy dog.

Pathetic, Kelley.

Entering the lobby of the old building, he found her standing near a guy wearing a baseball jersey for the Yankee's.

Seriously. Everyone knows the Red Sox rule, dude.

His annoying chuckle irritated Nick all the way across the room. When she smiled at something the chump said, his hackles rose in tempo with his pace. Nearing them, Nick could hear him asking her, "Does that guy know you, Sara? He looks like he's about ready to rip my head off."

Good call, buddy.

Forcing a polite smile as he joined them, one hand moved possessively to the small of her back.

She edged sideways, golden eyes still sparking with annoyance as she shifted, trying to dislodge his hand—unsuccessfully.

39

"This is my neighbor, Nick. Don't worry, he always has the brooding thing going on. Smiling would crack his jaw, I'm sure."

With a knowing smirk towards where Nick had placed his hand, the guy held his gaze in a contest of wills. "Ty Garrett, if you live in the neighborhood you must know my aunt, Tess. She rents a lot of the houses around there."

What was he doing? If she wanted to date every single person in this town, it shouldn't matter to him. He was only here temporarily, long enough to finish his therapy and maybe try to get his shit together. She had friends here, good people who seemed to care for her and her little girl. He had no place in that.

"Yeah, she's a nice lady; I'm actually staying in one of her houses." Cursing himself for an idiot, Nick looked down into her rosy face. "Listen, I'm going to walk over to the hardware store. I'll meet you at the diner in about half an hour, okay?"

SARA WATCHED his smooth stride away from her side, glad Nick's warm hand had dropped away from her back. Really, she was.

"Are you two—?"

Rattled because she'd forgotten Ty standing beside her, Sara turned away, determined to get a certain dark-haired devil off her mind. "No. Nick is helping your aunt with a few repairs around my house, that's all. We're friends."

And they were. He'd proven himself to be a good man. Always patient with Jessica. Fixing things around the house, like her rickety stairs. Or the day he'd stopped into the kitchen for a glass of water, seen her dripping tap, and fixed that too. All things Tom would never have dreamed of handling himself. And there was nothing wrong with the view either as Nick worked his magic with her yard, his muscled arms and legs bunching and flexing at his every command. On warm days, his shirt would stick damply to his chest, highlighting his abs and muscled back.

The man was seriously H O T.

In another time and place, she might even have been tempted, but after all the trauma of her life with Tom, she wasn't that girl anymore. Except, she couldn't seem to forget about that darn kiss.

"All right, so how about going out with me Friday night for dinner and a little dancing then? Come out and play, Sara, you won't regret it." Ty's warm voice broke through her meandering thoughts.

He was a good-looking man, came from a great family and had been asking her out for months now, with no success. Maybe she needed to try again. And it certainly had nothing to do with her silly attraction to Nick. As a matter of fact, the more she thought about it, the more it made perfect sense. She was lonely.

Already regretting it and not sure why, Sara nonetheless gave him the answer he was looking for. "What time?"

CHAPTER FIVE

Sara pulled up to the curb in front of Grits and Grace, and turned off a grumbling Mirabelle, all the while arguing with herself over saying yes to a date with Ty. She wasn't ready to jump back into the dating world. It'd taken her months after Tom to get to the point where she could even converse normally with a man.

She was perfectly satisfied with the status quo, thank you very much. Well okay, maybe not exactly...satisfied, per se. But she could certainly make do without men. Walter, her battery-operated boyfriend worked if she found herself desperate. The problem was Sara hadn't realized until *The Kiss,* how much she'd missed some of the intimacies to be found between a man and a woman. Maybe it'd do her good to go out and test the dating pool. Have some fun, before her ovaries shriveled up like year old prunes.

Ignoring Miss Doom and Gloom going on inside her head, she pushed open the door of the diner, smiling as bells above sang out a tinkling welcome. Stopping for a moment, she was hit with a sensory overload of frying bacon, coffee, the clang of the till and chatter of happy patrons. Popular with the locals, it was much like stepping into a past era. A beautifully preserved Jukebox stood sentinel in a corner of the room, a slightly scratchy rendition of *Teddy Bear* emitting from its large speakers. Red leather seats, Formica tabletops and black and white checkerboard flooring were all straight out of a fifties sit-com. Looking for Nick, she found him at one of the window booths. He reminded her of bad boy, James Dean as he sat there with an arm over the back of the booth, flirting with Grace Martin, the diner's owner.

One of her favorite people, Grace was every bit as tall as she was round. She epitomized the old adage, *Never Trust a Skinny Cook*. Blessed with a face that never seemed to age, she was one of those people you meet once and feel like you've known forever. Her diner was the perfect place to sit, have a thick slice of homemade apple pie topped with a generous scoop of slowly melting vanilla ice cream, and catch up on all the juicy gossip which made small town living so unique.

As she slid into her seat across the table from him, Nick cast those gorgeous lake blue eyes in her direction, and the sparkle lighting their depths reeled her in effortlessly—the man was lethal.

"Well, well, if it isn't my, Sara Sunshine. Where you been hiding, girl? Old Gracie hasn't seen you in far too long. And where is little, Jessica Bean?" Grace's smoky voice drifted over her like a warm blanket.

Dragging her gaze away from Nick, Sara smiled at her

friend. "Hi, Grace, and you're right, it has been too long. Jessica is over at Tess's house, probably baking up a storm." They both grinned, aware of Tess's infamous messes whenever she got it in her head to bake. No dish was safe. "I wanted to drop in and see Annie for the paint I'd ordered, and thought I'd better stop for some of the delicious food you always spoil me with."

"Well darlin', I'll get right on that, but first, who's this young stud muffin? He's been busy trying to sweet talk me into running away with him," she smirked, her cheeks rushing up to meet her eyes. "It's about time sugar-pie. I was beginning to think you needed me to find you a nice young man, but looking at him, you did a fine job all by your little lonesome." Grace grinned at Nick, and Nick grinned back, looking already half in love, and he hadn't even tasted the food yet.

"Oh no, it's nothing like that." Her cheeks warm, she hurried to clarify, "Nick's my neighbor. He's been doing some repairs on my house for Tess." She caught a look that flickered across his face. How did he expect her to introduce him? She squirmed in her seat as his gaze dissected her for a long moment, his eyes now deep, reflective pools.

Then his mouth quirked, "Sweetheart, you're going to give Grace here the wrong idea. You know I'm at your house more than I'm at my own." He lifted one of Sara's hands and ran his thumb in a slow caress over the tops of her knuckles, causing goose bumps to erupt and her nipples to tighten.

Oh, man.

Pulling her over-sensitized hand out of his, she crossed her arms over her chest and chastised, "Nick, quit goofing off and let's order. I'm starving."

His low, "Me too, honey, me too," sent quivers of lust shooting through her belly. She had a feeling he wasn't talking about food anymore.

Grace gave them both a "get a room" look, but thankfully refrained from commenting on it. "Okay chickies, specials today are Broccoli and Cheese stuffed Tilapia, My Grace of God Meatloaf, or a Sloppy Joe Grilled Cheese. And for dessert, we have To Die for Strawberry Rhubarb Pie or Momma's Recipe Pumpkin Bread Pudding with a warm caramel sauce drizzled over the top."

"Well, I can't turn down meatloaf, and the bread pudding sounds perfect. What do you think, Sara?" Nick asked, skimming a knowing look at her arms.

"I think I'll stick with a nice salad, maybe with some grilled chicken on top. I need room for your strawberry pie, Grace; you know I can't leave without having some of that." She laughed.

"No wonder you're so skinny, child. You need food if you're going to put some meat on those bones." Shaking her head, Grace waddled into her kitchen, no doubt intent on performing gourmet miracles.

Now that they were alone, Nick sat back enjoying the easy ebb and flow of conversations around him. A cute old couple in a booth across from theirs sat on the same side of the table sharing a mountainous piece of pie. A man about his age rested his back against the wall in the corner by the jukebox, green eyes flashing as he talked on his cell phone. And a group of men, ages ranging from fifty to about a hundred by the looks of the one shrunken old guy, were solving world issues at a booth in the back. One of the servers, he guessed a lifer by the coordinated ease that she lined loaded plates along her bony arms, sassed Grace at the kitchen window and got an earful for her trouble. He grinned, it'd been a long time since he'd felt so relaxed in a public place.

Even after being back as long as he had, he still sometimes suffered from flashbacks and night sweats, and knew he was one of the lucky ones.

Seeking lighter thoughts, he turned his attention to the woman sitting across from him, nervously twisting her cup in its saucer. He liked that he made her nervous. Lord knows, she did things to him, also. Things best not thought about in public places.

A painting of Grace's diner on the wall behind her caught his eye. The Cascade Mountains made a perfect backdrop for the little cafe. Its brick façade, complimented by baskets of summer flowers hanging between the windows, and on the walkway below, managed to convey a feeling of welcoming warmth. Squinting to make out the name, S. Reed, in the bottom corner, Nick realized he was sitting with that gifted artist right now. "Did you paint that, Sara? It's brilliant."

Flushing at the sincere compliment, she nodded. "When we first moved here, Grace and Tess were kind enough to take us in under their wings. I wanted to give a little something back, so I did a painting for each of them. Grace has had plenty of offers, but refuses to part with it. She said it's going with her all the way to the Pearly Gates." Her eyes lit up with laughter, her glistening lips tilted upward full of warmth and fondness.

She should do that more often. Smile. It lit her up from the inside out, making her truly gorgeous. She was attracted to him. The signs were there in the blooming color on her cheeks whenever she looked at him. How her gaze met his, and then flitted away.

And then there was *that kiss.*

He knew about passion, had been in his fair share of relationships. Hell, he'd even been married once. But their kiss? It'd done something to him. Purely, in a field of its own. He'd even forgotten there was a kid in the house, for crying out loud. And when she'd kissed him back? He couldn't have recited his own name, even at gunpoint.

The white picket fence and two-story house thing complete with wife and kids had never been for him. He'd seen, first with his parents, then later in his own life, happy-ever-after was mostly a lark. Didn't happen, at least not very damn often. And the kids were almost always the ones to pay the harshest for those screw-ups. He swore that wasn't going to be him. Not again. He was fine on his own, anyway. It was better this way. And if he was a little lonely occasionally, he could call a friend. He had his dog.

He was good. Fine. Perfect.

Thinking he should come clean and explain his short-term presence in Tidal Falls, Nick began, "You know..."

At the same moment, Sara confessed, "You know, I'm a..."

They both stopped. Looked into each other's eyes. Smiled.

"Ladies first." He offered, more than happy to put off

mentioning his looming departure.

"I was just going to say I think I'm something of a closet romantic. I think it's what drew me to this town. Everyone I've met has been kind-hearted and welcoming. I appreciate it so much."

"What about your husband? You must miss him." The more he came to know her and her daughter, the more he wanted her to confide in him. Tell him the truth about what was going on so he could help her. But watching her shoulders slump inward and her face lose its animation, he was sorry he'd brought it up.

She ignored him for a long moment as she stared out the window into her past. When she did begin to speak, it was almost in monotone, all the vibrancy sucked from her voice. "I guess I was too young and vulnerable when I met Tom—that's his name you know. Sounds harmless, doesn't it?" A choked laugh escaped, and Nick reached across to grasp her hand as it fluttered near the tabletop like an injured bird. Lost in the past, he didn't think she even noticed. He cursed his stupidity.

"I'd lost someone close to me that year, my foster father. And then Tom came along and swept me off my feet. He seemed like perfect husband material, charming, handsome, and intelligent. At first we had a good life together. We were happy, or at least I was happy. Then something changed. He changed."

She turned away from the window to stare defiantly at him, a trace of tears turning her eyes to glistening amber. "So, in answer to your question, I would have to say no, I do not miss him. In fact, I'd be grateful never to see him again. You must think me callous right?"

Actually, he thought she was pretty fricken amazing—and

beautiful. The sun streaming in through the glass shot her hair with strands of burnished copper and gold. Her summer dress gaped slightly on its way down to her breasts, teasing him with glimpses of soft, smooth skin, and a hint of lace.

He knew how hard it must be to admit to the breakdown of a marriage. He'd never even copped to his own. Preferring to push it under the table, hidden.

"No, I don't think you're callous. Love is a fickle bitch at the best of times. I think you probably gave it your best shot and it just wasn't enough, that's all."

SARA LOOKED AWAY, blinking rapidly. She couldn't believe she'd dropped all that on him. And he'd accepted it. Sometimes she still wondered if what happened was her fault. If she could have done things differently. She'd read about other victims of domestic violence saying the same thing, but hadn't really understood—until it happened to her. Maybe if she'd skipped lunch that day, or maybe if she'd taken the time to call Tom. Maybe. Maybe. Maybe. Thousands of scenarios had run through her mind since then. But, she was slowly coming to grips with the realization that even if those things were true, he'd still had no right to do what he'd done. It was wrong. Tom needed help.

Determined to set aside ugly thoughts of her marriage, she refocused on the man sitting across from her. The high-back leather seats accentuated Nick's dark, wavy hair and swarthy skin. He must have grabbed her hand while she'd been talking, though she couldn't recall it, and was now rubbing his thumb in a soothing motion as he smiled up at the shy young server who'd come along to refill their coffee cups. Nodding her thanks to the girl, she pulled her hand back, and received a soul-piercing gaze in return. Turning away she gazed out the window at the downtown core, absently listening as Nick asked about working at Grace's and received the server's enthusiastic response.

The street lay north to south like a flowing gray ribbon. Flowering Mayday trees, their elegant branches dancing in the slight breeze, lined the walk. The delicate white flower's perfumed scent drifted into the diner whenever the door chimed open. A meridian filled with an assorted rainbow of happy-faced pansies interspersed with impatiens and Gerbera daisies ran down the center of the street to the intersection, where they flowed into a roundabout highlighted with a sparkling fountain.

The downtown businesses all pitched in with hanging baskets and planters filled to the brim, a profusion of color and textures. Sara could see all the way to the front door of Annie Campbell's store, the Craft Shack. She'd been happy to find a kindred spirit in Annie, a potter and single mother. Chris was Jessica's age, a doll, with copper hair and freckles across his still chubby cheeks. They'd developed into close friends. She hoped it wouldn't have to come to an end.

"Hey, where'd you go?" Nick's baritone broke through, "Why don't you tell me what's bothering you and maybe I can help."

"It's nothing; I was just day-dreaming." She wasn't ready to share the horror her marriage.

"Okay, tell me about painting then. Where do you get your inspirations from?"

A slight smile curved her lips at his obvious ploy to pull her out of her funk. She toyed with her teaspoon for a minute, giving serious thought to her answer. "Did you ever read *National Geographic* when you were a kid?" And at his bemused nod, she continued, "I used to dream I was a photographer of theirs, experiencing all those different cultures. So many of the people portrayed between those pages cared little for material wealth, but what they had, they took enormous pride in. I guess that's what I try to show in my work. It's not what you have, it's what you hold dear that counts."

Nick squeezed her hand and she raised her eyes to his. Staring into the cerulean depths, she could see a innumerable thoughts chasing themselves around and wondered what she'd said to cause it.

"Nick, are you married?"

Well, that was blunt enough, wasn't it?

Her cheeks warmed as he burst out laughing. Several heads turned in their direction at the attractive sound.

"You're asking me that now? After you kissed me senseless the other day? For shame, young lady, for shame." He waved his finger back and forth like a pendulum, his eyes glinting with humor.

"Actually, you kissed me," she said, a smile breaking across her own lips. The sun seemed to shine brighter and the sky became an impossible blue. Grace returned to their table with fragrant dishes of steaming food, and suddenly, Sara was ravenous.

CHAPTER SIX

The room smelled of sex and perfume. The phone rang and Tom grasped the blond head between his legs, stopping her movement.

"Mr. Sheridan, it's Sam."

Finally. About fricken time.

"I was beginning to wonder what happened to you." He coughed to clear the rasp from his throat. The stupid son-of-a-bitch better have a good explanation for leaving him hanging this long.

"Yeah, well, I've been busy chasing your wife across the countryside. She's turning out to be a very smart woman."

He didn't know the half of it. "So...have you found her?"

"No, not yet. Listen, sir, I'm thinking we should let this go."

Tom yanked the phone away from his ear and stared at it incredulously. What the fuck was he talking about? Hauling in a hot breath of rage, he counted to ten, then let it ease out, before placing the phone back to his ear. "I need her back, Sam. You know that."

"Have you considered giving her some space? Maybe she just needs a little room to think or something, you know?"

He squeezed the phone until his fingers were a bloodless white, wishing it were someone's throat instead. He couldn't afford *time* for her to have a little *space*. He needed those goddamned files back. Now. Then he'd make sure his oh so *smart* wife, kept her pretty mouth shut. Permanently.

It sounded as if Samuel might know more than he was letting on. If he were thinking of double-crossing him, Tom would make him sorry he'd ever lived.

"Where are you, Sam? I'll come to you. We can sit down. Talk this over. Is it the money? I pay you very well. Well enough, I expect results. If you can't handle it, tell me now and I'll find someone who can."

So far, all his men had proven themselves less than useless. How hard could it be to chase down one woman and a child? "Sam, you still there?"

"Yeah, I'm here. Look, you know how women are. Hurt their feelings and they immediately go running off to their friends about it. I know you're worried, but I'm sure if you give her some time she'll come back, boss."

Did the asshole not know whom he was dealing with? "Time is not something we have a lot of, my friend. My... associates have been asking questions. They've been hearing rumors. I can't afford to piss these people off, Sam. If you know something and you're not telling me, I suggest you rethink your strategy. These guys play for keeps. You don't want to cross them, trust me."

There was a long pause, during which he could hear the muted sounds of clinking cups, laughter and conversation overlaid with what sounded like—was that *Elvis?* Sam came back online, his voice abrupt. "Yeah okay, I have a lead. They may be headed into New Mexico. I'll follow up and let you know."

Relieved now he'd won, Tom leaned back in his chair, the better to view the blonde kneeling at his feet. "Good man, I knew I could count on you. Keep in touch; I want to know as soon as you find her."

Setting the phone down, he tried to focus as Belinda went back to working him over. Time was running out. He needed to find Sara and get back those files, before she turned them in to some do-gooder cop. The campaign for the governor's office was already well underway. He'd worked too long and too hard to allow his wife's untimely disappearance to ruin his dreams. He couldn't afford to have even a hint of scandal attached to his name. He was on his way to the President's chair, and right now, the only thing stopping him was his pretty wife.

Disgusted, he shoved the minx between his legs away, gesturing for her to leave. Instead, she leaned back enticingly on her arms, her wide-open shirt showing off bare breasts, nipples puckered and inviting. Her legs bent spread-eagled under her short skirt, showed him she wore nothing underneath. He'd started using her for sex soon after hiring her to take care of his brat. Sometimes he liked things a little rough and she was more than willing to play those games.

Staring up at him with eyes like a cat, Belinda sucked a

finger between her pouting lips, then brought her hand between her legs and fondled herself, her long hair brushing the floor as her head fell back and she began to pant.

Slut.

Tom laughed and gave in. Falling out of his chair, he grabbed her around the neck and squeezed as he slid home.

CHAPTER SEVEN

Sara was at Grits and Grace, having coffee with Tess when Grace, pink cheeked and over-heated, shuffled out of the steamy kitchen to plop down beside her on the wide bench. The musty scent of cooking oil swirled around her as she heaved a heartfelt sigh of relief, leaning back to wriggle her toes. "So, Sara, where did you hide that handsome young man of yours today?"

"He's not *my* man, Grace." Especially since Nick seemed to be making a game of avoiding her ever since their lunch date. Bad enough she couldn't quit dreaming about him, all hot and shirtless, big leather tool belt riding low on his hips as he...grabbing the menu she waved it in front of her face.

Whew, was it warm in here?

"I don't know where he is, I haven't seen him in a couple of days." She swiftly changed the subject, no need giving her friend's any more ammunition. They were always trying to pair her up with the men of Tidal Falls, some of them old enough to be her grandfather. "Anyway, I have news. I'm going on a date tonight, which should make you two matchmakers happy. I wanted to ask if one of you can take Jessica for a while."

"Well of course I will, you don't even need to ask, child," Tess hurried to respond, and slid a triumphant glance across the table at Grace. The two of them had an ongoing competition over which one Jessica loved spending time with more. Truth was, she soaked up all the love and attention both women lavished on her, returning it twofold.

Passing a snarky look Tess's way, Grace offered, "Well then, maybe I could help you in another way. I have a closet full of dresses I've never even worn. I bet something in there would be perfect for tonight." Her eyes twinkling, she raised her right hand as though under oath. "I confess, I'm a shopaholic. I've tried to quit, but I just can't seem to stop." Laughing, her hand flopped down to the table with a thunk, causing Sara's cup to rattle in its saucer. "I'm always buying things I don't have a hope of ever getting into, if you can believe it."

"Oh, I can..."

Sara gave Tess a sharp kick under the table before she could finish the wisecrack, instead receiving a wounded look as if to say, "*What*?"

"As a matter of fact honey, I have the perfect one for you!" Grace grabbed onto her arm, pumping it enthusiastically.

Inwardly groaning, Sara took in Grace's plump figure dressed in a flowing orange tie-dyed tank dress covered with peace signs placed strategically here and there. She forced out a weak smile. "Thanks, girls. I can't believe how nervous I am. It's been years since I was on a date. Ty's going to take me out for dinner and maybe some dancing afterward. It might run a little late. Is that a problem Tess? Because I can call and cancel."

"Oh no, you don't. It's about time that nephew of mine stepped up to the plate. He's been making puppy dog eyes at you for months now." She chuckled. "Why don't you leave Jessica overnight with me. She'll be safe enough. Then, if you two kids wanna get busy..."

"Tess! I do not intend to get *busy*, as you put it. It's a night out between friends, that's all. I don't have any plans on ever getting *busy*, thank you very much." She winced at how loud she'd gotten.

Grace added her thoughts on the matter, "Well, hold on now, missy. That horse may have already left the barn, but that doesn't mean it won't ever want back in. As long as it's the right barn, if you catch my drift."

Tess and Sara looked at each other in shock, then at Grace who was now looking a little uncomfortable, and then laughter erupted all around the table.

"You're bad, Grace Martin, very bad." Sara smirked. "I can't believe I agreed to this but you guys are making it much easier. Thank you."

"No problem, sugar-pie, that's what friends are for. Okay, let's get on to more important stuff. Who wants pie?"

TURNING THIS WAY AND THAT, Sara tried to see her back in the floor length mirror attached to her bedroom door, entranced with the dress Grace had picked out for her. It was beautiful—if somewhat short on material. Backless and fashioned out of the softest oriental silk, it fell gently down her torso to end barely shy of indecent. The gorgeous mixture of turquoise greens and blues were breathtaking. Grace insisted it was perfect even though Sara wasn't so sure it was appropriate for a first date.

Too late now.

The chime of the doorbell and voices down the hall had her throwing on a pair of black velvet stilettos and rushing out of her room, only to slide to a stumbling halt at seeing Nick in the open doorway. The sudden flare of heat in his eyes when he caught sight of her was gratifying, and her pulse leapt in response.

"You're beautiful." His voice deepened and rumbled, stroking something warm and womanly to life inside of her. Not knowing how to handle the moment, she lifted her arms above her head and gave a little twirl, like the ballerina in Jessica's jewelry box.

"Grace did a good job, with what little she had to work with." Slowing her spin, she glanced over her shoulder, and caught his widened eyes on the open back of the dress. The little devil coaching her on from inside had her bending over on the pretext of checking if her shoes were properly strapped.

His muffled groan rewarded her as she slid her fingers enticingly up first one leg, then the other, checking her nylons before giving a little shimmy shake to straighten the short skirt.

"Something wrong?" she murmured, giving Grace a conspiratorial wink.

It wasn't often that anything ever left Nick at a loss for words. He was now. If he wasn't careful, he'd be picking his tongue up off the doorstep. He'd decided to drop over and see if Sara and Jessica would like to go see a movie with him, a peace offering of sorts. He hadn't been around in a couple days, and had missed them. He'd thought maybe some time and space would help him with the crazy attraction the two of them seemed to generate.

Guess not.

Remembering the day he'd seen her in those white shorts and yellow t-shirt, he'd found her heart-stoppingly pretty. The day of their little field trip, she'd been striking in a cute summer frock. Now though, now he felt gob-smacked. And that was before she bent her curvalicious body practically in half—sweet Jesus kill him now—to tighten the straps on a pair of come-fuck-me-up-against-a-door shoes. All the while showing him the long graceful curve of her bared spine and a perfect heart-shaped ass, all of which had his fingers tingling and his cock hardening. He was in so much trouble.

There was a knock on the doorframe behind him, and there stood what's-his-name, looking like a kid in a candy store.

What the Hell?

The dude cleaned up not bad, pissing Nick off even more. He wore a white dress shirt rolled up to show off most likely gym-toned arms and had tucked it into a pair of khaki colored chinos.

"Wow, doll-face, you look amazing." Ty grinned, looking way too pleased with himself. "We're going to have an incredible night together."

What the fuck did he mean by that?

Glaring from him to Sara, Nick expected her to send the a-hole down the road. Instead, she wore a welcoming smile on her very kissable lips as she picked up the little purse sitting on a side table in the hall.

There was no room for mace in that thing. And she should have a sweater on, her dress looked downright chilly.

"Ty, you're right on time. You remember my neighbor, Nick, from the post office the other day."

At the other guy's self-satisfied smirk, he wanted to plaster his pretty-boy face to the wall.

"Was there something you needed, Nick?" Sara enquired, the sound of his name pulling him from his funk.

"It can wait." He growled, shoving his hands deep into his pockets before they ripped the guy's face off. What the hell was she doing with surfer boy?

Ty bent his elbow, inviting Sara to place her hand in the crook. "Hey Grace, good to see you. Listen, if you're ready we better get a move on, I've made reservations at La Lune. You'll love it, great French cuisine."

What a Candy-ass. *French cuisine.*

As if Sara would be impressed because he was taking her to some fancy, shmancy restaurant. As she brushed by, he inhaled the fresh clean vanilla scent of her. It took all of his self-control to stand aside instead of pulling her into his aching arms.

SARA COULD SEE the tension tightening Nick's broad shoulders.

His face was an imperturbable mask, but annoyance flashed from his expressive eyes. She'd missed him the last couple of days. Had thought they were at least going to be friends after the lunch they'd shared. She wished now she'd called and cancelled her date, and hoped the rest of the evening would go better than the start. Ty did look nice, she had to give him points for that. But standing next to Nick's dark splendor, he faded into the woodwork.

Nick wore a pair of well-loved jeans and a much-washed soft looking button down shirt, the color an exact match to his cobalt eyes. He looked incredible, even with the scruffy stubble along his jaw, which had set her skin tingling. If only he'd been the one to ask her out.

Overwarm, she turned to Ty. "Yes, I'm ready. I've been looking forward to this. Your aunt tells me you're a terrific dancer." Forcing a smile for Ty she slipped first by Grace with her knowing eyes, and then Nick, inhaling his unique maleness on her way past. Man, if they only learned how to bottle that smell, there would be some very happy women in the world.

Glancing up as she passed, she met his intense gaze, and paused at something she thought she saw in the crystalline depths. Then the moment passed and he gave her a lopsided smile that failed to reach his eyes. "Have a good time."

"I will," she said, her heart not in the game. "See you tomorrow, Nick."

"Yeah, you will."

Feeling as though she'd made a grave error, but not sure what to do about it, Sara continued down the walk, her hand on Ty's arm. Before sliding into his fancy car she stopped to look back and wave at the two on the porch, but Nick was gone, leaving only Grace smiling and waving.

As they drove to La Lune in the sporty little coupe, she gave herself a stern lecture, only half listening as he described his day. She could tell Ty had gone all out tonight, the car sparkled and he looked very handsome. He'd booked them into *The Hot Spot* in Tidal Falls. He deserved her complete attention, and she was determined he would get it.

Pushing aside all Nick related thoughts, she was pleased when Ty hopped out, strode around front of the vehicle and opened her door for her. Manners, check. He guided her over the uneven cobblestones to glass entry doors, intricately etched with a harvest moon. Gesturing for her to enter, he spoke briefly with the maître d' before they were led to a secluded, candlelit table. Both men waited until she seated herself, the headwaiter then passing them menus and an extensive wine list.

After first deferring to her, Ty chose a Pinot Noir and they perused the exquisite menu choices as "Night and Day" by the great Ella Fitzgerald played from the nearby dance floor. She gazed after an elderly couple moving slowly around the room, eyes only for each other, and Sara's chest swelled as tears threatened to fall. Their love was almost tangible, wrapping them in protective layers of happiness and security. It was beautiful. She reluctantly turned back to the table only to find Ty watching her, a speculative look on his face.

"Nice couple. Kind of reminds me of my parents. They're always doing stuff like that, dancing around the kitchen, or sitting together on the couch, holding hands and hugging. It's kinda cute."

"You're lucky to grow up in a nice family, Ty. I think Tess mentioned you have a couple of sisters and a brother?"

"Yep, I do. All older and married off with kids now. I remember when we were youngsters though, whenever they wanted to play dress-up they'd rope me in—usually to play the baby." His smile said he hadn't really minded all that much. "But you're right; I wouldn't change a single day of my child-hood. How about you, is there some family out there some-where? I assume you and your husband are divorced?"

Sara looked down at the thick menu. "I have Jessica. She is my family." In the uncomfortable silence that fell over their table, she could hear the intimate murmurs of the other guests over the clink of fine crystal.

Ty changed the subject. "What looks good?" Pointing to the richly embossed paper she'd been staring at without actually reading, he laughed. "I have to confess, I've never heard of half of this stuff."

Relieved he'd let the subject of her marriage drop, Sara smiled as she tried to guess what some of the items were. "Me neither. I think I'll stick with a steak, though the Coq au Vin looks interesting. It's a beautiful restaurant Ty, thank you for inviting me."

Their server reappeared, and after placing their orders, Ty stood and held his hand out to her. "Dance with me, Sara?"

She placed her hand in his and as he led her out onto the dance floor "Home" by her favorite artist, Michael Buble, began to play. As they twirled around the room, she had to admit Ty knew what he was doing in the romance department. This should have been the perfect date. If only she could get a certain blue-eyed devil off her mind. Why had he shown up at her door tonight? She'd heard nothing from him for two surprisingly long days. Not that she cared where he'd been—or with whom.

Sure, you don't.

Ty's voice near her ear startled her. "Are you having a good time?"

Flushing, Sara answered with more enthusiasm than the question warranted. "Oh yes, I am. It's been a long time since I've been out dancing; you're very good by the way."

"Sisters, remember? They always dragged me along to dance classes with them. Guess I picked it up there. I do a mean two-step too," he joked, pretending to dip her.

"Oh no, Mr. Garrett, this is my limit." She giggled, enjoying herself more than she'd expected.

"Okay." He laughed. "But you're missing out on some serious fun."

They'd gone a couple more trips around the small area, weaving between the other couples when she noticed something had caught his attention behind her. "What's wrong? Someone you know?"

"Are you sure there's nothing between you and that Nick guy?"

"Of course I'm sure. Why do you ask?"

"Because he's here, and if looks could kill I'd be a pile of ash by now," he said as he twirled her around for a look.

Her heart gave a kick in her chest, and she forgot to breathe as she searched the room for him. "Why in the world would he have followed us here?"

"Oh, I think I can guess," Ty said dryly. "He's the big ugly one, over by the bar."

Sure enough, it was Nick all right. And he wasn't even pretending he was there for any other reason. Full of attitude, arms resting behind him on the bar, he was staring straight at her. Looking at his grim visage Sara should probably have been worried. Instead, excitement coursed through her veins. He'd followed her.

Did it mean he was jealous? She dropped a hand to her fluttering tummy, uncomfortably aware of how close Ty held her.

He sighed against her warm cheek, before releasing her and stepping away. "You know it's kind of providential he's here. I was going to have to cut this short anyway. I'd forgotten about an important appointment I have to keep. Unavoidable, I'm afraid. Maybe if I asked, he could give you a lift home?"

Distressed that he thought he needed to make excuses, she refused. "No, Ty, if you need to leave, I'll go with you. It's fine."

"Really, I insist. Stay and enjoy the meal. It's the least I can do for standing you up." He led her back to their table, and bending down, kissed her full on the mouth. "I had a good time tonight, Sara." He gave her a smile laced with regret before ambling across the dance floor to Nick.

Leaving her wondering what had just happened.

———

NICK WAS MORE than ready for pretty boy as he made his way across the dance floor after taking Sara back to their secluded little tête-á-tête table. It had been all he could do to remain in his seat as the asshole dipped and dallied with her out on the floor.

Garrett fired the first word as he came into range. "Listen, I don't know what you're doing here, but if you ever hurt that lady over there, you'll answer to me, got it? I must be out of my mind, but I'm going to leave now. The door's open. Do. Not. Screw. It. Up." Sketching a quick salute across the dining room, Ty turned and left the restaurant.

A little stunned that he was getting another chance, and calling himself all kinds of a jerk, Nick made his way over to the woman who had him tied up in knots. He had no excuse. He'd been compelled to follow them. Seeing them on the dance floor, the perfect couple, had about killed him, but he couldn't have stayed home tonight. Whether Sara wanted to admit it or not, there was something special between them, something he wasn't willing to walk away from.

The moron was lucky he'd been able to walk out of the building after kissing her like that. Nick had been ready to bust some kneecaps for a few minutes there. Seating himself awkwardly at their cozy little table, he was still working out how to explain breaking up their date when Sara beat him to it.

"Nick, what are you doing here?"

Yeah, Nick, what *are* you doing here?

He needed his head examined. He had no business showing up here tonight and ruining her date. He'd tried to go home after they left together in that POS, make himself supper and find something to watch on the boob tube. Nothing worked, she stayed front and center in his mind. Finally he'd given up and decided to take a little drive, blow off some steam. Yeah sure, that worked well. Next thing he knew he was parked in the La Lune parking lot, watching fancy dressed couples making their way inside.

Since he was here anyway, he might as well go in for a beer, right? The place was nice, he had to admit. Dining patrons encircled a gleaming hardwood dance floor. Soft lighting high-lighted an elderly couple drifting to an old-time melody. No sign of Sara yet, so he made his way over to a polished mahogany bar, found a seat, and ordered up a drink from a cute little barmaid. Turning to face the room, he rested his arms on the counter and scanned the room until he found them.

Scowling, he noticed studdly had reserved them a private little table for two with candlelight and wine. He grabbed his beer and took a long pull, annoyed with the little green monster riding his last nerve. The feeling intensified tenfold when the guy got up and invited her to dance.

They looked good together. She moved with grace, head tipped up smiling at her partner. The soft lighting caught in her hair, turning it to burnished gold. Beautiful. He watched as the bastard dipped her and she came up laughing like a schoolgirl, and something twisted inside, his jaw clenching on the pain.

"You okay there, buddy?"

The bartender. Shit. He needed to get out of here.

"Yeah, I'm good. Be out of your way in a minute."

"No problem. Take your time."

That's what got him into this mess in the first place. He'd been so busy trying to deny what he felt that he'd missed what was right before his eyes. Fuck.

He almost growled when the asshole led her back to their

table and kissed her. Slugging back the rest of his beer he set it on the counter, when he wanted nothing more than to wing it across the room. Throwing some cash down, he was about to leave when he saw Garrett cutting across the dance floor, headed his way.

And now here he was, sitting like a tongue-tied idiot while the woman of his dreams waited for an explanation. "I was restless, thought I'd come check out what all the hype was about."

"Really? You thought you needed to see how popular La Lune is? Tonight?" Sarcasm laced the words.

Well, at least she hadn't thrown her glass of wine in his face as soon as he sat down. That was promising. "You're right, I followed you. I guess I just wanted to make sure your 'date' behaved himself." No way was he admitting how lost he'd felt when she'd driven away with the guy.

"He was the perfect gentleman, you didn't need to worry," she said, gazing across at him with undeserved warmth, her eyes reflecting the candle's glow. "Besides, I can take care of myself, Nick. I have for a long time now."

"I know you can, but maybe you shouldn't have to." He decided to switch topics before he totally ruined the night for her. "What were you planning if he tried anything, stepping on his foot with those killer shoes you're wearing?" He smiled to show her he was teasing.

"That's not what I meant and you know it." The sound of her laughter popped in his chest like bubbles of champagne. "But thank you for watching my back, I appreciate it."

"My pleasure, and your welcome. Now what's for dinner?" He sat back and savored the moment. The music, candlelight, wine, and the beautiful woman sitting across from him.

Sara chuckled, her eyes still sparkling with mirth. "Your incorrigible. I feel terrible. Ty went to a lot of trouble for tonight."

He loved her laugh. Whole-hearted and husky, it slid its way down his spine like warm syrup. The candlelight high-lighted her lovely heart-shaped face and those honey-colored eyes. Her hair was twisted up in a complicated knot and a few loose tendrils had fallen out to caress the side of her neck. Giving in to the temptation, he stretched out and gently tucked the silky strands behind her ear, his pulse rioting when she leaned in to his touch like a purring cat.

"What are we doing, Nick?" The soft yearning in her voice made his chest tighten even as his thighs hardened in reaction. Good question, what *were* they doing?

He tugged the bottom of her ear before reluctantly letting go, satisfied as a visible shudder coursed through her. He sat back and contemplated whether to give the easy answer or an honest one. "I suppose we're here to enjoy this fabulous meal."

Easy, it is.

The server arrived with impeccable timing. "Brought together by the powers that be, I think a toast to good old Ty is in order, don't you?"

She gazed wordlessly at him for a long moment. Disappointment turned her mouth down at the corners and wiped some of the sparkle from her eyes. He was about to throw caution to the wind and admit how much he wanted to be there with her when she straightened her spine and tossed her head before replying, "You're right. A toast then, to a perfect meal."

She lifted her glass to touch his with a faint ting before taking a sip of the fruity tasting wine. "This is nice. A relaxing evening with a friend, no expectations."

Which one of them was she trying to convince? She could call what they had together friendship all she wanted, but it wasn't going to change a damn thing. Nick wanted her, and he was pretty sure she wanted him back.

He wanted to tell her about his past. He just didn't want to bring it up right now. Not with her looking like a dream come true in the softly flickering light. Tomorrow. He'd tell her tomorrow, for sure.

"Nick, tell me something about you I don't know."

Startled at how close their thoughts coincided, he kept it light, wanting to see that sparkle again, "Well let's see now...I shave in the shower. Kill two birds with one stone, right? And I abhor broccoli, actually anything green. If we were meant to eat green shit, we would be walking on four legs, that's my theory."

"Nick!" She chuckled, her lips tilting up so that her cheeks rounded out like two plump apples, and her eyes crinkled at the corners. "Don't tell Jess that, vegetables are very good for you. Makes a body strong, you know." Then, as her gaze wandered over him just long enough to make him sweat, "Okay, maybe not everyone needs them." She admitted, admiration glinting from her glorious eyes. "And what you do in the shower is your business. I was talking about something from your past. Do you have any brothers or sisters? Are your parents still alive? Have you ever been in love?"

It was easy to think they were two people out on a date, enjoying each other's company with no obstacles between them. He only wished that were true. "You should be a reporter. Okay seriously, I thought I was in love—once. It never worked out." His hands fidgeted with the wine glass. "No brothers or sisters. My old man ran off years ago, no loss there. And my mom lives in a senior's condo in Florida. She loves it; they have weekly Bingo nights, craft nights, singles nights. She never has time to get bored, it's good for her."

Wanting a chance to hold her close, he stood. "I'm not nearly as smooth as Romeo there was, but give me a chance and I'll try not to step on your toes?" He hadn't danced in years, and hoped like hell the music would be slow.

Hesitating only long enough to stop his heart, she smiled, and grabbing onto his hand, pulled him out to the floor as a great old song his mom loved, "Till We Meet Again", by Doris Day began to play.

She settled his arm securely around her waist and holding his other hand close between them, rocked from side to side, doing interesting things to his equilibrium.

"Listen for a minute. Do you hear that?" She hummed along with the melody, her sweet voice stroking him from the inside out. "That's what we're going to move to." She nodded towards an older couple he'd noticed her watching earlier. "Like them."

After a somewhat rough start, Nick began to focus on more important things than where to set his feet. Her body tucked up close to his, so close he could smell the citrusy fragrance of her shampoo as her hair tickled his chin, a couple of strands catching in his stubble. Her bare back, soft and silky as he ran his fingers up and down the gentle curvature of her spine. His other hand resting in heaven, enveloped between the pillowy softness of her breasts. It was all he could do to concentrate on where his feet were supposed to be. Wow, if he'd known dancing could be like this, he might have taken it up sooner.

"You're doing great. Not so hard, is it? I just love these old songs; they lend themselves to rhythm."

Nick could think of a few other rhythmical moves he'd love to be practicing right now. "Yeah, it's not so bad. Thanks, Teach."

SARA WAS FLOATING, safe and secure, tucked in close to Nick's warm body. One hand rested on his broad shoulder. The other was wrapped securely inside of his, resting between her breasts. They were so sensitized by the movement of their bodies, she needed him to do something. Anything.

Looking up, she became entrapped within the hooded darkness of his eyes. He wanted her. She knew it by the tension in his shoulders, and the hard brush of his body as it rubbed against hers.

It'd been almost two years since she'd lain with a man. On that nightmarish day, she'd had no chance at all against Tom's anger. It was that, as much as the actual act, which had frightened her the most. And maybe he'd felt guilty for what he'd done to her. She didn't know, or care, but was grateful when he moved out of their rooms and never bothered her again.

One of the first things Sara bought upon their escape was

pepper spray, and she made sure there were hard case flash-lights in both her car and every room of their house. She'd learned they were an effective way to fight off an attacker, at least long enough to escape.

The dance had ended. Angry that she'd let stupid thoughts of the past waste the precious moments, she returned to their table to pick up her purse. "I'm tired, Nick. Mind if we go home now?" The evening was destroyed. Once again, Tom had managed to assert his mastery of her. Would she never be free of him?

She tried to smile as he searched her eyes. "Sure honey, just let me pick up the check. Why don't you go wait for me by the doors?"

Off-balanced and emotional, she moved to stand by the entry. Gazing through the moon etched glass into the starlit night, she realized either she could spend the rest of her life jumping at shadows or she could take this chance at a new beginning.

She knew which one she wanted to choose.

Nick's big body joined hers, reflected in the glass as if the two of them were an actual couple. Nick, so tall and dark, standing protectively behind her smaller, slighter form left her feeling both sheltered and loved.

She chose to live.

He guided her to the parking lot where his big four-by-four truck should have looked out of place among all the fancy imports. Instead, it looked safe and trustworthy, much like the man who owned it.

Opening the passenger door for her, he grimaced at the left

over takeout bags and coffee cups. "This truck's not really meant for classy dressed ladies. Hold on while I make some room."

Watching as he collected the empty coffee cups and chocolate wrappers, carrying them to a nearby garbage can before striding back to move some power tools into the back of the pickup, Sara couldn't help but note the differences between her ex-husband and Nick.

Tom always had to surround himself with the best of the best. From the cars he drove, to the meals at upscale restaurants and expensive suits he wore. Nick, on the other hand, was comfortable in his own skin, wearing jeans and button down shirts as if they were of the finest cloth.

"Okay, ready, but there's no way you're going to climb up there in that dress. I'll give you a boost up." He dropped his arm behind her knees, and wrapping the other around her waist, easily picked her up.

Breathless at the contained strength in those hard arms, she grasped Nick around the neck, bringing their lips millimeters apart.

"I would cut off my own arm before I ever hurt you. I hope you realize that." He said, the eyes holding hers, a crystalline blue.

She sighed, not surprised at how their thoughts had overlapped. "I do know. It's..."

"What? Talk to me sweetheart."

She knew he sensed something stood between them from her past. If they were going to move forward, she would have to trust him with the truth. Soon.

"Take me home, Nick." Wanting to forget, she bridged the

gap between her lips and his. The shock of his warm, perfect mouth on hers made her gasp, and her hands tightened their hold against his neck.

A deep, hungry groan was her only warning before he took control, kissing them both half senseless. A muffled cough and a giggle nearby broke them apart and it was hard to say which one of them looked sorrier.

Choking out a giggle, she said, "Wow, you're pretty good at that." She smiled into his eyes. "Maybe you'd better, um...set me down now?"

"Hmm? Oh, yeah. I guess we should probably go." As he settled her carefully into his pick-up, her hand caressed the side of his face down to the pulse she could see pounding in his neck.

"I want to go home, Nick. With you."

CHAPTER EIGHT

Gripping the steering wheel, Nick stole sideways glances at Sara as she sat biting her nails and gazing out the passenger window. As far as he was concerned, they couldn't arrive at his place quick enough, but he had a feeling she was second-guessing her decision.

He needed to get himself under control. Even to his own ears his breathing sounded like a freight train. For crying out loud, he wasn't some callow teenager looking to get lucky here. He'd better get his shit together. She was different, special to him. Whatever happened between them, he wanted her to know she would be safe with him—he'd never hurt her.

"Nick I hope you..." Her voice drifted across the dark cab.

"Sara, are you...?" They looked at each other and laughed, releasing some of the growing tension. This was becoming a habit.

"You first, this time." She smiled.

"I was just going to ask if you're sure, about you know—this. You and me? I don't want there to be regrets between us, so if you've changed your mind, I'm fine with that. Well maybe not, but I'll live," he teased, hoping to ease her mind a little.

"Wow, Nick, that's pretty noble of you." She giggled at his pained expression. "I'm kidding, of course I'm ready, or I wouldn't have made the offer. I just wanted to make sure this meant more to you than a simple fling. Because, it does to me. Mean something, that is. I haven't done this sort of thing before."

He pulled to a stop in the driveway of his rental and threw the truck into park, cutting the engine. Listening to her hesitant little speech had him almost reaching for her right there. Instead, he shot her a quick glance before hopping out to stride around and open her door.

"Honey, I can guarantee there isn't anything simple about this. Sometime soon, we're going to have to be open with each other. There are things about me I want you to know. And I think it would do you a world of good to get whatever is bothering you off your chest. If there's going to be something between us, I think we should talk."

His attention zeroed in on her pearly white teeth chewing her luscious bottom lip and he groaned under his breath. Leaning in, he gently kissed it better. Pulling her towards him, he let her slide deliberately slow down the length of his body. Letting out an inaudible growl at the soft warmth of her against his hardness, he nibbled along her smooth jawline up to her ear, breathing in the essence of sunshine and roses that was so much a part of her. Giving a little bite to the lobe, he smiled against her throat as she moaned and dropped her head back to give him access. He tucked back a stubborn strand of silky hair, before cupping her warm cheek. "I've dreamt of this, you know. Of us being together like this. You're so damn beautiful. But—I don't think we should rush into something you might regret, so how about we go inside and I'll make a nice hot cup of tea. We'll take things slow and see where we end up, okay?"

The gratitude swimming in the golden depths of her upward glance told him more than words ever could. "That sounds perfect. I guess you noticed how nervous I am."

"Don't be, honey. We won't do anything you aren't ready to do." He stroked a finger down her cheek, enjoying the feel of its velvety smoothness.

"What if I want it all, Nick? What then?" she murmured into his chest, her innocent directness almost unmanning him right there.

"Well, then I'll die a very happy man," he only half bantered. Jesus, he wanted this woman. More than he could remember ever wanting another.

Only when, and if she's ready. Don't rush her.

He led her through the back door, smiling as she looked around, glad for once the Navy had drummed cleanliness into him. He lit his stove and placed the kettle on to boil. Searching through the cupboard he found a bag of Oreo cookies, and a couple of delicate looking porcelain teacups, and set them on the island counter behind him. Catching her amused expression, he shrugged. "They came with the place, and what's tea without cookies, right?"

She snickered, the sound a sweet chime, and moved to hike

herself up onto one of the wooden bar stools. "You're right, tea is meant for dunking. You know, you're not at all what I expected after our first meeting."

"Yeah, I wasn't too sociable." He grimaced.

"And then you almost decked me."

"Hey now, that was purely accidental." Serious, he reached across the counter and caressed her cheek. "I would never hurt this pretty face." Unbidden, a tear slipped down her face and he cursed under his breath, his careless words leaching the warmth from the room.

"He did, you know. My husband. He did," she whispered, the color fading from her skin, leaving her face pale and almost translucent.

Freezing at the anguish oozing from her voice, he dropped his hand and wrapped her ice cold fingers in his. He was going to kill the son-of-a-bitch. He swore roughly, aloud this time. Keeping calm was the hardest thing Nick had ever done, but Sara needed comfort right now, not more violence.

Reaching behind, he turned off the stove, and then, keeping her hand in his, circled the island to her side. "Come on honey, let's sit in the living room and get this off your chest." Tugging her up gently, he led Sara down the hall into the semi-darkened room. Sitting in a big, leather rocking chair he pulled her down onto his lap, and turned her so her head rested on his shoulder and her legs stretched out over the side.

He rubbed up and down her ribcage trying to infuse some of his warmth into her chilled skin. His chin rested on the top of her head. For a while, there was only the squeak of his old chair and the tick of the clock in the hallway, hypnotizing them both as it slowly counted the minutes.

When she began to speak her tone was careful, controlled. "The night I met Tom, I'd recently lost my foster father. I was lonely, he was handsome and charming, and said all the right things. Before I knew it, he'd swept me off my feet. And when he told me we should get married, I stupidly believed he loved me." She snorted, "More fool me."

Gazing up at him with despair, she continued, "I thought things were good between us, and they were. Until I found out I was pregnant. I couldn't wait to tell Tom. I thought he'd be thrilled with the news. Instead, he accused me of trapping him into fatherhood and ordered me to have an abortion." Her voice hitched on the words, and Nick gave her a little squeeze of reassurance, his blood boiling at the disappointment she must have felt. Guilt plagued him. He wondered if his wife had thought the same of him with his seeming indifference.

"After that he changed. Became oppressive. Domineering. I couldn't do anything without him. He cut me off from my friends, told me I needed to meet a better class of people. He even kept me from my studio, saying I needed to quit wasting time with my painting. I guess I should have known then, but we were married. I thought we could work it out. When Jessica was born, he insisted on hiring a full-time nanny, even though I begged him not to. He made sure I hardly ever saw my own child."

Nick's jaw clenched, furious at what she must have endured. It sounded as though she'd married Jekyll and ended up with Hyde. He nuzzled her forehead. "Shh, baby, it's okay. It's over now, I've got you." He wished there was something more he could do, but knew she needed to get this out before she could move forward in her life.

"Fiona, my friend who owns the gallery I had a showing with, called and somehow managed to get through. She asked if I'd like to go shopping, a girl's day out. The nanny had Jessica, Tom was out somewhere on business, and I was lonely, so I jumped at it. We had so much fun, gossiping and laughing like school friends. We stopped for a late lunch downtown and she tried to talk me into another showing, I didn't want to admit how unlikely that would be, so instead I told her how busy we'd been getting the campaign ready. Tom planned to run for Governor in the next election. Of course, then she wanted to hear all about our 'exciting' lives. What a joke. Anyway, it was later than expected by the time I returned home." Her head dropped back to his shoulder, as if too heavy for her neck to bear.

Her voice when she continued, was so low Nick had to strain to hear it. "Tom went psychotic, screaming and swearing I'd been with another man. I tried to explain, but he wouldn't listen. I decided to give him time to calm down and told him I was going to lie down for a while. But he followed me, and even though I tried to stop him, he—he hurt me." Tears were coursing down her face now and her whole body shook. "He was my husband and he hurt me. How could he do that? How?" Sobs wracked her body, and she buried her face into Nick's neck.

His blood boiled even as his soul cried with helplessness. Pulling her closer, he wished to God that he could take her pain upon himself. It'd been hard enough watching his mother go through this kind of shit for years when he'd been too young to help her, but with Sara, it was torture.

After a while, her sobs slowed down to hiccups. "Af...after that day Tom never touched me again. I think he knew it was over for us, but he still refused to let me go. Said he needed me, and I could never leave him. He even kept Jessica away to make sure I stayed." Her fingers played distractedly with the buttons of his shirt.

"One night I overheard him on the phone in his office. It proved what I'd already suspected. He'd been aiding his clients dealing in drugs and gunrunning for years. I didn't know who to trust. I didn't feel I could take a chance on calling the police. My husband has a lot of important friends." She stopped for a moment, wiped her eyes with impatient fingers.

"Then he prosecuted, and won, a high profile murder case. He said it was his ticket into the governor's chair, and hosted a celebration dinner party. I took the opportunity to sneak away and copy the files I knew he had hidden on his computer. Then I grabbed my little girl, and ran. Fiona met up with us, gave me a vehicle and enough money to get by with. I owe her so much." She lifted red-rimmed, weary eyes to his, her voice raspy, "I don't know what I was thinking. I only took the files as leverage. In case he tried to make us go back with him. I just wanted him to leave us alone. But now, with what I know, he never will."

Needing to ease the fear and pain he could see in her tear-swollen eyes, Nick tenderly kissed first one lid, and then the other closed. "Hush now, rest. We'll figure something out in the morning. You're not alone in this anymore. Okay, Sara? Do you hear me? You're not alone."

He sipped at the tears running down her cheeks, and catching at the corner of her mouth. She, in turn, wound her arms around his neck, drawing him down, even as he would have eased away.

"Please, Nick. For one night, help me to forget. Just kiss me."

He knew she was defenseless right now and didn't want to take advantage of that, but sweet heaven, he wanted her. More even than the sex, he wanted to ease her pain, erase what had happened to her. But since that could not be—he at least wanted to prove to her that all men were not like that asshole.

Her moist lips touched his in a tentative invitation he was more than willing to accept. Tasting her bottom lip, he licked into her mouth before tangling his tongue with hers. God, she was so responsive. Nick could feel her softening for him even as she kept his mouth sealed to hers. Her seductive hands combed through his hair, massaging his scalp, until he couldn't contain a hungry groan, whispering, "Oh baby, you taste so sweet. I want to savor all of you, every honeyed inch."

His words seemed to release something almost desperate within her. She slid her hand down his chest, over his pounding heart, to the bottom of his shirt, slipping under to touch his overheated skin. Her teeth nipped at his neck as her other hand joined the party working to get his shirt off. As Nick lifted his arms to toss it aside, she licked and kissed her way to his rigid nipple, and he tensed as her lips closed over his skin.

He was in danger of embarrassing himself if he didn't slow this down a little. Hands trembling, he cupped the side of her face, lifting it to his own. "My turn," he whispered, as he closed his mouth over hers. At the same time his fingers were doing the walking, skimming up the inside of one silken thigh until his thumb could rub her sex through her lacy panties. Sweet hell, she was already wet, ready for him. He groaned and eased aside the leg, his fingers flicking and teasing her honeyed softness, even as his tongue copied the motion above. Sara's sexy little cries showing he was on the right track.

He slid his lips from the heat of her too tempting mouth, and stopped to lavish attention on her silky neck. She moaned and dropped her head back to give him more access as he worked his way down to feast on her luscious breasts. Pushing aside the neckline of her slay-me-now dress, he paused to suck in a hard breath at her beauty in that moment, "Sara."

His shaking fingers moved to caress one hardened nipple as his mouth latched on to its twin, suckling softly at first, and then with more force. She tasted like candy, sweet and succulent.

"Please, Nick, I need you." Want filled her husky voice, turning him inside out. She ran her hand up the hard length of his arousal, stroking upward from the base to his head through his jeans, and his whole body followed as if on strings.

Anxious now, his hand joined with hers, fumbling to get his zipper down. He wanted to howl with the restraints he was placing on his body. He'd wanted her to have control, lead the way, but wasn't sure how much longer he could hold back.

"Easy baby, we'll get there." The very last thing he wanted to do was freak her out because he couldn't control himself.

He helped her tug down her panties, and then turned her to face him, her legs straddling the outside of his. The sight of his rough jeans against the insides of her pale thighs invoked memories of their first kiss, something he wouldn't soon forget. His hands slid from her slim waist, down over her hips to her shapely ass. He slid his fingertips down her crease to her sex and up again, spreading her open for his touch. Fierce pleasure filled him at the rough pitch of her breathing, showing her desire. For him.

Sara again took his length in hand, stroking him with more enthusiasm than experience. Hissing, he lifted his hip and growled, "In my pocket, my wallet, I think I have a condom."

Her slim fingers digging in his pocket had him shuddering and cursing under his breath as her breasts swayed forward brushing against his chest. Eyes dark with want she lifted the wrapper to her mouth, licked her lips and grabbed a corner with shiny white teeth, ripping one end open. She tried to slide the rubber over his cock, but only succeeded in driving him mad without accomplishing much.

He placed his hand over hers, stifling a throaty groan and stared into her glowing face. And just like that Nick found himself ass-over-teakettle in love. He couldn't wait any longer. They'd take it slower next time. Right now, he had to feel her around him before he exploded. He made short work of getting the condom on, then lifted her up. Slowly she slid down the length his cock, and his eyes practically crossed at the pulsating warmth and tightness of her.

She'd captivated him. And as she took over from him, sliding up and down, her breasts swaying, her head thrown back, her hair falling out of their pins, she looked like a warrior and he was more than happy to call himself her prisoner.

She was so beautifully responsive, hot and inviting. As she brought them close to completion, Nick ran his palms along her hips. His fingers stretching between to thumb her center, caused her to contract around him. And then it was he throwing back his head shouting as he came at the same time she cried out her release.

———————

SARA CLUNG to him as she trembled with the aftershocks, sliding slowly back down to earth after the most amazing sex of her life. She wasn't sure what to say or do now. What was Nick thinking? What in the world was she thinking? Her life was way too complicated already—and now this. She appreciated Nick wanted to help, but worried about Tom. Bad enough that Fiona knew, and was in danger because of them. He would kill Nick for sure, and she couldn't bear that.

Reluctantly levering herself up and away from his hard body, she worked on straightening her clothes, looking everywhere except at him. After a futile search for her undies she pulled her messed hair back and into a rough twist, and grabbed up her handbag. Backing towards the door, anxious now to escape, she glanced at Nick as he lounged in the chair watching her through narrowed eyes.

"I'm going to get out of your hair, and um...walk home, so

don't get up okay?" He looked like sex on a stick. She wanted to stay, but knew she had to leave.

He put his hands on the arms of his chair and seemed about to say something so Sara turned and hurried out, racing across the street to her own little haven. Closing the door, she slid to the floor, right there in the entry, covering her face with her hands.

She couldn't imagine what he thought of her running out like that. They should have been spending a passion-filled night together. Instead, she'd messed up by telling him her whole sad story. Nick wasn't the type to let it go. And while she cherished the fact that he wanted to protect Jessica and her, she was more interested in keeping him alive.

Nick didn't know what Tom was capable of, but she did. All too well.

Thoughts of when she'd found out about her husband's illegal activities flashed through her mind. After he'd forced himself on her, Tom had taken to treating her like the dirt under his expensive shoes. Her new 'job' as he called it, was to bring him his evening meal in his office, where he spent most of his time when at the house. On that night, as Sara reached the half open door, she heard Tom talking angrily to someone on the other side.

"You better not be threatening me, Ramos. I could make your life very difficult. I know everything there is to know about you, even where you hide that pretty wife of yours. And your children, you have very cute little kids, my friend. I would hate to see anything happen to them, Si? Now you make sure everything is prepared on your end and I'll handle the rest. Don't

forget who's running this little show, or you won't like the consequences. The Phoenix plays for keeps."

Frightened, Sara had turned, wanting nothing more than to
run away to her room and hide, but the dishes rattled, alerting
him to her arrival. Peeking around the door, she'd seen Tom
slam down his cell and type furiously on his keypad.

Her hands sweaty and with a pounding heart, Sara had
entered with the tray of food.

At the clatter, Tom glared up at her and snarled, "Well, if it
isn't my mouse of a wife, coming to feed me. Bring it here,
woman, before you drop the damn thing." With a snap of the
wrist he shut down his computer from her curious gaze.

Nervous and scared, she'd hurried to his side. Just as she
went to set the tray down in front of him, he'd lashed out, grabbing her wrist in a painful grip, and pulling her down to the
floor in front of him, the dishes crashing to the carpet.

"What did you hear? How long were you standing there
snooping around in things that are none of your goddamned
business?" The tone of his voice had climbed with each word,
until by the end he was screaming, spittle forming on the corner
of his mouth.

Crying out as he grabbed onto her hair and gave it a vicious
tug, forcing her head back, she'd pleaded, "I didn't hear
anything! I swear. Please, Tom, you're hurting me."

He'd shoved her and stared derisively as she fell backward
and scrambled away from him. "You're such a child, what did I
ever see in you? Go. And you'd better keep quiet about this
night, or the next time I might not be as nice. Get out of here.
And close the fucking door."

The coolness of the floor anchored her and brought her back to her hallway. Shivers racked her body with remembered terror of that night, one of many she had endured from her *loving* husband. She didn't know what her next move would be, only that it couldn't involve Nick.

CHAPTER NINE

Nick fell back into his chair with a grunt as Sara went racing out the door as if her hair were on fire. That was new. Usually he was the one looking for excuses to leave after doing the deed. He understood she probably needed some time alone to process everything that had happened tonight, not the least of which they'd had sex. S.E.X. A small word to encompass a life-changing event.

The knot in his stomach, which had been there since she'd shared her story, tightened painfully. What Sara had gone through mixed with that of his mother all those years ago when he'd been a child and couldn't do much to stop it. He'd failed to protect his mom. He couldn't fail Sara.

Rubbing a weary hand over the scar at his temple he gazed at the shadows dancing on the wall and his mind slipped back to his time overseas. His team, Adam, Jared, Frank, Steve and him, had just finished a brutal thirty-six-hour mission in Iraq. They were overtired, wired out on adrenalin, and looking to blow off some steam. So, they'd gone into town to a local watering hole, and were working hard at getting pie-eyed drunk.

Jared, Frank, and Steve, their invaluable medic, were sitting in on a game of poker. Frank had a nice stack building in front of him, Jared not far behind. Jared, their technician, was a master at electronics. There wasn't anything with wires attached, that he couldn't take apart and put back together again, probably twice as well as it was to begin with. Frank was their leader, SEAL Team Chief, and his solid steadiness when under fire kept the whole team focused and alive. The two of them had been roomies since joining with Uncle Sam, and seemed to know each other's thoughts without a word ever spoken. Which meant the other three sitting at the table, were going to be hurting by night's end, without a doubt.

Adam, Nick's best friend since joining the team, was over in the corner, back to the wall, nursing a beer as his eyes roamed the room, ever watching. His golden boy looks garnered him plenty of attention from the hookers lined up in front of the bar, but he either wasn't interested, or didn't notice them. Most of his attention remained focused on the three Iraqis and an American sharing a pipe in a booth near the back. Nick could barely make them out through the smoky haze.

He kept his back planted to the bar, his gaze on the room, as a leggy brown-haired young woman sidled up to him.

"Hi there, handsome. You look lonely. Care for some company?" She kept her voice warm and welcoming, but her eyes when he glanced at her, spoke something else entirely. There was a world of pain and weariness in those spheres. She set her slender hand onto his forearm, stroking up and down, making it clear what kind of *company* he could have. For a price. How had she ended up in this godforsaken place? She should have been at home, maybe going to college, dating frat boys, not peddling her wares in this hellhole.

Every few seconds, she would send anxious little glances over her shoulder at the men sitting in the corner. Nick could practically taste her desperation.

Much as he wanted to help her, he wasn't interested in sex with a kid. "Well, honey, I can't say as I've ever had a nicer offer, but I'm a little too tuckered out to party. How about I buy you a drink? You can sit and tell me a little bit about yourself, instead."

Gratitude leapt into her eyes. Then, with a frightened look over her shoulder at the back booth, she whispered, "Thank you for your kindness, but I must go now." Head down, she scurried over to the men's table, where the American grabbed her arm and yanked her down to his lap. She tried to shift away, but he reached around and gave her breast a hard squeeze, laughing when she cried out.

Nick started up off his stool in anger, but caught the Chief's brief head shake. He knew the rules, no interference, but shit, something needed done. Sinking back down, he frowned.

This is bullshit.

A sudden commotion at the poker table caught everyone's attention. Jared pushed back and stood, his chair wobbling on its uneven legs. He waved his arms in the air, showing everyone his shitty hand of cards. Next thing you know, he'd reached across the table and pulled Steve out of his seat, accusing him of stacking the deck. Of course, then the Chief had to step in and suggest they calm down before he slammed some heads together. Meanwhile, Adam rose from his chair and strolled over to the guy in the corner. Nick wasn't sure what he said, but after listening for a brief moment, the creep cursed and pushed the girl off his lap to the floor, then dug into his pocket and pulled out a pile of cash, throwing it her way.

Nick grinned as he saw the Chief putting his cell back into his pocket. He must have called it in. If there was one thing the man hated, more even than losing at poker, it was seeing a bully in action. Something to do with his kid brother, Nick had heard through the grapevine.

The American—shit, it was the guy they'd been assigned babysitting duties to—pissed off now, said a few words to the men he'd been sitting with, slid out of the booth, and grey eyes flashing to the girl on the floor still gathering bills, then to Adam, stomped out of the bar. Good riddance, asshole.

Blinking, Nick refocused on his still shadowed walls, dawn's first blush just starting to lighten his blind covered windows, grateful the headaches he used to get with the slow return of his memory had tapered off. For the first couple of months they'd all but crippled him, the pain was so intense. Then as he learned not to force the recollections, to just let them happen, it became easier to bear. That was the first time.

The second time he'd found out while in hospital, his back swathed in bandages, how close he and his new team had come to being toasted. Thanks to Jake, who'd smelled out the bomber, they were alive today. Not everyone had been so lucky. Those were the memories he could have lived without. Seeing a member of his team blown to hell because he'd stopped to help a village child—one who happened to be wearing a bomb—was a nightmare he couldn't escape. Cliff was one of the best. He'd left behind two little girls who'd never get the chance to walk down the isle with their daddy.

Stiff, he rose out of the chair he'd ended up spending the night in, and wandered over to the window facing Sara's house. His still undone jeans hung low on his hips, reminding him of last night's pleasure.

He didn't regret it. He couldn't. But he wondered what thoughts had been going through her mind, as she rushed to get her clothes on, and get out the door. Was she sorry for confiding in him? Or was this about the two of them?

Wishing now they would have waited, he turned away from the darkened house across the street. Moving towards his room, he stepped on something soft and silky, and bending to pick it up, found Sara's panties. She'd been in such a rush she hadn't even grabbed them. They were going to have to talk this out later. He'd give her a little time to rest and then he was going to be at her door, hoping she'd answer it. He threw on a pair of sweats and running shoes and headed out into the brisk morning, Jake by his side.

SARA WOKE to the rich aroma of fresh coffee and—was that cinnamon? Rising, she threw on her robe over her bare skin, trying not to notice the still faint marks on her hips made from Nick's fingers holding her in place last night. Last night. If not for those prints and her borrowed dress resting over the end of the bed, she could almost believe she'd dreamt the whole thing.

She'd enjoyed herself with Ty. He'd been sweet, and fun. But then Nick had shown up, like some kind of misplaced white knight come to save the day. Sara had never thought of dancing as a type of foreplay, until last night. Even though Nick had not been the most skilled of partners, he'd swept her away.

Then later, confiding in him about everything—maybe she should have been embarrassed for crying all over his shoulder like that, but instead all she could feel was relief. It'd been bottled up inside, waiting for too long to explode. There had been no time for self-pity. She'd been too busy trying to stay ahead of Tom and his men.

Nick inspired feelings in her she'd never felt before. Even though he aggravated and frustrated her, he had also shown her he could be patient, kind and giving.

The lovemaking had been transcending. Even now, hours later, thoughts of it sent goose bumps shimmying up and down her spine. Sara had always played a passive role in sex. Tom preferred it that way. But with Nick, she had found herself being the aggressor, and she liked the sense of control it gave her.

He'd given her back her self-esteem, and she loved him for it. There, she'd admitted it. She loved him. She'd been sure Tom had killed her ability to care about any other man. Then Nick came into her life and blew that right out of the water. Sitting on the edge of the bed before she fell down, Sara clasped her arms around herself and squeezed.

I'm in love.

Nick was everything that Tom could never be. Honorable, honest, trustworthy. Caring, kind and sexy. No doubt about that. Picturing him sprawled in that rocker last night with his big body sated, lips swollen, shirt off and jeans undone had her warming up all over again. Wanting to apologize for her abrupt departure, which she admitted now had been emotional overload, Sara left her room and headed down the hall to the kitchen, wondering how he'd gotten in.

When she entered the room, instead of a tall, handsome handyman, she found it taken over by her friends, Grace and Tess. They were sitting at the table eating huge cinnamon buns, cups of hot coffee steaming away. That made more sense, if she would have been thinking clearly. Nick couldn't have gotten in without a key.

"About time you climbed out of there, missy. Or maybe there's a reason you'd like to share with your good friends, about why you slept in for so long?" Grace teased.

Sara couldn't help the blush that stole over her cheeks, or the hint of a smile that ghosted across her lips. "Hush you two, Jess will hear you. Where is she anyway?"

"She's fine, don't worry your pretty little head. She's out back playing ball with the dog and a certain blue-eyed hottie we all know and love," Tess sighed. "I heard a little rumor that things got interesting at La Lune last night. Come on girl, spill."

Floating over to the coffee machine, Sara poured herself a cup, staring through the window as Jess and Nick played toss. Nick looked as if he had just returned from another run, in sweats that hung low on his lean hips and a sweat-soaked shirt that lovingly hugged his abs. Jess was laughing at something he'd said, as they watched Jake chasing his tail a few feet away. Her heart swelling, Sara turned back to her friends, catching them grinning at her knowingly.

"You have it bad, don't you, baby girl?"

"What in the world are you talking about, Grace Martin? It was a first date, and Ty was a true gentleman."

"Oh, I'm sure my nephew was," Tess replied. "His momma done raised him right. But we're more interested in what happened *after* Ty was called away. My yogi happened to be there last night and saw the whole thing. She said it was the hottest thing since *The Notebook*. Details, we want all the juicy details."

Sara wasn't sure whether to be more embarrassed, or annoyed that her personal life was gossip central this morning. "So, should I take out an ad in the paper? Dumped woman catches ride home with handsome escort. Kind of catchy, don't you agree?"

"Oh, come on now, honey. You know we care about you, and want to see you happy, that's all. We're a couple of nosey old ladies, trying to live vicariously." Grace apologized.

"Hey, watch who you call old, you old coot!" Tess countered.

Crossing the room, Sara leaned in and enfolded each woman in a hug. "Neither one of you are old, you're ageless. I love you both. I'm sorry for jumping down your throats like that. I guess I'm still not used to small town gossiping. In the city no one cares whether you're injured or not, much less who you go out with."

"Well then, I say thank God for small towns. I'd hate to go

through life without my good friends watching out for me," Grace said, reaching out to pat Tess's thin arm.

"It's fine if you don't want to let us in on it, we'll sit here and have a nice cup of coffee with you and then be on our way," Tess agreed.

"So...what's new?"

Sara burst out laughing. They really were priceless.

CHAPTER TEN

F rank Stein was having a very bad day. It had started bright and early in the a.m. with a phone call from Jared. It seems there'd been a miscommunication when security for the Vegas casino he was in informed him they didn't allow card counting.

Who knew?

Ol' Jare thought they would appreciate him showing them their weaknesses. Turned out he was wrong. They sent him on his way, but only after some three on one time. That should have been a clue right there. Normally, casino security companies don't go around roughing up the clientele. Whether they're cheating, or not. The idiot should have considered himself lucky not to be wearing cement shoes and called it a day. Except Jared hadn't appreciated getting the shit beat out of him. As far as he was concerned, he'd only been helping them out, and making a little dough as a reward for his trouble.

Unfortunately, they hadn't seen it in quite the same way,

and that's where the trouble began. Ordinarily, Jared was the easiest going person you could ever meet, but get him pissed, and all bets were off. He'd limped back to his hotel, logged on to his computer, and proceeded to raise a little hell through a back door entry into their mainframe computer system. He triggered the fire alarm system, which in turn set off the sprinkler systems. At the same time, he messed with the slots so they all started shooting out winning tickets, making for some very happy, if a little bit damp, customers.

Metro PD picked him up not long after as a person of interest and now here was Frank, six and a half friggin' hours and two airplanes later, cooling his heels in their dismal little waiting room. Happy, happy.

A few minutes later, a fresh-faced rookie stepped out from behind the counter and nervously approached, "This way, sir, they've gone to get him now."

Frank came to his feet, more than ready to kick Jared's no doubt already bruised ass, just on principle. The rookie's eyes grew round and he jumped back a couple of paces. Gesturing, he turned and started down a narrow hall, and Frank's black mood turned even grimmer. He'd developed a real aversion to closed in places, after spending a good part of his Navy career in gloomy little holes on the lookout for drug runners, bombs, or gun-laden insurgents. He craved wide-open spaces and blue Texas skies these days. Sure enough, the little person in front of him led Frank right into a broom closet, disguised as an interrogation room. Man, Jared was going to owe him big for this.

As the rookie backed out and closed the door, Frank sat in one of three dinky little chairs pulled up to a pitted steel table that had seen far better days. He'd felt the eyes on him ever since he entered the shithole, and turned his full attention to the one way mirror in front of him. Placing both of his big hands face down on the scarred tabletop, he leaned in and mouthed, "Come on, let's get this show on the road."

THE MAN STANDING on the other side of the mirror grinned. Good to see the chief hadn't changed much in the past few years. He still commanded attention with no effort at all.

It could be because the man was built like a brick shithouse, six-five, and somewhere around two hundred eighty pounds, none of it extra either. On the other hand, maybe it was those steel grey eyes of his. If he ever had cause to reprimand his men, usually a slicing look stopped even the most pugnacious of them.

He hated that he had to stay standing there, behind that glass. He wanted nothing more than to go in there and shake the hand of one of the men who had been instrumental in saving his life.

"You can't." The other person standing in the dark room commented. She'd read his thoughts perfectly, which is why they'd made such an unbeatable team for the past five years. "If you go in there now, you risk everything. Don't be an idiot."

She was right. It sucked, but she was right. "Fine, go in there and find out what they know then. I'm telling you they're clean. They're being set up, and you know it."

"I know no such thing. They're your friends, not mine. Besides, people change. You know that better than anyone."

He watched her leave the room, regret a lodestone around his heart. They'd once had a hot and heavy fling, but his own asshole attitude had destroyed that. He was lucky they'd managed to overcome it and remain partners, and more importantly, friends. She hadn't deserved half the crap he'd put her through, but he was more glad than he could say that she had stuck by him through it.

FRANK LEANED BACK as the door opened and a woman walked in. Okay, this was getting interesting. Either she'd made a wrong turn on her way out of lockup, or he was receiving an early Christmas gift. He was hoping for the second, but figured on the first. "I think you made a wrong turn there, sweets, bail paying is down the hall."

He'd been away from women too long if a prostitute was going to turn him on, but shit. He figured she was tall, maybe five eight or so, hard to tell though with those screw-me-now leather boots she was wearing. He traced the zipper he could see running up the inside of her leg, almost to mid-thigh. Licking suddenly dry lips, Frank admired the micro mini skirt in a hot pink and the impressive swell of her full breasts, barely covered by a slinky white top and three different lengths of a chunky beaded necklace that made him literally sweat as they draped across her nipples.

Her hair was raven black, long and straight and matched her

boots for shine. She'd painted the pillowy softness of her lips in the same hot pink of her skirt. When he finally made it up to her eyes, the brilliance and intelligence he could see lurking there let him know what he had already guessed. This was not your average floozy.

"Mr. Stein, my name is Maggie Holt. I have a few questions to ask you while they are working on the release of your friend, it won't take long."

Crossing his arms, Frank contemplated the charming Ms. Holt. What in Sam-hell did Jared have himself into this time? She was obviously no ordinary cop. The way she carried herself spoke of authority and he could tell from her toned body—which was no hardship to look at—that she was in great physical shape. He wasn't sure what the get-up was all about, but he wasn't complaining any. He knew he should have ignored that damn phone this morning.

"Sure, babe, anything you want, gotta say the uniform's a winner by the way. I'll need to see some I.D. though, and maybe a hint of what's going on? Last time I checked card counting wasn't a capital offense. What exactly are you holding my friend in for?"

JUST WHAT SHE NEEDED TODAY, a hard-ass. Maggie had already put in a fifteen-hour day. Her feet were killing her in the boots Stein admired so much. When she'd heard that Jared Martin, a person of interest in their case had been detained by the local PD for the destruction of property and computer hacking at a Casino, she'd called her partner. The two of them beat feet for the precinct, hoping to get a jump on the Feds who were sure to be on the way, before they had everything tied up in acres of red tape.

For almost six years now, they'd been on this case without it going much of anywhere. They needed to catch a break.

Maggie already knew plenty about the good Chief. She was aware that he'd grown up on a Texas cattle ranch, which he now ran himself. She knew he had a younger brother who'd been the victim of abuse over his sexual preferences, and that Frank had beat the living shit out of a group of five boys for it. He'd been in high school at the time. All charges were dropped on the condition Frank join the Navy and get some serious anger management.

Cameron, blaming himself, disappeared from home. No word since, though Frank had soaked money and time into the search. During his stint with the Navy he'd enlisted with the SEALs, and soon climbed ranks to Chief Petty Officer.

Looking him over, Maggie was reminded of a big cat preparing to pounce. She worked with alpha men every day and had never been the type attracted by a man's looks. Something about him drew her though, whether she liked it or not.

His sable hair gleamed under the harsh fluorescent lights, picking up hues of red and gold among the dark strands. He had eyes that looked steely now but she could imagine them a softer, warmer color. Like, maybe during sex. Shifting, she told herself to get a grip.

He could be a possible suspect in an ongoing case. A case that she had put heart and soul into, and wasn't about to mess up due to some unwanted attraction. Her team had been after the men in this crime ring for a long time. This was the closest they'd come to a break and she was determined to get something useful out of this meeting. There was something big in the works. The trouble was, they were getting nowhere with the where and the when. Maybe with the help of Stein and his friend Martin, they might finally get a chance to close these assholes down.

Maggie enjoyed undercover work. The rush of excitement. The opportunity to play a part. The danger. This time though it'd been different. The things she'd seen in the past few months had twisted her insides. Not being able to stop it was heartbreaking. She'd vowed then to take these jerks down, and this man could be the key to everything.

Frank's gaze on her as she reached into her shirt and brought out her badge from its resting place between her breasts made the natural act suddenly feel like something illicit. Her body responded to his male sensuality, and she had to grab the chair on the other side of the table, her legs unaccountably weakened.

Pissed off with her reaction to him, Maggie became all business. "I'm with the DEA, Mr. Stein. My team and I have been working this case for a long while now and unfortunately we are not as close to catching these men as we would like to be. We have reason to believe one or more members from SEAL team five, which is your old team I believe, are, and have been for quite some years, involved in the trafficking of humans, cocaine, heroin, and guns. These are big players we're after, Frank." She hoped to bond—professionally—and read from the report she'd carried into the room.

"For the past several years, there has also been a growing use of, and interest in, synthetic cathinones, which as you may know are stimulants/hallucinogens, sold under the guise of "bath salts" or "plant food." Marketed under names such as "Ivory Wave," "Purple Wave," "Vanilla Sky," or "Bliss," these products are comprised of a class of dangerous substances perceived to mimic cocaine, LSD, MDMA, and/or methamphetamine." She looked up briefly, saw his gaze glued to her face, and hurried on.

"Users have reported impaired perception, reduced motor control, disorientation, extreme paranoia, and violent episodes. The long-term physical and psychological effects of use are unknown but potentially severe. Recently one of my trusted sources tipped us to a huge exchange in the pipes, taking place within the next month.

"The problem is, we don't know where, and we aren't sure who all the players are. Yet. That's where we hope you come in. We need your help, Frank. We can't let this stuff hit the streets, we have to stop it." Pausing to give him time to let it all sink in, Maggie glanced behind her at the dark glass. Their career was on the line here, but more important than that, the lives of all the young people affected by these drugs if they failed.

"Look, you don't know or trust me, I get that. But, I've been led to believe that you were an outstanding leader of your men. All I'm asking is for you to think it over. If there was a bad seed among them, we need to know who it was."

FRANK COULDN'T BELIEVE what he'd just been told, or that they expected him to narc out one of his own men. They'd trusted each other with their lives. They had to. He was pretty damn sure they all knew the color of each other's shorts, they were that close. How could he possibly point a finger at one and say him, it must be him.

There's no friggin' way, that's how.

And if they were thinking of landing this whole thing at Jared's door, as they were leading him to believe by this whole setup, hell no. The two of them had been through fire together. They had a bond that no pretty-eyed fed was going to break, that's for sure.

Frank ignored the indrawn breath from the woman in front of him as he stood. His chair scraped like nails on a chalkboard across the cement floor, as he moved around the table to stare into the glass. He wasn't sure what the hell was going on here, but he had a strong feeling it had to do with whoever was behind that window.

"If we're done here, I'd like to collect my friend and leave. I'm just a simple rancher trying to make a living. My days of working for Uncle Sam are long gone. I haven't seen or heard from any of the men except Jared in a couple of years at least, so there's not much I could tell you even if I would, which I wouldn't. You need to get your pretty butt out pounding the pavement instead of bugging the average guy. You might actually get somewhere that way."

On that parting shot Frank turned and grabbed the doorknob just as it opened from the other side. Jared walked in followed by the rookie cop, whose mouth dropped at the sight of Ms. Holt. Frank could sympathize with the man, that'd been his first reaction too. It was too bad she'd turned out to be a fed, definitely on his to-be-avoided list.

"Hey, Franco, my man, you came. Thanks, bud. I thought I was going to be spending the night in the crowbar hotel." Jared grinned past the swollen lip and black eye he was sporting, no doubt courtesy of The Golden Ring Casino. The man never learned. Frank was relieved to see the damage was minimal. His ugly mug would heal.

"Wow, who's the babe? You've been holding out on me, old man. Hello, pretty lady, I'm Frank's better-looking and much more charming partner."

Frank shook his head. Jare never knew when to keep his big trap shut, which is how he always got himself into shit. "She's got way more class than to hang out with the likes of you, now let's get out of here. I could use a beer." With a last look at the woman sure to be occupying his dreams that night, Frank etched a salute at the shadow behind the glass and pushed his friend out of the room.

"What the fuck was that about?" Jared griped, and sent the young officer a back-off stare, his humor disintegrating now that they were almost alone. His aggressiveness was so out of character that Frank took a better look. Other than the bruising, he looked wrung out, his green eyes murky, hiding his true thoughts. Frank didn't like it, not at all.

"They wasted a shitload of time down in holding with the release papers. At first they didn't even want to give me my phone call, until they found out I was calling you, then they couldn't move fast enough. I thought they were just being jack-asses, but now I'm guessing there was another agenda. This whole thing stinks. I didn't do anything wrong. Well, not much at any rate." He let loose a mischievous grin. "Those guys over at the Ring need to get a sense of humor. They are way too serious. That'll give a guy lines, you know?" He pointed to Frank's less than smooth forehead. "Case in point."

The idiot was a giant pain in his ass, but Frank thanked his lucky stars every day for putting him into that barracks room with Jared all those years ago. After Cameron disappeared from home, Frank had gone near crazy looking for him. He'd always taken care of his younger, frailer brother. Cam was special. Ever since he opened those green eyes and looked up into Frank's misty ones, they'd been inseparable, or at least that's how his mama liked to tell the story.

Their father, Frank Sr., had been the rock in the family, strong and silent but always there to lean on. He'd died in a freak accident out on the range not long after the incident with the Muldoon boys and Cam. Cameron blamed himself, and no one could change his mind about it. It festered until one day he just up and disappeared, breaking their Mother's heart. Bad enough she'd lost her husband, but now her baby was gone too.

"Come on, buddy, I owe you a couple for coming all this way to bail me out. Who's watching the spread?" Jared asked, slinging an arm over Frank's shoulders, jarring him back to the present.

"Spencer's there, he can handle it. Ma'll keep him in line."

Frank answered, shrugging Jared's arm off. The ass knew he wasn't a touchy-feely sort of guy.

"Spence get her to agree to marry him yet? That old codger's had a thing for your Mom pretty well ever since I've known you." Jared laughed.

"Not yet, not for a lack of trying though. The old bugger's persistent, I'll give him that." Spencer was as reliable as the day was long. He'd been Frank Senior's foreman, and was an invaluable help to Frank when he had to pick up the reins and carry on in the wake of the family's double tragedy.

Thanks to Spence's urging after his father died, he'd been able to continue his career as a SEAL for a couple more years. Actually, it had been both his and Cam's dream. Cam was all Army though, and the boys had often argued good-naturedly about the perceived values of one over the other. Frank often wondered if his little bro' had gone there when he'd disappeared, but had never found any trace.

Spencer had been in love with Emily, Frank's mom, for years. After Frank Sr. died he'd stayed on at the ranch to help the Steins out in any way that he could. If his deepest desire was to have Emily finally take note of him, Frank couldn't blame the man. His mother was a fine woman, one who deserved a second chance. She was too young to be burying herself along with her husband.

Leaving the coolness of the precinct behind, the two men ambled across the hot-enough-to-roast-a-chicken parking lot towards Frank's car, a beige four-door sedan.

"Vegas and you rent this piece of crap? What were you

thinking, man? This isn't a chick car; it's barely a step up from a walker," Jared complained when he caught sight of the wheels.

"I was *thinking* that I might need my hard earned cash to pull you out of the clink, asshole. I'm not here to go joyriding."

"Take it easy, I was joshin' ya. It's cool, lots of leg room, see?" He pushed the front seat all the way back and stretched out his long legs. Tipping the mirror down, Jared looked at his beat up face in the glass. "Those creeps did a bang up job of messing with my pretty face. So what do you think that Fed wanted?"

"How'd you know she was a Fed? DEA by the way. What did you get yourself into this time?" Frank put the key in the ignition and wound down the windows, the wind a dubious relief. He couldn't count the number of times he'd come to Jared's rescue. The man was a walking trouble magnet.

"Me? They were asking you all the questions. Of course she's a Fed, didn't you notice her eyes? Cold, man, ice cold. What were they after, anyway?"

Cold? No. Intelligent, yes. Frank knew there was no way Jared would knowingly get himself tangled up in smuggling of any kind. However, unknowingly? That was a whole other ballgame. He was more than a little worried about what kind of trouble his friend might have gotten himself into.

"Besides your friends at the Casino, who've you been hanging with? Someone out there is setting one of us up for a big dive and we need to figure out who it is, quick like. If the DEA is in on this, you can best believe we're soon to have the whole friggin' alphabet soup up our asses, and I don't know about you but that makes me a wee bit edgy."

"I haven't been up to anything, Frankie. I swear it on my father's grave. Since I saw you last year out at the ranch I've just been bouncing around, playing a few games here and there, to keep the cash flowing, you know. Until the meet and greet with those goons the other night things have been pretty copasetic for a change."

"Well, that agent thinks differently. We're going to have to come up with a game plan, and fast. There's some serious shit going down, and apparently, we're right in the middle of it. She said something about drug smuggling, cathinones. Also, gunrunning and human trafficking. This is bad Jare, very bad," Frank said grimly. "She believes it's someone from the team. We need to find them ASAP, and find out what the hell's going on."

Franks' phone let out a little burst, *you are my Sunshine*. Looking over at Jared's grinning face he growled, "Not a word, not one single word." He couldn't believe his mom had messed with his phone, and now he couldn't figure out how to change the blasted thing.

"Stein," Frank barked, putting a stop to the offensive sound.

"Chief, how are you, sir? It's, Nick. Nickolaus Kelley."

Funny how that worked, he couldn't count the number of times he'd thought of someone he hadn't heard from in forever and wham, there they were. "Kelley, no kidding. Jared and I were just talking about you. Yeah, he's here. I had to come rescue his sorry ass out of the slammer for messing with a casino in Vegas. Their mainframe computer no less, same old Jared." Turning sideways, he smirked at the sour grimace on his friend's kisser.

"It's great to hear your voice, Chief. It's been too long, I should have kept in touch. Fact is I've got a situation brewing here. I'm in Tidal Falls, Washington. I could use a hand, if you can spare the time?" Nick's deep voice carried through the cell phone's receiver and reverberated in the air between them.

"No shit. Yeah, we can be there by tomorrow. Funny you should call. I was just getting ready to look you up for the same thing. I'm looking forward to seeing your sorry ass, Kelley, and it's Frank now."

As Frank closed his phone down and drove towards the nearest gas station, thoughts of the team ran through his mind. It would be good to see Nick again. He'd better give the ranch a call though, make sure his mom and Spencer had everything under control. He didn't like to be away for very long, though truthfully, Spence didn't really need him there. He handled the men and day-to-day stuff fine without Frank around. Shit, he'd been the one that had taught Frank most of what he knew in the first place.

"Well, how's that for fate stepping in and giving us a big high five?" Jared chuckled. "Guess we're going on a road trip, hey buddy?"

Rolling his eyes he turned his attention to the road while a flare of adrenalin flowed through his body, electrifying the air and exciting the thrill-seeker inside him. He loved his home and enjoyed making a success of the farm, but it couldn't compare to the do or die of day to day in the SEALs.

Now, if he could only find some duct tape wide enough to tape yappy's mouth shut.

CHAPTER ELEVEN

Nick jogged through the early morning streets, Jake trotting by his side, enjoying the peace and quiet before the town woke for the day. Little songbirds greeted him as he passed a cedar hedge on his way to the park. The air was fresh and cool at this hour. He was glad his strength had returned, his breathing even and stride long. It'd been an uphill battle. For a while after the ambush he'd shut down. Closed everyone out. He wished now he'd made it his business to keep in touch with all his old teammates. The faint sounds of a dog's bark had Nick looking down at Jake, loping alongside. He'd healed up well, and only flinched at sudden loud noises these days. His hip had taken the brunt of the damage. When the explosion had thrown them, Nick worried he'd need to put him down, but he'd pulled through. Tough mutt.

After his run, he would head over to Sara's and have a look at those files, see what they were looking at here. Nick had a bad feeling that Tommy boy was into some heavy shit. They needed to solve that first, before there could be a chance for him and Sara.

A sudden sharp pain stabbed him behind the eyes, causing him to falter. Jake whined, sensing his distress. Squinting through slit eyes he spotted a nearby bench, and slumped onto the seat. He pushed a shaky hand through his hair, and then using his thumb and middle finger squeezed in towards his nose, relieving the pressure. "It's okay, boy. I'm fine. Let's just take a little break, hmm." The doctor had explained in excruciating detail while he lay in that hospital in Germany, how lucky he was. The explosion had hit him and sent him flying right up against the stone wall of a nearby house. Shrapnel had gouged a deep line on his forehead, right above his old bullet wound. A centimeter farther to the left and it would have been lights out, of the forever kind. Unfortunately, it'd taken his short-term memory away from him. He'd been told it would come back in dribbles, or one big slam—or maybe not ever. Nice. It angered him that he couldn't break through the fog to discover the truth of what happened to him and his team. There was something there he could feel it.

He supposed he should be grateful he could remember his childhood, though those memories he could have lived without. Years of mental and physical abuse at the hands of his old man had sent him down nothing but a path of trouble during his high school years. Alcohol, substance abuse, vagrancy, you name it he tried it. His motto had been *if you're not living on the edge, you're just taking up space.*

Then he'd met Kendra in one of the few classes he'd decided to show up for and they'd fallen in love. She'd been the only child of lawyer parents, sweet and innocent. The odds had gone against him when they'd had unprotected sex on a hot summer's night. She'd gotten pregnant. At least he'd done the right thing and proposed. And though her parents of course hated him, they agreed the marriage should take place. Maybe if they'd stopped it, or if he'd just walked away, Kendra and his son would still be alive today.

They'd been too young, and in the end, it tore them apart. He couldn't even recall what the fight had been about—no doubt his lack of a 'respectable' job. He'd been working at a local garage at the time—all he did remember was getting up to answer the door, only to see two uniforms on the other side. Devastated, blaming himself, he spent the next couple of months shit-faced drunk. Coming out of an alcohol-induced daze one day he saw a poster for enlisting in the marines. Not caring much whether he lived or died at that point, he'd signed up. They sent him to Lackland Airforce Base in San Antonio, where he met Jake. They'd been inseparable ever since.

The searing pressure eased enough for him to open his eyes. Jake sat with his head cocked to the side, his ears laid back in commiseration. Nick nudged him with his knee and gave his sides a good hard rub, Jake groaning his thanks. "Okay, big guy, what do you say to finishing our run?" He'd learned a long time ago that pushing through the pain was often the best medicine.

He had that in common with Sara. She'd gone through both a physical and a mental trauma that would have crushed most. She was doing great, but he bet a violation like that was something from which no woman ever fully recovered.

It humbled him that she had trusted him enough to allow

him to make love to her last night. Nick would never hurt a hair on her head, but there was no real way for her to be sure of that. He hoped and prayed no one would ever crush her again, and swore to do everything in his power to make sure of that, starting with Sheridan. If those files contained half of what Sara had intimated they did, he'd need some help. Checking to make sure no one was around, he pulled his cell out of his sweats and made the call.

"Hey, Chief, how are you? It's Nick, Nickolaus Kelley. Long time, sir, too long. Shit, I've missed the team. How's the whizz kid?" A big grin split his face as he listened to Frank describing Jared's latest and greatest.

"No kidding, trust Martin to take the term, *Land of opportunity*, to a whole new level, right?" He laughed. Man, it was good to talk to the chief again. Why did people always let the important ones in their lives fall to the wayside, while they went about the business of life?

He could well believe Jared had almost shut down the strip; the man was scary good with electronics. "I understand that you're out of the loop these days, sir, but I was hoping I could ask you, and Jared if he's still with you, for a helping hand. I have a situation here and could really use your input."

Relief coursed through his veins at the quick response to his plea. "I'll tell you all about it when you arrive. Tomorrow then, and thanks—Frank."

AFTER THEIR BREAKFAST OF CHAMPIONS, fresh grilled

cinnamon buns and hot, black coffee, Grace left Sara's to get the restaurant up and running and Tess said she was going over to her sister's. No doubt to try and get the dirt on last night from Ty. Shaking her head, Sara picked up the cups and carried them over to the sink. Glancing out the back window to check on Jess, she was surprised to see Nick still there. He and Jessica were tossing the baseball.

Nick was pointing out her in painstaking detail, how to grip the ball, and then the correct posture to take before making that all-important throw. Sara's heart swelled until she could barely contain it watching the two of them playing together. The dog ran in circles while the sun shone down, banishing shadows and seemingly placing a protective shield around them.

This. This is how a family should be. Tom had certainly never taken time out of his precious days to stop and play ball with his little girl, and although that was his loss, in a very real way it was also Jessica's.

Even though they had only known Nick for a few short weeks, he'd become more of a father to Jess than her own ever was. Listening to their joined laughter, Sara wished things could be different. He hadn't said, but she had the sense that it hadn't been easy for him as a child, either. As if he sensed her gaze upon him he stilled in the middle of all the chaos that was child and dog, and turning toward her dropped the ball he'd been holding to stride across the green grass toward the back door, followed by his entourage. A sunbeam infused him in a warm glow, and though he was certainly no angel, to her he was undoubtedly divine.

Turning away, Sara dabbed at her eyes and fixed a

welcoming smile upon her lips just as Jess burst through the doorway talking a mile a minute.

"Mom, guess what? Nick showed me how to throw a curve ball. He said that I could strike anybody out with it. Can I join a baseball team?"

"We'll see, honey. Now go wash up, and I'll make us all some breakfast." Sara wished more than anything that Jessica could join a ball team. Be like other normal kids. She knew they couldn't keep running. It was hurting them just as much, in its own way, as staying in that monolith of a house with Tom had ever done.

Nick came through the doorway and raised his brow upon seeing Jessica's little shoulders hunched over as she headed down the hall. Sara shrugged and gave him a reassuring smile.

"What's up?"

"It's nothing, she'll be fine. Want some of my world-famous waffles?" As he came close, she breathed in the fresh, clean, spicy scent radiating off his skin, and almost moaned. It took her straight back to his darkened living room of the night before. All she'd done. To him.

Suddenly shy, she turned toward the stove but he caught her chin in his sun-warmed fingers and lifted her head to his.

"Hi." His beautiful voice rumbled a soft greeting.

"Hi, back," she whispered just before he sealed their lips together. He kept the kiss tender, sweet. Her eyes slid closed, her arms wrapped around his neck and she hung on for dear life as the world spun on its axis.

A giggle had them lifting their heads, to look into Jessica's grinning face.

"Mommy and Nick, sitting in a tree, K I S S I N G, first comes love, then comes marriage, then comes Nick pushing a baby carriage!" She laughed and danced around the small room, Jake trailing behind her, barking his joy with the world.

Sara smiled somewhat ruefully, and shrugged her shoulders before turning to her daughter. "Okay, brat, settle down. Nick and I were only saying hello. How about blueberry waffles for breakfast?"

"That's not how Nick said hello to me," Jess snickered.

"You know what, munchkin, you're right. I knew I forgot something this morning, come here." With that, he chased her around the house, dragging his leg, and scrunching up his shoulders in an imitation of the *Hunchback of Notre Dame*, as Jessica went squealing away.

Sara turned back to the stove to begin the promised meal, her heart overflowing with tenderness and warmth. She couldn't remember the last time there had been this much laughter in their home, it filled every corner of the room, chasing away the shadows.

After sitting down together for breakfast and knowing Nick wanted answers for why she'd left the way she had the night before, Sara called Annie to see if Jessica could spend some time with Chris. As she expected, Annie was quick to agree, and drove right over.

Hugging Sara, she said, "This is perfect. Chris has been driving me crazy, he's so bored with it being spring break and all. Jessica can stay for the day if you want, then we can both get a break!" She laughed.

"Thank you so much, Annie. I'll repay the favor soon, okay?

Jess, you listen to what Ms. Campbell tells you, and be a good girl. I'll see you later."

Jessica was already skipping down the sidewalk towards Chris waving from the back of Annie's minivan. "I will, Mom, don't worry. Chris and me are going to make a fort in the back with a bunch of old blankets. Then we can tell ghost stories. It's going to be fun." Jess smiled back over her shoulder before sliding the van door open and hopping in.

"Those were the days, eh, Mom?" Annie chuckled. "Okay, gotta go. See you tonight," She looked behind Sara at Nick who'd come to stand behind her, before grinning cheekily, "or maybe tomorrow?"

Sara could feel the heat stealing into her cheeks as she glared at her friend. "Tonight, I'll see you tonight."

Annie laughed and gave a quick wave as she sprinted down the stairs, following in Jess's tracks. "Whatever."

Sara gazed after them until they drove out of sight, more than aware of the large male warming her back. She closed the door and began re-engaging locks, her nerves clenching at the thought of sharing what she knew. Nick's large hands rested upon her shoulders, turning her to face him. "Guess you want to talk, right?"

He moved closer, sandwiching her between him and the door. "Yeah, we could talk." His hands slipped down her arms and intertwined with her fingers. He slowly lifted them to bracket her head as she leaned back against the smooth wood. "Later."

CHAPTER TWELVE

Tom sat in the dark car feeling like a common criminal, staking out Nirvana, the art gallery of his wife's best friend. His half open window let in all the nighttime sounds of the city. Far away sirens screamed, counterbalanced by laughter, music, and the never-ending roar of traffic.

"Don't be ridiculous, there's nothing common about me." He giggled, then glanced around to make sure no one heard him talking to himself. It should have clicked much sooner. If he had not left it up to idiots to do the searching, it probably would have. He couldn't believe he hadn't thought of it before and would have to thank Sam when he caught up to him. And he would catch up to him, it was only a matter of time.

He was becoming more and more certain that Willets had led the rest of Tom's men on a wild goose chase with that tip about New Mexico. He didn't know why, but he was sure as hell going to find out.

Sam had given him one useful bit of information though.

He'd said, "You know how women are, get their feelings hurt and they run to their friends. That's probably where she is now."

Good point, Samuel. Very good.

So now here he sat. One quick call to that dealership confirmed what he'd already guessed. The car Sara had traded in was registered to a Karl Radcliffe, the lovely Fiona's little brother. It had only taken a short little heart-to-heart chat with him to find out Fiona had *borrowed* the jeep, but never returned it. Instead she'd bought him a fancy new Mustang.

After taking care of Karl he'd driven across town to the Nirvana gallery, and now he waited, fingers drumming the steering wheel, for the place to close. Socialites wandered the floors, fake smiles on their overpainted faces, glasses of bubbly in their manicured hands, the silks and satins of their dresses forming an ever-evolving rainbow of color. The rich cadence of classical music filtered through the partially opened door, probably left that way to allow fresh air into a room overwhelmed with the scent of a hundred different fragrances.

He'd once been a part of that boring crowd, though he'd never asked to be. There was more to life than who was screwing whom, or who'd lost a bundle in the stock market last week. He'd never had time for all that annoying drivel. And then came Sara.

One look into those topaz eyes and he'd fallen hard. She was different, a rare and unique butterfly amid all the moths of Boston's high society.

They'd gone to Fiji, gotten married, and spent their honeymoon screwing like bunnies. On their return he'd brought her home to Balmoral, ready to show her off in his world. Tom tried, he really had, to refine her and teach her the demands of her new life. He bought her a complete wardrobe of acceptable clothes, got her to quit with the painting, and made sure his staff knew calls from her old friends were not welcome. Then one day, Sara came to him with news of her pregnancy, and what for her caused tears of joy, for him caused a deep ball of choking dread.

His own childhood had taught him children were only good for one thing, carrying on the linage. He wanted his to end with him. Raised by a succession of nannies with only a vague memory of his father, mommy dearest was much too busy running the family's shipping company to have time for a lost little boy. Just as well, her rule was children were not to be seen nor heard. She'd taken great pleasure in meting out punishment using a thin leather belt on him for breaking the ordinance.

He could still see it coming at him sometimes in his dreams, a leathery black snake, unwinding at her urging, from talon-like fingers. It slithered and snapped as it flew across the room, catching him across the back when he turned to run and hide. Repeatedly, it bit into his neck and arms as he cowered into a ball in the corner, crying out he was sorry, though not sure what it was he'd done.

No, he hadn't wanted children, and even when Sara presented him with the squalling little red bundle in the hospital, Tom had felt nothing but anxiety, a bone deep urge to run the other way. Though he knew Sara was disappointed, he quit spending time at Balmoral. He hired a nanny, and then tried to make it up to Sara by taking her out to different functions, buying her nice things. None of it helped. He felt them sliding away from each other. Angry and frustrated, he drank, and when his darling wife turned him away at night, he slept with Belinda, the new nanny.

During this time, with his personal life a mess, Tom received a commendation to the U.S Attorney's office and the case that would change the course of his life. Ramos Guerra, a Mexican rebel leader with the Sinaloa Cartel, charged with the sale of heroin to some undercover feds. And drugs were only the tip of the iceberg for Ramos.

Under too much stress, his company floundering, Tom saw an opportunity to reinvest in the black market he had begun while overseas, and managed to get the charges dropped. Guerra, returning the favor, told him about a sweet deal on a shipment of cocaine Tom knew his contacts in Iraq would willingly pay to acquire.

Their partnership worked out well for both of them. Tom had a steady supply of weapons from his pals overseas, and with his cargo ships the means to purvey them. Ramos needed the weaponry for the ever-expanding war between the Sinaloa Cartel and their enemies, Los Zetas. The Mexicans loved their guns, and the drug trade in the Middle East was still going strong. The Sinaloa Cartel had a strong foothold in Chicago's drug and prostitution rings and Tom, through his connection with Guerra and the Iraqis, used his cargo ships for ferrying between the two countries.

It was surprisingly easy to keep his activities discreet; his job gave him the perfect cover. He began to look towards the governor's chair, his thirst to become the best, the most powerful, coming from the dark place inside of him that begged for his mother's approval, even though she was now long gone.

Thinking back, Tom realized he should have known everything was going unrealistically smooth. Instead, he'd taken the money and run with it. What an idiot. Then came the day of reckoning. The day he found out how little of his life he actually had control over. That same day he learned of his wife's duplicity. He could still hear her crying her innocence, but he'd known, from the lingering excitement in her eyes and the glow on her cheeks, she'd betrayed him. She probably thought he'd left her alone after her lesson because of guilt, when the reality was much more basic than that. Sara had fallen off the pedestal Tom had placed her on. He'd thought her perfect, so to find out she was a deceitful woman, like all women, he lost all sexual interest.

He might have let her leave, if she hadn't overheard him talking to Guerra. After that there was no turning back. She was a danger to everything he wanted to accomplish. He'd been working on a plan to have her quietly disappear when she copied his files and ran, taking her daughter with her.

The rumbling clap of thunder in the distance had him peering out the window at the gloomy, billowing clouds marching over the tops of the nearby buildings. Between flashes of forked lightning, he observed the steady flow of people as they hurried to exit Nirvana, before the softly falling tears could become a torrent, soaking their expensive finery.

Opening the door to his Lexus coupe, Tom silently slipped through the stream of humanity and entered the now nearly silent building. His senses were bombarded by a bouquet of leftover wines, the still faint scent of paint, cologne, and the musty smell of moistened dust coming through the still open door.

The tinkling of fine crystal in the back room let him know where his quarry was. Perfect. He double-checked to make sure they were alone, carefully latched the door, and dropped the shades to seal themselves in before making his way to her office. There she sat, her back towards him as she ran the numbers from tonight's little soiree. Careless of her.

Fiona Radcliffe—the bitch—with her fiery red hair and pixie-like frame, had managed to be a thorn in his side for far too long now. If not for her, his Sara would never have wandered. Ms. Radcliffe was going to wish for a set of those fairy wings before tonight was over.

"Hi honey, I'm home."

CHAPTER THIRTEEN

S ara awoke to the raspy glide of Nick's tongue stroking her breast where the navy-blue cotton sheet had fallen away. The warmth of his solid body lying alongside hers, filled her with happiness and contentment. He'd taught her so much about her own sensuality. She'd had no idea her toes or the backs of her knees were erogenous zones. Returning the favor, she'd soon had him moaning, nibbling her way from his ear all the way south.

Erotic thoughts from earlier blended with what he was doing to her now and had her squirming as she came fully awake. Lifting her head slightly off the pillow, she became a voyeur to her own pleasure as Nick's dark hand worked one rosy nipple, while he nipped and fondled the other.

When he noticed her attention on him, a sly grin split his face before he focused on inching his way down her body, tasting every bit of silky skin along the way. Her bottom lip caught between her teeth when Nick grasped her hand in his and brought it along on an exploration of her smooth flesh. As their combined fingers swept away years of repressed urges, Sara let go of any embarrassment as Nick proved to her that her body was gloriously made for this, and pleasure was meant to be given as well as received.

A laugh escaped, freeing the last vestiges of darkness from her soul as Nick turned onto his back and lifted her above him. She gazed into his precious face and let herself sink onto his stiffened cock, gasping at their connection.

"I hope you're not laughing at my technique darlin', my ego is frail you know." He panted as they both let out a gratified groan.

"Your ego is as massive as...other things." Sara smirked, leaning over to kiss his bristly jaw just as she tightened her inner core, causing Nick to swear as he pumped into her.

"Do that again," he gasped, "and they're both going to be deflated."

HER FLUSHED face and whiskey colored eyes filled with passion and laughter directed towards him was the biggest turn on Nick ever had. Her beautiful breasts, limned by the light peeking through the gap in her bedroom blinds, bounced in synchronicity with the motion of their bodies. Her skin glowed dusky pink with a fine sheen of sweat, and as he gazed down at their joined bodies all he could think was, Mine. He wanted—needed—to stake his claim on her. One that couldn't be denied.

A Child.

Holy shit. He realized what was different. No protection.

"Ah...sweetheart, God, we need to stop this. Sara, no con... dom," Nick croaked, his eyes almost crossing as she did that twist and tighten thing that about drove him wild.

"It's okay, I'm on the pill. Are you okay...with that?" Sara panted, close to the edge now.

"Hoo-yah, babe, better than okay." He looked into her glazed eyes, "Come on honey, let go for me. I've got you." Stretching between them, he lightly brushed her core back and forth a couple times. Her whole frame tensed. She dropped her head to his chest, and sucked back a cry as she came, in turn triggering his own massive release. Hooyah.

They lay boneless together for a while, then arose and climbed into a long-drawn-out shower spent scrubbing each other's one hundred and one parts. Afterward, reality intruded and they sat at the kitchen table, the purloined file open on the laptop in front of them. She'd been right. Tom was into some heavy shit with several very powerful men. Reading down the list of names and dates was like checking back issues of front-page news stories. It contained everything from the ongoing trouble south of the border, to the escalated drug and trafficking trade right here in the U.S.

This file could shut down a major corridor between their country and overseas black market avenues. "Wow, honey, you weren't kidding, this is big." He turned away from the computer and looked at her sitting beside him, lost in that old bathrobe of hers. She resembled a turtle sinking into its shell. As if seeing that file open on the table had made her shrink into her own skin.

"I want it to stop, Nick. I only took those reports in case I needed to use them as leverage against him." She whispered, and the pain in her tone broke his heart. "I had to make him stop. Instead, now he won't leave us alone."

Feeling like an ass for not noticing how upset she'd become while he'd been pouring over the information, Nick hastened to assure her. "I know, sweetheart, I know. It's going to be fine, don't worry. I called some friends for help. These are good people, Sara. They'll be able to figure out the next steps to keep you and Jess safe, okay? Trust me, it really will be all right." He leaned over to give her a lingering kiss, pleased with her immediate response.

"Listen, honey, why don't you lay down and have a rest? You didn't get much sleep last night." Thinking about all the reasons why, had him hardening all over again. He didn't think he'd ever get tired of gazing at her beautiful eyes opening next to his on their pillow every morning. A thousand conflicting emotions inside fought to escape. He wanted to shout it from the rooftops.

I'm in love.

He wanted to slay all her dragons. He wanted to lock her and Jessica away somewhere safe where nothing could ever take them away from him. He wanted to give them anything they could ever wish for. His chest swelled until it was almost painful. It'd be over his dead body before her ex came anywhere near her or Jessica ever again.

"Mm-hmm, I am a little worn out," she murmured, setting her chair back and rising before leaning over to give him a warm hug. His throat closed, trapping all the emotions racing around his chest. His arms tightened their hold, and he buried his face in her soft bosom. When she pulled away, even though it'd been his idea, he felt the loss.

Nick watched until she was out of sight, and then turned back to the computer with renewed resolve. He needed to find the key to snap this ring. A bio on the asshole would be a good place to start. With that in mind he opened up a search on Sara Reed and didn't have long to wait for the results to come pouring in.

She'd married a shipping magnate who was a U.S Attorney, currently running for governor. Was there anything the prick wasn't into? He ran down the list and noticing an interview in a society column, hit the link. A grainy picture popped up and when Nick enlarged it, he fell back in his chair.

Well, son-of-a-bitch. Tom Sheridan.

Sara's no-good ex happened to be the very same American they were assigned to protect. The American from the bar in Iraq. Crazy. No wonder Tom had been so chummy with those sketchy men, all those years ago. So he'd been doing this for quite some time. Making a fortune on the backs of innocent victim's like that poor girl Nick had tried to help.

It made him furious, but it also scared him to death. These people knew Sara had this file. He no doubt had a whole army of men out searching for her. It made Nick doubly glad he had made that call to Frank yesterday. They should be arriving sometime tonight, and not a moment too soon, according to this. The deeper into the files they'd gone, the more they became aware of how far her husband's duplicity ran. She'd tweaked the monster's tail by getting away from him. He hoped they could find a way to slay it.

After her nap they spent what was left of the afternoon talking and making out on Sara's comfortable old chintz sofa, knowing that after today it would be a lot harder to find any alone time, at least until a resolution was found.

They both decided Jessica would be better off staying with the Campbell's for now, so Sara set the phone on speaker and called over to the craft store. After ascertaining the kids were getting along and not causing trouble she asked Annie if her offer still stood.

"Are you kidding me? I would love to take care of the munchkin. She keeps Chris from boredom. Do you and that handsome man of yours have something special planned?"

He only wished. It'd be great if the only thing they had to think about was plans for a romantic evening together. He'd love to take her out, his choice this time. Maybe a moonlit drive through the countryside. Find a nice private spot for a picnic and stargazing. Love-making. Hooyah.

"Oh Annie, I'm not even sure where to start. I'll try to explain everything when I come for Jess tomorrow. Better put a big pot of coffee on. It'll take a while." Sara sighed.

She'd just hung up the phone when a sledgehammer like pounding began at the door. Jake jumped to his feet, barking up a storm. Sara recoiled before running to the replica Quaker style end table, and opening the drawer, pulled out the can of mace.

That won't stop a bullet, my love.

Shushing the dog with a quick upward hand motion, he waved Sara back to the kitchen, which she of course ignored, then moved to check the viewer in the door. Relief swamped him when he saw who was putting up the hullabaloo on the other side. Rushing to flip the locks, he swung the door wide, and only had time for a quick salute before Jared grabbed him up off his feet in a bruiser of a bear hug.

"Nick. Good to see you buddy. It's been way too long. I was wondering what the hell you've been up to all these years. Now I see you went and got yourself a little woman. Shit man, you've put on some pounds, too." Jared laughed as he set Nick back down and pretended to hold his back in pain.

Nick grinned so hard he felt his jaw pop. "Hey Jare, I hear you have been up to the same old, same old. Great to see you too, bro."

Turning back to the door, Nick took in the chief. He knew as he gazed into the proud man's eyes that Frank still, even after all this time, held himself responsible for Adam getting shot and killed.

Giving his mentor a sharp salute, Nick held out his hand and Frank latched on, hauling him into a tight clinch.

"I've missed you, sir. It's been too God-damned long." His throat closed, filled with hot emotion. These men were his family. How had they let themselves drift apart for so long?

"Nickolaus...ah man, I'm so sorry. Every damn day it sits there in my guts. I know how close to Adam you were. I wish..."

The Chief would have taken those bullets himself if he could have. Nick never once blamed the man for what went down. It tore him apart that Frank had been castigating himself all these years. He should have kept in touch. Some friend.

"There was nothing you could have done, sir. We all knew

when we signed up that there was a chance that some of us would go home in body bags. It's the way it is."

"That it is, I should have made an effort to track you down when I got out. Things happen, time passes, and before you know it here we all are, five fucking years later." As his gaze moved past Nick's shoulder, he bowed his head slightly. "Begging your pardon, ma'am, been out on the range with only the cows for company for too long, I guess."

————————

THREE DIFFERENT SETS of eyes zeroed in on her, and Sara's cheeks warmed. Holy testosterone, she felt like a midget at a Globetrotters game. These men were huge.

Nick had described his chief to her as larger than life. He hadn't been kidding. The Man filled her doorway with his shoulders, and had to duck as he entered the house, instantly dwarfing the entry. She liked his craggy, lived in face, tanned a deep red, no doubt from the hot Texas sun. Coffee colored hair hung slightly shaggy around his ears, highlighting silver eyes. Those eyes had seen too much of the wretched side of life. They made Sara wish that she had a sketchbook handy; she wanted to catch all the little nuances she could see in them, stunning.

Nick's friend Jared was lean and lanky, with sandy blonde hair and multiple tattoos marching up and down his arms. Between the beat up leather coat swinging by a finger over his shoulder and the fading bruises on his face, he reminded her of a biker. Nick had depicted Jared as an easygoing, brilliant man, but after seeing him in person, she sensed there was a lot hidden inside his good-old-boy vibe.

"Sara, honey, come and meet two of the best guys you could ever have on your side. Chief, Jare, this is Sara. She and her little girl need your help; she's up to her beautiful neck in some heavy shit."

These men looked what they were, fully capable of creating some major chaos on those that crossed them and theirs. As she went about the business of making enough food to fill an army, the men sat at the table with big mugs of strong black coffee, looking over that ugly file and strategizing their next move. She placed a plate piled high with the roast beef she had started earlier in the day, a mountain of mashed potatoes with a bowl of thick, rich gravy, and the requisite green vegetable, beans, on the table in front of them.

Nick caught her hand as she pulled back, and turning it over, kissed the inside of her wrist as he gazed up into her eyes. The sudden flare of awareness between them spiked her blood and if it were not for Jared's smart aleck voice reminding her of their company, she knew Nick would have liked nothing more than to lay her out on the table as his own personal banquet.

"What do you see in that ugly face gorgeous? Come run away with me, I'm way more fun than old Mr. Responsibility there." He began to sing in a horribly off-key but compelling voice, "*sweet dreams are made of the year, who are we to disagree. Come on sugar; I'll be your sweet dream.*" He wagged his eyebrows, Groucho Marx style and his turquoise eyes high-lighted by glasses and a dark tan were quite mesmerizing.

Sara laughed at his silly antics, sitting beside Nick who

retained a firm hold on her hand as if she might actually go, silly man. Her heart already belonged to him, no matter how cute his friends were. Not that she'd told him yet, she was still adjusting to it herself. She was almost sure Nick felt the same way about her too, after the way he had held her and made love to her this afternoon. His eyes glowed whenever they landed on her and he touched her often, as if he could not get enough of her.

"This is roast beef the way my mama does it, tender and juicy, thank-you for the nice meal, ma'am." Frank frowned at Jared before sending a careful look her way, taking note of their linked hands.

So he wasn't as ready as his friend to accept her into their little fold yet. That's okay, she was a little overwhelmed by them also. "Sara, please, and you're more than welcome Mr. Stein. I cannot tell you how deeply I appreciate Mr. Martin and yourself coming all this way to help my daughter and myself. When we began this journey, I knew it wouldn't be easy. I guess I thought that Tom would conclude that it would be easier to let us live our lives. I should have recognized, especially after seeing the contents of his file he would never give up until he found us."

"Why did you take it ma'am, if you don't mind my asking?"

"No I don't mind. When I copied that folder, all I was looking for was a little advantage, something to make him leave us alone. I knew it was a record of his transactions, but I never guessed it was full of names and dates. Important names. Now that I've read it, I understand it was the worst possible thing I could have done. He'll never stop now, he can't afford to. And I haven't been able to stop running because whom would I trust this to? The names listed in there are some of the highest-ranking officials in our country." Frustrated and angry with the whole situation, she jumped to her feet.

"I know you're wondering how I could have been married to the man for nine years and not known what he was involved with. The only thing I can say in my defence is the man I married who was gentle and caring, changed. He became secretive, stayed late at the office, went on business trips without me. At first, I thought he was having an affair. My marriage was floundering when I found out I was pregnant but I was optimistic this would bring us closer together again, however when I shared the news with Tom, he was distressed. He began to drink excessively and turned into someone I didn't know or like very much."

Gazing soberly at each of the men around her table, Sara admitted, "Things got bad, bad enough that I felt I had no choice but to run. Tom was once a good man, Mr. Stein. I don't think I can say that anymore." She patted Nick on the shoulder to assure him she was fine, and began clearing plates from the table.

An awkward silence filled the room punctuated by the dripping of the tap from the old sink and Jake noisily slurping up the gravy from Nick's discarded meal. She could practically slice the tension in the room. Each one of them were going over as much of what she hadn't said as what she had.

"I guess that explains why the dipshit liked to spend all that time with the locals over there, and it wasn't to be a good citizen. What an asshole," came Jared's blistering proclamation.

"Wait until you get a load of what our old pal Sheridan has

been up to, you won't believe it," Nick said as she came and slid under his arm. Then it sunk in.

Old pal.

Shock had her standing frozen as the men laughed and talked over her head. They knew Tom. Betrayal rose up her throat, ugly and corrosive. How could she have missed it? She'd trusted him. Loved him. How stupid could she possibly get?

Her cell phone rang out from where she'd left it on the coffee table when her and Nick...stopping that thought in its tracks, she escaped his hold to answer. It was probably Annie calling to let Jessica say goodnight.

Swallowing rapidly to conceal her tears, she picked up, "Hello, peanut."

"You still care, how refreshing." Her husband's pompous tone in her ear had her sliding in a boneless heap onto the sofa behind her.

"What do you want, Tom? How did you get this number?" The sudden silence in her home was deafening. Unable to help herself, her gaze locked on Nick, begging for support. He hurried over and sank down beside her, his warm palm settling over her thigh. She turned the phone to speaker with shaking fingers, and tried to regulate the tremor in her tone. "I would have thought you'd have figured out by now I want nothing to do with you. It's over between us. Leave us alone. Please, Tom." She couldn't help it. Entreaty filled her voice. Even after being away from him for this long, the sound of his silky voice still brought frissons of anxiety skating over her skin.

"I think you must be confused, my dear. Since when do you

get to give any commands in this relationship? I've missed you, Sara. It's time for you to quit this insanity and come home."

"That's not going to happen. The only thing you've missed is your precious file. I've read it, Tom. If I turn it over to the authorities, you're going to jail. You and I both know it. All I want is for you to give me custody of Jessica, and a divorce. In return, I'll give you back your precious flash drive. Take the deal; you won't like the alternative." Her teeth threatened to chatter themselves right out of her head as shock began to set in. She wrapped her arms around her body. She was cold, so very cold.

"Au contraire, I think the best would be if you did as I God-damn asked for once in your stupid, insipid little life." The octaves rose, his power indisputable even through the airwaves, had Sara shrinking back as if he were right there before her. "I've asked you nice, but as per usual, you aren't listening, so I'll let someone else convince you to pay attention. I plan to win, Sara."

"Don't tell him anything, I'm so sor..."

"Oh my God, Fiona. Are you okay? Fiona!" Sara sobbed. Then in the background they heard a slap, and a choked off cry along with the wounded screech of a chair overturning and hitting the floor. Hard.

Tom's manic laugh rang through the room. "Sorry my dear, she's temporarily incapacitated. Your pretty friend was very forthcoming with your number when she realized just how much I've been missing you. We've been spending a little time together, getting to know each other. She's quite the firebrand, must be all that red hair."

"What have you done? You monster. Fiona did nothing to you. Let her go, Tom, right now. If you've hurt her in any way—"

"You'll what? Snivel and cry. That's about the only thing you're any good at. I'm tired of the childish games you've been playing. They have gone on long enough. I need that file back and I mean to get it. You get your ass back here within the next twenty-four hours or Ms. Radcliffe here will have to pay the price for your tardiness."

"That would be a very grave mistake on your part, Sheridan. The police don't look too kindly at kidnapping." Nick squeezed her thigh in reassurance, and she almost forgave him. Almost.

"Ah, Nick Kelley, is that you, my old friend? I'd heard you were out. It's been a while. Return her to me and you will be well compensated. I always knew I could count on you."

Shit, shit, shit, Nick knew as soon as Tom uttered the words, how Sara would construe them. He felt her stiffen within his arms, the shudder that ran through her body, and then she pushed away, regarding him through hurt-filled eyes, as if he were ten times worse than her prick of a husband.

"You win, Tom; it seems you hold all the cards." Sara spoke in an eerily empty voice, her expression as she stared at Nick, frozen with betrayal. "Your lackey here can call you back with the travel plans. Don't hurt Fiona; I swear to God, I will make you pay if you do."

"I don't believe you are in a position to swear anything my dear. Well played, Nick, well played. I will see you soon, wife. We have a lot of catching up to do." She could hear his sickening chuckle as he closed the line, and then there was nothing but the loud ringtone reverberating through the room.

Nick stared at her with entreating eyes, as if begging her to understand. "Honey, I know that sounded bad, but it's not what you're thinking."

"Really, Nick, because I'm thinking that sounded like my ex-husband just hired you to bring us back. It sounds like you came here and introduced yourself under false pretenses." Her voice rose with each sentence, shaking with hurt and anger. "And then you insinuated yourself into our lives, made us care about you. All for what? How much did he offer you Nick? How much did he God-damn offer you?"

———————————

Before he had a chance to explain the misunderstanding, Sara jumped to her feet and dashed down the hall to her room, slamming the door as she entered. Nick could barely grasp how this had gone from being the best day of his life to the foulest, all in the space of twenty-four hours.

He didn't regret speaking up, but he was sorrier than he could ever say that he hadn't explained the situation to Sara sooner. Though to be fair, how could he have known fate would play such a huge cosmic joke? Nick wanted to follow her, make her listen, but he had a feeling that she would discount anything he had to say right now. Better to give her some time to calm down. He hoped she would realize if he'd been here to turn them in, he could have done that weeks ago.

Avoiding the sympathy in the eyes of his friends, he went

back to the kitchen and the still open file. "Have a look at this. You're not going to believe who Sara's ex is, I can hardly believe it myself."

Jared shook his head as he read the top pages. "Well, looky here. Tommy's joined the big leagues. You were right man, this is some heavy shit. There are names in here that are going to stir things up but good."

"Seems so," Frank replied. "This explains a lot. Look how far back this goes, six years at least. A man has to wonder how many assholes he's helped keep out of jail in all that time. He's been courting the system as he climbed the ladder on the backs of every cop out there trying to do his job. This kind of bullshit is exactly what is wrong with almost every country out there. Power and corruption, it's an ugly fact of life."

"Way to be positive, big guy. Always looking at the bright side. You should tone that down some." Jared said drolly, ducking when Frank's big fist came at his nose. "You're slowing down, old man. Better quit lazing around on the back of your horse and hit the gym once in a while."

Nick had to snicker; there wasn't an ounce of spare flesh anywhere on that huge frame. Both men had hearts the size of Frank's home state. It felt amazing to see them again. He'd forgotten how well they clicked together, like pieces of an over-sized puzzle. Well except for Sheridan, he was the piece they wished they'd lost.

Right from the first day when he'd shown up in the mess tent and made clear he was there under special orders from General Baker, an old family friend. When he'd demanded his own quarters the chief informed him as long as he remained under the protection of SEAL team five he would stay where he was told to stay, and the animosity between the two men grew. Frank, for the most part, remained his stoical self. In a couple of memorable instances, Sheridan went his own way, ended up with a sharp reprimand and landed himself KP duties. He lodged a complaint and the higher ups informed him that the Chief was, well, the Chief, and he needed to follow all direct orders or find himself on a long flight home, general or no general.

Tom began spending more and more down time with the locals. Which worked well for them, as none of them, especially Adam, who'd drawn the short straw and shared his tent, liked the guy. Guess he was the smart one, and if he were here in this room, right now, they all would have bowed before his brilliance. He would have liked that, the bugger.

Right from deployment he and Adam were inseparable. Adam's golden movie star looks had the women flocking, and his rakish smile charmed them out of their panties. Nick had always done okay for himself in the women department also, but Adam had that special thing, catnip for the female species. He missed the asshole.

"We need to find out exactly how far up the ladder Sheridan has gone and then we need a way to bring all the players together. There are a number of familiar names on that list. People we had under surveillance while on ops. I'm not sure how far this goes but we have to assume, going by the fact that Guerra is involved in this, the Sinaloa Cartel has a stake in getting this file back. It could cause them a serious headache if the DEA gets a hold of it."

"This explains why they held you until I arrived; they were on a fishing expedition." Frank said, and then for Nick's benefit, "a member of the DEA grilled me when I arrived in Vegas to pay numb-nut's bail. She fed me some cockamamie story about one of my men supposedly trafficking everything from drugs to humans back in Iraq. I thought she was pointing a finger at Jare and pretty much told her to kiss my ass but now it's making a whole lot more sense." Frank's voice roughened with anger. "I can't believe Sheridan played us right under our noses, and we never picked up on anything other than what an asshole he was."

"Wait, this could work in our favor. If the DEA's already looking into this, why don't we turn the whole thing over to them and let them chase after Sheridan and company?"

"Yeah, we could do that. Except once they get involved they're going to tear into every aspect of all our lives, including Sheridan's, do you want that, Jared? What about what they will do to Sara and Jessica? I don't want their lives dissected by the feds just as they're getting back on their feet."

"Fair enough, buddy, I don't blame you for wanting to protect your family, but then we need to come up with a way to round them up ourselves. Anyone have any ideas? Woohoo good times, you sure know how to liven things up, Nick, my man." Jared chortled.

"Don't get too excited, this isn't going to be a walk in the park. These guys are big league. We're going to have to strategize for every contingent because there is no way in hell that I want Sara or Jessica anywhere near that asshole again." Frustrated, he combed rough fingers through his hair.

"I agree with Nick. We need a strong plan in place. But I think that it would be better for us if we did a little, you show yours, I'll show mine, with the DEA. We could keep it controlled. Tell them we'll only deal with the agent and her partner I talked to in Vegas, and it has to stay under wraps, or no deal. The more I think it over, the more I believe we're going to need all the help we can land, especially if we end up with the Cartel up our asses."

"Are you sure you don't just want to get the uber-hot Ms. Holt back in your orbit where you can woo her with your staidness?" Jared teased, ducking another hard fist.

"I'm going to go check on Sara while you two lovebirds twitter away. Be back in a few. If we put our collective brains together, we should be able to come up with one good idea. I hope." Nick said as he came to his feet. Jake startled awake, jumped up also, his nails scrabbling on the faded green linoleum. "Maybe between us and the DEA, we can drop a net over their ugly asses and be done with this shit. I want Sheridan behind bars for a very long time gentlemen. Now how are we going to accomplish that?"

CHAPTER FOURTEEN

A tornado of emotions whipped through Sara. She'd opened her arms and her heart to Nick, trusted him with the safety and wellbeing of herself and her child, and look where it landed her. Betrayal was a living, breathing entity in her chest. She wanted, *needed*, to avenge it.

Swiping angry tears from her face, she spun away from the sight of her bed with its recently messed covers, locked her door with a satisfying snap, and flung open her closet doors. Dropping to her knees her shaking fingers peeled back the thick old wallpaper to reveal the loosened wallboard. Sara pulled out the stash of money she'd hidden there, along with their fake ID's and passports.

She grabbed the go bag from the floor filled with their essentials and stuffed everything inside before stopping to make sure Nick wasn't on his way down the hall. Déjà vu, a bad habit, listening at doors. Nick's deep tones mixed with the low rumble of voices coming from the kitchen.

He's not coming.

Her breath stalled in her chest. Fine.

I don't want him to anyway.

She pushed away, crossed to the window, and lifted, glad she'd kept the frame well oiled. Sliding the fire escape rope ladder from beneath the bed, she threw it out the opening, making sure it landed noiselessly against the side of the house. With a last, sad look around the room she'd grown to love, Sara breeched the windowsill and began the short climb down, pulling the go bag along with her.

She hit the ground in a low crouch and prayed Jake would stay sleeping inside with the men, then raced through evening shadows to jump the white rail fence to Tess's house. She ran to the backdoor, knocked, turned the latch, and slipped inside.

The rich yeasty smell of bread welcomed her as she entered the kitchen from the little mudroom. "Tess, I need help." Tess stood at the counter kneading dough and jumped at her voice. "Sorry, I didn't mean to startle you. Listen, I have to leave for a few days and have a big favor to ask."

"Anything honey, you know that. What's wrong, baby girl? Is Jessica okay?" The worried look on Tess's face as she turned, rubbing her fingers together to rid them of flour, made Sara realize she'd better calm herself down before she picked up Jessica or she'd have her scared.

"Jess is fine. It's a family thing, that's all." The stress of the past couple years, and then Nick's betrayal caught up to her. Overwhelmed, Sara crumpled. Tears flooded her face, her shoulders shook and big gulping sobs forced their way out of her mouth.

"Oh, sweetie. Come here, come on now. Let me hold you, Sara. That's right, honey, let it out, I've got you." They stood together that way for quite a while, Tess humming a soothing little melody until Sara's sobs became hiccups and she pulled away to grab a tissue from the table.

"I can't do this anymore. I'm tired of lying to everyone I care about." She sank onto one of Tess's colorfully quilted cushions gracing the old wooden chairs. "I have something I have to tell you. I can't hold it to myself anymore."

"I think I can guess some of it. You were in an abusive relationship, weren't you?" Tess came over and joined her, reaching out to link hands with Sara's frozen ones.

"How did you know? I thought I hid it pretty well. Obviously, I've been fooling myself all along."

"You did fine, angel. I just knew. I never told you this before but I had a daughter also. She grew up beautiful and vivacious. All the young men used to chase after her, but she only had eyes for one. He worked at the bar downtown, was a little rough around the edges. I think the bad boy image attracted Vivian the most. They ended up living together, and things seemed good for a couple of years.

"Then he got restless, started staying down at the bar even on days off. When she asked him about it he laughed and pushed her around a little. I never heard until later or I would have brought her home with me then. I wish to God I'd known." The heartbreak in her friend's voice broke Sara's heart. No mother should ever lose a child.

"She followed him down there one night. I guess she wanted to see what the big attraction was. Well, she found out.

He was in the back with some hussy pinned up to the wall. Vivian told him to pack his bags and get out and then she left, crying. He chased her out to the parking lot and beat the crap out of her. It was late, and at that time there were no lights in the lot, which has since changed, thankfully. My little girl pulled herself into her car and tried to drive herself to the hospital, but crashed into a tree and died. A rib had punctured her lung."

"Oh, Tess. I'm so sorry." More tears rushed to her eyes, thinking of what her friend had been through.

"None of that now." Leaning forward, Tess tightened her grip on Sara's hands. "It happened a long time ago and I've made my peace with it. That's not the reason I told you. I just wanted you to know I'm here now, and I'm listening this time. So talk to me, okay? We'll figure it out. I don't want to see what happened to Vivian ever happen to you."

"I had no idea. I'm so sorry." No wonder Tess seemed so pensive at times. Fate had brought them together. They both loved the grandmotherly woman and it was obvious that Tess cared deeply for them as well. They were good for each other. Locking onto their linked fingers like a talisman, Sara let it all out like a purging.

"I have a husband. Well, an ex-husband, Tom Sheridan. We were married for nine years. Half that time seemed like a never-ending nightmare. He didn't trust me and held me under constant surveillance. He's a U.S. attorney in Massachusetts with ties to some very bad men. It was always about the power with him, he has to have complete control over everything. It took a long time, but finally things fell into place. I had a chance to escape with Jessica and grabbed it." She took a moment to gather her thoughts, relieved to talk about it with someone, even if that someone couldn't be Nick. The betrayal rose up again, a giant fist smacking her heart.

"But now he's tracked me down. He called a little while ago to tell me he's kidnapped my best friend and is holding her as a ransom to get me to go home." Sara gazed at Tess through anguish filled eyes. "Don't you see, I know what he's capable of, I have to go. Fiona helped through everything, even our escape. I can't just abandon her. I'm going after him. It's my responsibility, he needs stopped before anyone else gets hurt. Will you keep Jessica for me if anything happens? It's essential to me she's safe, and I know she will be with you."

Tess shook her head so fiercely her silvery topknot started a slow slide south, giving her an elfin appearance. "You can't go after someone like that by yourself, you'll be killed. We should go to the police. One of my nephews, Ty's older cousin, is the chief of police here, he'll help us. And what about Nick? It's as obvious as the nose on my face that boy is in love with you."

"Oh, he knows. Tom hired the inestimable Mr. Kelley to drag me home. He's been playing some sick game with me all this time, getting his money's worth, I guess. Nick must be laughing at what a dumbass I was. I trusted him, cared about him. Now all I feel is played, first Tom, then Nick. I am sick and tired of being used by men; I want control of my own life, so I'm going to go see that a-hole husband of mine, give him what he's after, get my friend back, and then find a solution to world peace. Should be easy, right?" Sara grinned, half-heartedly.

"I think it might be easier to solve the world's problems than to corner your ex. What you're considering is too dangerous to do alone. You're going to need some help, whether you want to admit it or not. If anything happens to you, that sweet little girl of yours is going to be sent home to her daddy. You don't want that to happen, do you?"

A crushing wash of despair threatened to drag her under. Of course she wouldn't risk Jessica that way. Blinded by her righteous anger, she'd once again overlooked the big picture, which could have had tragic results for both of them. How stupid could she get? She couldn't go off half-cocked without a real plan in place. Tom was exceptionally smart. He'd see through any trick in half a second. How did she think she could go up against him and win?

Sara thought they had a real chance when Nick told her he was there for her and called in his military friends for back up. Obviously, she'd taken a tour to Fantasy Island, and should have known better. Life wasn't some kid's fairy-tale.

Wasn't she the pessimist these days?

She had to protect Jessica at all costs, and that meant stopping Tom. Those files needed to go to someone who could see him put behind bars. It was the only way any of them would be safe.

Tess was right, she did need help. This meant going back to Nick and his friends. Now she'd had time to calm down some—the sweet tea had worked its magic—she could see if Nick had been in it for the cash he would have turned her in long ago. So maybe he had developed feelings for her after all. And maybe she could use that to barter for their freedom, because for her, that was the endgame.

As far as she was concerned anything they had was over. She refused to be with anyone she couldn't trust, been there, done that, had the scars to prove it. When she went back home, she'd let Nick know it was only for business, anything else was off the table.

"You're right, Tess, I'm not thinking straight. Nick's called some military friends of his; they arrived a little while ago. They seem ready to help, so I'm going to take them up on it."

"What about Nick? I think you should at least listen to his explanation. He's a good boy, I can tell. You should give him a chance."

Shaking her head, Sara had to smile at Tess's description of Nick as a boy. It was hard to imagine his six foot something, muscular body, and lean face as that of a young soft-skinned boy. Her hand unconsciously slid to her flat tummy, rubbing it as she imagined a baby boy with his dark hair and her brown eyes.

CHAPTER FIFTEEN

Nick stared out the window at the darkening yard as his friends pored over the files behind him. They'd already been at it for a couple hours now but with the chief's contacts they'd managed to track down most of the people on the list. It read like a who's who of government officials, high-ranking cartel members, and someone only referred to as Phoenix. It forcibly reinforced to him the cunning Tom portrayed. It had not only kept the man alive, but also allowed him to profit from dealing with the likes of the Sinaloa Cartel and the Iraqis.

Had Adam known something was going on? Maybe that was the reason he'd spent so much time watching Sheridan. Nick had assumed it was because the two men had taken an instant disliking to each other, hell they all had, but Adam carried it further, practically becoming Sheridan's shadow. If only he would have confided in someone. Maybe, he wouldn't be dead now.

Nick gripped the edge of the counter so tight it groaned

from the pressure. The scene outside the window changed from a softly lit summer evening, Jess's bike laying on its side, baseball glove discarded from their earlier game, to one of chaos, with blasts of mortar, and screams of women and children.

He could see the Chief, Adam, and Jared across the village square. They were pinned down behind the town well. Suddenly Adam popped up; shooting his favorite HK-MP5K. "Get down, get down, you idiot." Nick chanted the litany under his breath, a prayer to keep his buddy safe.

Next thing he knew Adam took a couple hard shots to the chest, his gun flying from his hands as his body folded to the ground. Frank and Jared rushed out and pulled him behind the well amid a flurry of bullets. Nick laid ground cover, hoping to give them time to get the fuck out of there. Jake crouched beside him, low growls emitting from his throat. They were fubared. He didn't see this ending well for any of them, there had to be twenty insurgents out there, compared to the four—now three— of them. Jared dug inside his Kevlar and came out with what looked like a frigging cell phone, and Nick got ready to beat feet. Sure as hell, thirty seconds later there was a low rumble at the other end of the street, then the real party started.

Jared had done what he was best at, namely saving their sorry asses. He'd set up a bunch of flash bangs, probably as they worked their way into the village, and now they were going to reap the rewards. Bam, explosions rent the air, and villagers ran screaming, creating the pandemonium needed for them to ghost out of there, quick fast. He took flank position so Jared and the chief could pack Adam as they raced for cover, their fricken ride over a mile away. They were almost in the clear when something popped from the shadows and Nick felt a searing pain along his scalp just before he passed out. When he came to he was in a German hospital and his best friend was in a pine box. They told him he was lucky, he didn't agree.

"Nick, I think we've got a plan, come check this out." Jared's rumble brought his head around, back to Sara's pretty kitchen. It reminded him of her, warm and sunny. God, he hoped he could make things up to her; he didn't want to lose what they had.

"You okay, man? You look as if you've seen a ghost."

"I think maybe I did. You guys remember the night Adam died? I think I know who the shooter was. I'm almost sure now it was Sheridan. Over the years, I've had fragments of that night creep up on me but never enough to put it all together. Then tonight when Sheridan called, it triggered more memories. I think the cocky bastard killed Adam and winged me. He probably figured I was too fucked up ever to remember it. He's probably been laughing his ass off all these years. Stupid, messed up Kelley, can't even remember his own fucking name."

"Are you sure about this? That's good for a court marshalling; his sparkling career in politics is going to come to a crashing end. I confess I always wondered what went wrong that night. It was supposed to be a simple surveillance and all the sudden we found ourselves ass deep in rebels" Regret laced the chief's eyes and tone. "Then Adam disobeyed a direct order to stay down and was killed for it."

Jared stood and began pacing the room, looking grimmer than Nick could ever remember seeing him. "This is such bullshit! If we'd have got our heads out of our asses, maybe we would have noticed what that prick was up to, and Adam would still be with us today."

"It's no one's fault, Jare. We went there to do a job. How were we supposed to know someone on our own side would be a threat to any of us?" As always, Frank's was the voice of reason. "All we can do now is use what we know to take this mother-fucker and all his buddies down. Hard."

"I agree, we need to put an end to this once and for all. I hate that Sara and Jessica are in the middle of this shit-storm. I need them safe, even if what we had is over."

"She'll come around, don't you worry. All you need to do is spread some of that famous Kelley charm around, she'll realize what a sweetheart you are. Man, if I moved in that direction, I'd marry you myself." Jared moved towards Nick, arms wide, making kissy noises.

"If you two are done spreading the love, we'll get down to business here. I think I have a plan to bring all our players to one arena, and then with the DEA's help, we can go in and round them all up at once. The way I see it," as Nick and Jared pulled up chairs on either side of him, Frank laid out the bullet list he'd made. "We already know there is a big deal about to go down, maybe even the granddaddy for our boy here. The DEA wants in, and I'm willing to bet they'll give us whatever we need, if it means collaring these guys. I have a feeling Sara inadvertently took the single most important piece of evidence the Feds will need to build this case. That puts us in a position of power, boys. I say we bring all the players here, to us."

Frank leaned back in his chair as Nick pushed his back and stood, too agitated to remain seated. "Pardon my French here, sir, but are you fucking crazy? The last thing I want is that asshole and his friends anywhere near here. I want Sara and Jessica protected, not thrown right into the lion's mouth, for Chris-sake."

"Calm down buddy, you know the chief better than that. Give the man time to explain." Jared placated.

"No he's right. My plan will be dangerous for Sara. We'll make sure her little girl is under protection, but Sara's the key. We need her to lure Sheridan in, and with the right timing, his associates also. Look, we know from this file the deal is set for next week, and Sheridan's part in it is to have the guns he's already collected from overseas brought to a port for transfer to one Ramos Guerra of the Sinaloa Cartel. In exchange for the arms, Guerra is supposed to turn over twelve shipping containers of the precursor drug, methylamine. Twelve, men. We can't let that happen."

He looked them each in the eye, "I say we force his hand. We know Sara is his weakness, so we get her to call him. Tell him if he doesn't bring her friend here by next week, crunch time, she'll turn everything over to the local authorities. I'm betting Sheridan, being the pompous ass he is, will think he can out- maneuver her by bringing his colleagues here to stop her and take care of business all at the same time. We are only a few miles from the pacific so it makes sense. But with the DEA's assistance we'll be here, ready for them."

"I can't let her do it, it's too dangerous." Nick growled the words, knowing it was the only way but desperate for another answer.

"You don't get to have that choice." They all turned as one

to the sound of Sara's voice as she opened screen door. "You gave up the right to have a say in this when you withheld the truth from me." Sara avoided his eyes as she entered the room, turning instead to Frank. "I overheard your plan and agree. We have to try. But first you need to promise me by all you hold dear my daughter will be safe. That's a deal-breaker for me."

"Sara, you don't have to do this, we can find another way." Nick pleaded, lifting his hand to touch her, only to let it drop when she spun around, hurt and anger radiating from her form.

"Don't you get it? There is no other way. He's too powerful. Tom has spent years building himself up to be unreachable. He holds so many dirty secrets on important people no one can touch him. I was there; I saw what a word from him could do. He took great pleasure in squashing anyone who tried to vilify him. I won't stand by and let it happen anymore. He's ruled over me for too many years already. It's time to end this."

Ignoring him now, she turned back to the others, "He's very perceptive gentlemen, so we'll have to be precise setting this up or he'll just smell a rat and blow the whole thing apart on us."

Nick couldn't decide if he wanted to strangle her or applaud. He was fully aware of how dangerous Sheridan could be, that's why he wanted her nowhere near the guy, couldn't she understand that? She'd been crying, her eyes red and swollen, her voice husky, and yet she stood there before his friends, unbowed, ready to grab a dragon by the tail if it meant protecting her daughter. He'd never seen anyone braver, or more compelling.

"I know you're angry with me, and you have cause to be. But I need you to know I never meant to deceive you, and I sure as hell was never going to turn you over to Sheridan. I didn't even know who he was until you showed me those files. Shit, Sara, what are the chances the same S.O.B. we knew from overseas would be your ex-husband." He moved to stand in front of her, and gently placed a hand on each side of her face to make her look at him. "Honey, think about it. If I were only here to take you back to him, wouldn't I have done it already? He's playing you, Sara, and you're letting him."

Nick didn't care about their audience. All his focus remained on the courageous woman who held his heart firmly between her tiny little hands and was currently squeezing the living shit out of it.

She still wouldn't look him in the eye, her posture remained stiff and unyielding. He wanted to ask how she'd managed to get from her room where he'd watched her disappear a couple of hours ago, to coming in through the back door minutes ago. He hoped to Jesus that she'd not been about to slip town on him. The thought of what could have happened, constricted his already tight throat muscles. She was determined to follow through on this course of action, he couldn't stop her. He hoped she would at least listen to the voice of reason, namely Frank, and obey every precaution.

SARA COULDN'T BRING herself to meet Nick half way. She still smarted over his possible duplicity. Needed time to assimilate it before she decided anything. She wished she could set it aside and forget it, but it wasn't that simple. She'd fallen in love with him, put her trust in him, and he had let her down. For right now, she needed to focus all her attention on what needed done to get Fiona out of Tom's clutches and him behind steel bars. Her priority couldn't be whether Nick had lied to her, or how she wished she could lean against his broad chest and find the comfort she so badly needed. Instead, she was going to have to stand on her own, as she had always done. After all these years, she should know by now, you can't count on anyone but yourself.

She couldn't remember a time anyone ever cared how she felt. The nine different foster families she'd been assigned to took care of her basic needs, but no one ever tried to create a bond with her. Then she went to a new family the year she turned fifteen.

The Bakers were a middle-aged couple; Mrs. Baker worked at the local bank, Mr. Baker owned a car lot and spent most of his time at the office. Sara had a list of duties posted to the stainless steel refrigerator in the couple's upscale condo, and was expected to have them done by the time they arrived home each night.

She remembered coming home early from school that day, her tummy cramping, head aching, and laying down on the cool leather of the sofa. She awoke to clammy hands pushing her tank top down over her newly budded breasts, grabbing and squeezing even as a heavy weight settled over her prone body and a wet mouth ground her lips against her teeth.

Her eyes flew open and she began to struggle as Mr. Baker panted in her ear, "Come on honey, open your mouth for me, you know you want it. You've been flaunting your sexy little body in front of me since you arrived here, time to share it."

Sara panicked as his hands roved over her, pushing and prodding. She tried to knee him in the crotch but only succeeded in letting him settle deeper between her thighs, his disgusting hard-on pushing against her panties where her skirt had ridden up in the struggle.

He laughed, "That's it, baby, I knew you wanted me. We're going to have a good time, you and I."

"Get off me, you asshole." Sara cried as she bunted him in the face with her head. "Get off! I'm going to scream this place down in two seconds if you don't get the fuck away from me."

"Tsk, tsk, is that the way young girls talk these days? No wonder no one wants to keep you, you have no respect." His hand slipped down between her legs while his other hand restrained hers between their bodies. When she peeled her lips back to scream his slimy tongue entered her mouth, and Sara began to gag in shocked terror.

At that moment, she felt something hard hit her cheek and then a muffled thwump as it connected with the creep's skull. As he rolled away from her, Sara could hear the screeching tones of Mrs. Baker freaking out at both of them, as if Sara had asked for this. Mr. Baker, the asshole, stood there calmly straightening his shirt and slicking back his comb-over hairdo.

The authorities took her away the same day, with a big black mark on her reports. After that no one wanted to let her in their homes, as if she carried the plague or something, until Frank Harley, the art teacher at the school she currently attended, stepped up to give her a chance.

Sara, starved for affection, yet leery of trusting anyone, slowly came to realize Frank's heart was every bit as big as his body. The two of them spent hours together while Frank taught her the joy of painting in his workshop studio. She loved learning the techniques and found she had a natural talent for it. The next few years flew by, with Sara for the first time in her young life, thriving under the love of a parent figure. Her grades went up, her friends increased, but more than that, her confidence grew.

Frank was justifiably proud of her and encouraged her to pursue a career as an artist. He had a number of influential friends in the industry that thought Sara gifted. One day he introduced her to Fiona Bradshaw, the owner of a very swanky art gallery downtown. Fiona, only a couple of years older than Sara, was a human dynamo. A pixie, with peaches and cream complexion and fiery red hair that flowed to the bottom of her waist, Fiona had made herself a name in the art world by finding new up and coming artists to catch the attention of Boston's elite, and she wanted Sara.

The two women became fast friends, and spent hours gossiping and laughing together as they prepared Sara's work for exhibition. Then a few months before the big night, Sara came home from the gallery to find Frank sprawled out on the floor of the living room. Even as she fell to her knees beside him, frantically calling 911 on her cell, she knew it was too late he was gone.

The slamming of the back door and a wet nose nudging her hand brought Sara crashing back to her kitchen. Jake seemed to sense all the turmoil in the room and whined. Sara patted him absently and gazed after Nick's retreating back, realizing she hadn't answered him. He'd probably taken it as a rejection. She wanted to follow, explain how his betrayal made her feel, but the words caught in her aching chest and her feet stayed rooted to the floor.

CHAPTER SIXTEEN

S ara woke late the next morning after a fitful sleep, not surprised to find an empty echo to the house. She wandered out of her room after attempting to revive herself in a long hot shower to find someone had left a full pot of coffee for her. She gratefully poured a steaming mug full before heading over to the slim phone hanging on the wall.

"Hey, Annie, it's me. How's my baby girl doing?"

"Oh, she's great. I haven't seen the two of them all morning. They're in the back room painting, hopefully not my walls!" She laughed.

A picture of her friend going back to a room painted all the colors of a rainbow sprung to mind and a grin lit her face. Poor Annie.

"Okay then, I'm going to finish my coffee and then I'll be over, I could use a good laugh."

"Well, I'm your girl, see you soon."

Sara replaced the phone in its cradle and leaned against the wall, nuzzling the warm mug against her cheek. She noticed the printed out files and notes spread all over her table from last night were gone, replaced with an enormous bouquet of bright yellow sunflowers, their cheerful stems rising from the old glass pitcher she'd made ice tea in that day, was it only three weeks ago? So much had happened since then, good and bad.

She guessed both the flowers and the coffee were from Nick, an apology of sorts. She believed him when he said he never wished to hurt her. But how could she be with a man she couldn't trust?

Curiosity had her rolling away from the wall to walk through her living room to the only set of windows, which looked out over her pretty front yard to Nick's place across the street. She pushed aside the heavy cotton curtains the house had come with, and yes, there it was. His oversized truck took up most of the space on the road. A plain Jane brown four door sedan sat quietly in its shadow.

She'd missed him last night. Talking to him, laughing with him, making love under him. His presence filled her home, from the tap he'd stopped from dripping in her kitchen, to a discarded jean jacket on the back of the sofa, and the still faint pine-fresh scent of him on her sheets. She'd ended up hugging his pillow last night as she tried to settle down to sleep, tears clogging her throat, but all that had done was make her yearn for him. His husky voice as he whispered what he was going to do to her. His bristly chin as it rubbed against her aching breasts while his teeth nipped and lips sucked, his muscular body molding her slighter one close. The feel of him when he'd filled her, the moans and sighs as they strove to breach this world, and enter one made only for them. The knowledge that she was his, and he hers. Yes, she missed him.

Brushing away tears she hadn't even realized were falling, Sara let the curtain slide closed, scooped up her keys and went out the door to Mirabelle. A few false starts later, she coughed and choked her way to life, sounding like a three pack a day factory worker, and they were off in a hail of blue smoke. No sneaking away in this old girl. She caught sight of Nick and Frank through her rear view mirror as they walked out his front door and almost braked. Really though, what was there to say? So instead she goosed the gas, and with a burp and a fart, Mirabelle gave a gratifying leap away.

Pulling up in front of The Craft Shack a few minutes later, Sara sat for a second and admired the new window display. Annie had played well on the country theme by placing an old provincial wooden rocking chair in one corner draped with a beautiful handmade wedding ring quilt done in soft rose and white. An antique side table covered by a crocheted tablecloth edged with pink roses, and an English tea set beside an old, leather bound book looked warm and welcoming. A Tiffany table lamp finished the display. Its shade threw prisms of light made of many different colored pieces of glass shaped into drag-onflies.

Sara could see herself rocking that chair as she sipped tea and enjoying the mountain view.

Annie's shop was a beacon to the women of Tidal Falls and maintained a steady business going by the flow of traffic through its doors. Some of that could be attributed to her sunny personality though. To be around Annie Campbell for a few minutes was akin to a day at the fair, it brought a smile to all.

Sara opened the door and stepped through, catching a little tinkle from the bells set above and the cheerful chatter of at least ten women browsing the shelves for the latest patterns or most colorful wools. Towards the back, Sara could see Annie's brown bob as she bent over one customer showing her the intricacies of knitting. She glanced up at the sound of the bell and, seeing Sara, motioned over her shoulder to the door tucked neatly in the corner of the room.

Smiling her thanks, Sara navigated the busy front end and ducked through the back to see Jessica and Chris up to their elbows in colors of blue, green and magenta as they endeavored to cover every square inch of the giant poster board Annie must have laid out on the floor for them. The leafy, lemon smell of children's paints filled the room with the aroma of simpler times.

"Yes Chris, like that, that's a perfect tree. Now you should put a house underneath it, one like you hope you and your Mom can have one day. How about a castle?"

"I was going to do that, but I'm going to make a tree fort instead, way cooler."

Sara chuckled under her breath as Jess rolled her eyes at the obvious boy answer.

"That's silly, how are you going to live in a tree house? It'll be too small for all your stuff."

"Then I'll make a giant one, and it'll be the best house in the whole wide world. If you're not nice to me I won't let you in."

"Oh yeah, well I'm making a pretty pink house filled with

dolls and boys aren't allowed because they're dumb." Jess replied, standing and putting her hands on her hips for emphasis, immediately tie-dying what once were pristine white shorts.

Before the war could start, Sara moved further into the large shop-like space, her heels click clacking on the cement floor bringing the children's heads around.

"Mommy, look what we made, Chris helped too." Jessica held her arms wide, ever the drama queen, all the friction gone in an instant.

"Looks like you two have been busy. Good job, you guys. I think you're going to put me out of work one day. Everyone will be buying your paintings instead of mine."

"That's okay, Mom, Chris and me will take care of you." Jess said and tears welled as Sara realized she wasn't alone in this world at all. Instead she'd been blessed to have the most beautiful child to ever grace this planet, with real friends such as Fiona, Annie, Tess and Grace. She even had the support of Nick and his friends, at least until this nightmare with Tom were over.

"I'm going to go and have a quick cup of coffee with Chris's Mom and then we'll get going, alright, Peanut?"

"Sure, Mom, we need to finish this anyway so it can dry. Come on, Chris, I was thinking, what about a dog, maybe like Jake?" They turned and ran back over to their masterpieces. Sara swiped at her tears—now they'd started she couldn't get them to quit— and went in search of the coffee machine in Annie's cluttered office.

"Hey, sorry about that, I've just started a new class on beginner knitting, which by the way you should come to, it's a blast, and had to help Mrs. Robinson learn how to make a slip knot before casting on." Annie blew into the room; a mini tornado in a handmade moss green tunic stretching to slim thighs covered in black leggings and ballet flats.

She grabbed up her favorite coffee cup, a bright yellow with a giant black happy face, and set it under her well-loved Keurig machine. Picking a capsule, she set it in its slot, pushed the button, and closed her eyes, inhaling the fresh ground smell as the liquid splashed into her mug.

"Mm heaven, nothing quite like a good cup of Joe on a busy day, is there? So tell me all about it. How did you and Mr. Irresistible spend your evening? Laundry, dishes, mowing the lawn? Yeah, I didn't think so." She grinned at the bemused look on Sara's face. "I'm kidding, I don't want to know, and besides my virgin ears couldn't handle the details. I wouldn't know what to do with a man if I had one."

Sara burst out laughing. "Well you must have known one at least once, the proof is in the back room." A shadow darkened her friend's eyes for a brief moment before disappearing away, the usual sunny look filling the bright green orbs.

"True that, but we're all allowed one mistake, not that I'm sorry, I won the lotto with Chris."

"Funny you should say that, I was thinking the same thing a minute ago, we are lucky, aren't we." Sara sat on the edge of the overflowing desk, store samples, a leftover donut box and papers galore fighting over the small space with Annie's oversized ancient computer system. "If you have a moment, I'd like to fill you in on what's been going on. I don't want to keep it hidden any more."

"That sounds ominous. Yeah, I have as much time as you need. Chief Garrett's daughter, Tina, is helping me out right now, so I'm good. Let me catch the door so we have some privacy first." She used her foot to close it and then plunked down in the room's only other seat, a squeaky rollaway vinyl office chair that threatened to break at any moment.

"Okay, shoot."

"I don't really know where to start. I was in a bad marriage. My ex-husband is a very powerful man in Boston, a U.S. Attorney. He's made some very influential friends over the years, not all of them on the right side of the law. When I found out what he was involved in I knew I had to get out of there. He didn't agree, so we ran, all the way across the country to here." She looked down at the floor, absently noticing the scuffmarks and donut crumbs before settling on a blue crayon scribble on the opposite wall, reminding her why this was so important.

"Long story short, he called my cell last night and said he's taken my best friend as a hostage until I return something I took from him. I'm scared he'll hurt her the way he hurt me. And before you ask, I also found out Nick knows Tom, my ex, from a long time ago, and conveniently forgot to mention it to me. He did call in some of his friends to help me, but I don't know. I don't think I can trust him anymore."

"Honey, that sucks. I thought you and Nick were going to last, he has that look whenever he sees you. Maybe after all this gets sorted out, you could sit down together and talk? I think he's a good guy, Sara, unlike some." She muttered.

"As to that creep you married, it sounds as if he needs a comeuppance and I'd be willing to bet Nick is the man for the job, so take him up on it. Listen, why don't you let Jessica stay with Chris and me for a while? We're happy to have her and it would free up your time for more important things, like nailing the sucker." Annie grinned ferociously.

"Oh, Annie, are you sure? That'd be such a relief; I'd know she's safe. I was going to ask Tess but with her right next-door I'm scared Tom might find her. I don't think he'd ever discover her here, but then I didn't think he would find us in Tidal Falls either."

"I'm sure, we'll be fine. Who's going to look in a little craft store for her? It's a good plan, don't worry."

CHAPTER SEVENTEEN

Nick stared after Sara's wreck of a car as it hiccupped and belched its way down the street. Had she noticed the flowers he'd begged old Mr. Abraham down the block to part with? He'd never brought flowers to a woman before, well discounting the dandelion and daisy bouquet he'd proudly picked for his mother as a child. Hurt and frustrated last night when she'd refused to acknowledge his apology he'd stormed out as if he was still that little boy not getting his own way. After another sleepless night, his second in a row—though he couldn't complain about the first one—he didn't know what was up and what was down. He understood her hesitancy, but at the same time, was she going to give up on them at the first bump in the road? That didn't bode well for their future. He'd spent half his life believing love was a myth. Then came Sara. Now he was afraid she was sliding through his fingers, and he wanted to grab and hold on for all he was worth.

The hard, heavy clap of Frank's hand as it landed on his

shoulder reminded Nick why they had stepped out the door in the first place. Right, luggage.

"She'll come round, give her some space. Sorry if I created some discord between you two, that wasn't my intention. I'm open to anything you can come up with that will work better. But know this, if she does help us, we'll make double damn sure nothing goes wrong, okay?"

"I know, Chief, I get what you're saying. Sara needs to feel she has a part in this too, so she can put an ending on that piece of her life. I'm just scared shitless something will go wrong and she'll get hurt. I don't think I could handle that." Agitation propelled him to the back of the sedan.

"Believe me, I understand what you're going through, but if you don't give her the room to make her own choices, you're smothering her, and you'll lose her."

Nick heard the regret in Frank's voice and it made him wonder again about the chief's history. Frank reminded him of the lonely Mesquite trees standing sentinel on his land in Texas. He hoped to repay the big guy one day. Nick meant to make sure they stayed in touch after this.

The car, a four-door beige Chevy Impala, was plain as can be, but Nick would bet his bottom dollar under the unassuming hood lurked a monster, probably an LS7 pushing about 505 ponies if he had to guess. Frank popped open the trunk, and Nick had to grin at the mismatched luggage within, kind of like the two men who owned them. One was an old army duffle still meticulously clean though it had obviously seen better days, the small rip in one corner tacked with precise even stitches. The other, as flamboyant as its owner, a rich coffee colored leather satchel, straining the zipper open to overflowing with striped cotton shirts and high-end jeans, Jared's.

Hefting the case out—shit, did he have bricks in there or what? —Nick grinned at Jared's bragging from the doorway, "Careful there, mate, that case is going to net us a whole school of bottom feeding scum."

"Humble, isn't he?" Nick mumbled, and Frank let out a rusty bark of laughter as he lifted his own bag effortlessly before slamming the trunk closed.

"I can't rightly say I've ever heard that in connection with Jared. Now if you wanted to call him immodest, conceited or egotistical, I'd know who you were talking about."

Nick lugged the heavy bag up to the house where Jared stood, shirt undone soaking up the morning rays. He'd missed the camaraderie of these people. He'd made a few good friends over the years, but nothing compared to the connections between those who go through fire together, literally, and come out the other side changed, some for the good, some not.

"Hey, thanks man, I could've grabbed that. Let me change my shirt and then I'll treat you guys to the best breakfast to be found anywhere on the west coast. Is Grits and Grace still open downtown?"

"Yeah, it's there. You've been here before?"

"I grew up here. Left to go to college and never came back. Small world, hey." A somber look stole over his face, and he grabbed the first clean shirt to jump out when he unzipped the suitcase, heading down the hall to the can.

Frank shrugged, grabbed his own change of clothing and disappeared into the spare room to change, leaving Nick to ponder the craziness of the last few days. He wanted to see Sara again, talk to her about what happened. He hoped she would be more amendable to listening to him today. He hated the distance that had sprung up between them.

He should have told her as soon as he'd made the connection, instead of which he'd given her dickhead ex the chance to play a stupid mind game with her. He knew she was hurting, had wanted nothing more than to follow her to her room last night and force her to understand and accept his apologies. Not let one mistake tear them apart this way.

Who was he kidding? How much could she really care if she was so willing to take her a-hole husband's word over his anyway? Maybe he should forget it. Help her get her friend back, send dick-wad to jail for the rest of his natural born days, and then blow this place, move on.

Jared came back into the room tucking a western style charcoal grey dress shirt into the waist of his jeans, the color highlighting his weird eyes glowing behind his glasses in the ambient lighting, a teal blue. He'd wet his hair and slicked it back, and when he noticed Nick watching him he grinned, "Gotta look good for the babes, you never know." Frank moved up behind him and gave him a cuff across the head. "Hey, don't mess with the goods. Just because you took a vow of celibacy doesn't mean we all have to." He smirked, easily blocking the next shot.

"Just because I'm a lot more discriminating than some people I know," Frank threw a pointed look in Jared's direction, "it's got nothing to do with being abstinent."

"Oh, is that what you call it? I thought you were saving yourself, or maybe you're impotent, I hear that happens as you get older. They make little blue pills to help you out with that you know. Come on, we won't tell, you can trust us, your bosom pals." As he went to give Frank a commiserating hug, the pained look on the chief's face made Nick snicker.

"Okay, before he kills you and I get no breakfast, let's hit the road. I want to get back here before Sara does so we can figure out our next move."

"Why don't you give her a call, maybe she'll come and meet us, help break the ice?"

"Yeah, that's a good idea, safety in numbers, right." Nick grinned doubtfully.

"There you go, buddy, positive thinking, that's the way to win the girl."

"Okay, Dr. Love, if you're done handing out advice on that of which you know absolutely diddly-squat, we'll get out to the car and leave the man in peace to make his call. Come on, let's go." Frank bullied Jared out the door squabbling all the way to the car, man he was glad they were here.

Screwing up his courage, he woke up his cell and speed dialed Sara's number, hoping she would at least pick up and give him a chance.

———————

THE TWO WOMEN were in the back on the floor with the kids. Annie had brought the donut box half full of slightly stale offerings, and a couple of juice boxes, along with an obviously much-loved old wool blanket and they were now all enjoying an impromptu picnic. Amid the laughter and the teasing, there were lots of oohing and ahhing over Chris and Jessica's art. They had managed a more than credible job of depicting their own ideas of a perfect house down on paper.

Jessica's work had the requisite two story pink mansion built like her dollhouse at home, the back open to show each of the rooms cluttered with furniture, and Jake guarding the entry with a big smile on his doggy face. Chris's picture depicted a tall bushy tree, a ladder attached to the trunk led the way up, and he had actually done a masterful job of hiding the tree-house, with a wall here and a window there peeking out from behind the leafy branches. The kids had painted their families beside their homes. Both featured two adults holding hands with a child in the middle, causing lumps to form in the women's throats as they looked at each other and silently acknowledged their children's deepest wishes laid out in watercolor.

After finishing the snack, the kids jumped up and began running around the cavernous room, pretending to be airplanes dive-bombing the various pieces of pottery equipment and crates of craft supplies, convincing blasts coming from their small throats.

"It's none of my business, so please don't feel you have to answer, but is Chris's father a part of his life?"

A cloud fell over Annie's usual sunny disposition. "Chris never met his father. He left here the night after he got me pregnant, and he's never been back." She spoke matter-of-factly but her feelings manifested themselves with the darkening, bruised look of her normally green apple eyes.

"Oh honey, I'm sorry I opened my big mouth, let's forget about it, okay?"

"No, its fine. I learned a long time ago I could only count on myself, so no worries. He and I should never have happened anyway. He was the high school quarterback and I was the geeky girl. Half the time I wore whatever art project Mr. Hammond had going on, and he, he always had his choice of adoring fans. I thought he was nothing more than a pretty face. Art was the only class we shared, thank God, because I couldn't stand listening to all those simpering girls vying for his attention. Then one day a couple of boys had me pinned by my locker, they liked to tease me a lot because I was kind of chubby back then. No, really," At the disbelief on Sara's face.

"Anyway, they'd grabbed my hair; it was a lot longer back then, and was trying to drag me to the guy's bathroom, when he came out drying his hands. As soon as he saw what they were up to, he grabbed the one holding my hair and did some kind of trick, because the kid let go, squealing like the pig he was and the both of them took off. He made sure I wasn't hurt and then went on his way as if nothing had happened. I figured, okay, the guy's not a complete loser, but then the next time we had art, he made a point of stopping by my table, checking out my work, asking for advice. I didn't know what to think, I mean me, chunky Campbell, in the same orbit as the hottest male in school? It was beyond weird, but kind of wonderful at the same time, and I fell headlong into my first crush."

She watched the kids for a few minutes, a faraway look in her eyes. "I think he knew, but he never needled me about it. We hung out at lunch whenever he wasn't flirting with the co-ed's, and we started going to each other's houses a couple times a week studying, when he wasn't at a game or out on a date that is. Then high school was over and he was heading to college while I was staying here, getting a job. Mrs. Hammond owned the craft store back then and took me on as an apprentice, so I was happy.

"Whenever he came to town during his breaks, he'd call and we would meet up; catch up on all the news. Then one day he phoned from college, and I could hear by the excitement in his voice something big was up. I'm pretty sure I died a little, thinking he was about to say he'd found someone he was serious about, but it was even worse than that. He planned to join the freaking Navy. I, and I'm sure his mother too, tried to talk him out of it, I mean it's noble and brave and everything, but not for him, you know. All we did is succeed in pushing him away, he quit calling, never came home on his leaves, and I thought that was it, I'd never see him again."

As the whooping and hollering continued on the far side of the room, Annie looked at Sara with melancholy eyes. "I never heard a word for four long years, not a word. I lost some weight, had my hair styled, and even started dating, but I still missed him every single day. Then one night, I came home from work and there he was, sitting on my doorstep, looking the same and yet so different. His gorgeous hair was gone, replaced by a buzz cut that only accentuated those killer eyes. He seemed both taller and broader to me. And when he looked up, there was an instant when everything narrowed down to him and me. It felt as if the whole world held its breath. Silly, huh."

Sara's throat clogged with emotion. "No, not silly at all, pretty much perfect actually." She shared a goofy grin with her friend.

Annie sighed, filled with memories, and then continued on, "We hugged, I tried not to cling, and then we went out for dinner, and came back to my place where he filled me in on the last couple of years. Seemed he'd become a Navy SEAL, he always was an overachiever, and was only in town for a couple of days to try to mend fences with his Mom. It was so great to see him, I felt like my heart was going to burst right out of my chest. He asked me...me, Sara... if I would like to go to a party the next night his old school friends were hosting. Said he really wanted me there, that I was his best friend. Yeah," At Sara's commiserating look, "so anyway I went, and actually had a pretty good time. Most of them didn't even remember me, ouch, but at least it solved any awkwardness, well except for when they asked if I was his girl and he hurried to correct them."

"He would have been lucky to have you, you're gorgeous." Sara grabbed onto Annie's tensed hands and squeezed.

"Where were you when my confidence needed a boost?" Annie smiled and gave her a quick hug before checking again on the children who were now working on Chris's Litebrite machine.

"So then what happened? Did you meet some guy at the party and have wild monkey sex with him?" Sara teased, and then seeing the look on Annie's expressive face, "oh, you did meet someone. Was he hot? Was it bad, what?"

"He was hotter than sin and it was the most enchanting night of my life. Everything I always knew it would be."

"Oh, my God. You nailed him, your friend. That's who you ended up with?" Sara half-laughed in amazement.

"I'm still not sure how it happened. One minute we were

talking and laughing about the evening and the next minute he had me pinned up against the back door of this very store. Both of us drank too much, but no, we weren't drunk by then, that wasn't why. I know, because I've gone over it at least a thousand times since then. He, of course knew I was still working here, and asked if I had a key, so we could rest a bit before finishing the trip, even though it's only five blocks, but hey, I was more than willing." She stopped for a moment, lost to nostalgia.

"It was perfect. He was perfect, and even though he was gone the next day, without a word, I can't be sorry because he left me with a very precious gift." They both swiped a few tears, as they watched their bundles of joy arguing about whose go it was to turn on the colored picture from their game.

Shaking her head, Sara had to smile at the paths that had led them to this moment, so different, yet so much the same. Her cell began to sing "Sweet Home Alabama" from the front pocket of her pants and she pulled it out to see Nick's name lighting up the screen, a beacon calling her to him, as sure as if he were standing right there in front of her.

Determined to keep her personal feelings hidden, she answered with a calmness she was far from feeling. "Nick, I'm kind of busy at the moment, what do you need?"

Her heart went skittering when he sighed softly in her ear. "I miss you, Sara. Is it so wrong to want to talk to you? Don't shut me out, okay? Anyway, that's not why I'm calling, I'll save that conversation for face to face. The guys and I were heading to Grace's for breakfast and thought you might like to join us. Come on, Jared's buying, and that only happens once in a millennium, so we should make it count, right?"

She smiled at the boyish delight lighting his voice. Maybe they could at least come out of this as friends. The thought of losing him completely made a hard fist twist in her stomach. "I am kind of hungry this morning, and Grace's does sound good." Sara watched as Annie turned away to begin the cleanup process from their spur-of-the-moment party. "I need to finish up here and then I'll meet you, say fifteen minutes?"

The relief was evident in Nick's warm tenor, "Okay good, I'll see you then, and Sara—"

Her hand tightened its grip on the cell held to her ear, "Nick—" she breathed.

"Don't forget to order big." He clicked off, leaving her smiling. She was coming to the realization that the heart wanted what it wanted and her head was only along as mediator.

"So, that was Nick on the phone," and at Annie's knowing smirk, "he wants me to join him and his friends for breakfast at Grace's. Why don't we bundle up the rug-rats and all go?"

"Oh no you don't, missy, you are not going to put me in the middle of your lovers spat, no, no, no. You go, show him that you're no pushover and the kids and I will stay right here doing what we do best, making a mess." Annie looked amused at Sara's obvious discomfort. "You'll be fine, honey. Give yourself a little time to process, and then put it behind you. Life is too damn short to stay mad or hurt, ask someone who knows. If you get a second chance then for God's sake, take it. He's a good man, Sara. Maybe he did screw up, but then, don't we all? None of us are perfect, my friend, well except for those two." She waved her slim hand at the kids as they went zooming by on scooters, one blue, one red, laughing like banshees.

Sara's heart swelled as she watched the uncomplicated joy the children exhibited. She'd never had that as a child and it had hurt unbearably to see the light dying in Jessica's eyes the longer Tom forced them to stay. She was fiercely glad they had found this town full of kind, caring people and she vowed to do whatever necessary to ensure her daughter continued to thrive and grow here.

She agreed with Annie, life *was* too short to waste, and as soon as this situation with Tom was over, she would sit down with herself and figure out exactly what she wanted to do about Nick. For right now though, she had a date with a trio of gorgeous, sexy men for breakfast. A girl had to do what a girl had to do.

"Okay I'm going. If you need me for anything I'll have my cell on me at all times, and Annie, thanks for everything." She leaned in and gave her friend a long hug, soaking up the scents of citrus, sunshine and the faint sugary sweetness from the donuts, which were as much a part of Annie as her smile.

"Jessica," Sara called, trying to be heard above the whirr of the scooter wheels, and the ooga-ooga of the attached horns as the kids raced towards them, looks of determination lighting their cherubic faces. "Jess, stop for a minute, I need to talk to you."

With a satisfying squeal of rubber, Jessica came to a sudden halt right in front of her Mom. "Did you see us? We were flying like the wind, right Mom?"

"You sure were, honey. Listen, I'm going to leave now," at her daughter's moan of sadness, "not you, you can stay for a few days and keep Chris company, how does that sound?"

"Wow, really? But who's going to take care of Jake?" She had a good point, in all the upheaval of the last forty-eight hours Sara had forgotten all about the poor dog.

"Listen, we have plenty of room at our house for Jake. Why don't you run home, grab him and bring him back here? The kids will love it. It'll give Fitzroy some company too."

"Fitzroy's our cat; he's old now so all he does is sleep." Chris informed her in his solemn little voice. "I bet Jake and him will be friends, like me and you." He said as he looked to Jessica.

"I'll see what Nick says, it's his dog after all. Annie, I don't know what to say, except thank-you so much, I owe you."

"You're welcome, that's what friends are for."

"Don't forget Jake's leash, it's hanging on the peg by the door, like you told me to do. Organization is very important, Chris, a place for everything and everything in its place." The two women burst out laughing at this piece of sage advice, the storage room looking as if a tornado had recently gone through.

"Thanks o'wise one. Okay, I'm off then, give me a hug." As her daughter raced into her arms, Sara's closed around her protectively, tears springing up. The next few days she would once again be apart from the most important person in her life. It wouldn't be safe for her to come over or even to call after they put into motion their plans. She knew Tom would do everything in his considerable power to stop her, including using his own daughter to achieve it.

CHAPTER EIGHTEEN

Jared pushed the car door open and hopped out the moment Frank pulled up in front of Grits and Grace, his lanky legs carrying him to the glass doors.

"Hey man, where's the fire? Don't worry, Grace has plenty of food, you don't have to race us for it." Nick joked through the open passenger window, shooting a look sideways to the chief, only to notice he wasn't getting out as he stared somberly out the window after his friend.

"Um, am I missing something here?" Silence. He decided to try again. "Frank, you want to tell me what's going on?"

"I think you're about to find out."

Jared sent them a what-the-hell's-taking-you-so-long look, coupled with a distinct plea for support that had the two men scrambling to catch up. Nick didn't have the faintest idea what was going on but if his buddy needed him, he was there.

They waited as Jared drank in a deep breath, let it whoosh out, squared his shoulders and stepped through the doors. The first thing to hit them were the smells, maple from the bacon and the ham, rosemary and sage from the turkey that had more than likely been cooking for a couple of hours, the rich beefy smell of gravy, and the aroma of fresh brewed coffee mixed with the tang of orange juice. There was a cacophony of noise, jukebox playing Hank Jones, the rise and fall of conversations from the nearly full breakfast crowd, and servers calling out orders to the kitchen.

"There she is, out from the back to schmooze the customers, her favorite part of the job she always said. Keep 'em happy and they'll come back." Jared's tone was a complicated mix of love and frustration. Nick, who was standing close because of the small entry, could feel the tension in Jared's body.

She skirted from table to table, sharing a kind word here, a pat on the shoulder there, and then she stopped in front of them, about to ask where they would like to be seated when she froze, a stunned look of joy transforming her face with joy.

"Hi, Momma."

Her mouth dropped open in shock, her green eyes just like Jared's, welling with happy tears. "Oh my good Lord. Jared." She brought shaking fingers up and hesitantly set them against his lean cheek. "Well, would you look at you? You grew into a fine looking young man. I always knew you would though, good genes."

At his shaky laugh, Grace held up her soft arms and he wrapped his own arms around her rotund figure and lifted her right off her feet, swinging her around in a King Kong hug before setting her down.

Blushing at all the amused looks, Grace grabbed up his

calloused, scarred hand, kissing it as if it were sacred, and lifted her voice to be heard above the din. "Hey all, this is my handsome boy. He's come home to see his momma," ending on an almost whisper, "he's home."

Everyone whistled and clapped as Jared wiped the wetness from her still soft, rosy cheeks, and forced words past an obvious baseball-sized lump in his throat. "I missed you, Mom, every damn day, I missed you."

"Oh son, you could have come home anytime, if you weren't so dang stubborn, just like your Pops, but enough, let's save that talk for later. I want to soak up the joy of having you here, it's been far too long. Come on now, let's get you fed." She retained a death grip on his hand as she led them to a man-sized booth for six set near the back, close to the kitchen, as if she was afraid to let him out of sight.

"Momma, I'd like you to meet some good friends of mine. Chief, this is the woman who I judge all others by, which is why I'm still single." He laughed as he turned to Nick, "Nick, I want you to meet the best cook to ever grace, pun intended, God's green earth."

"Well, if that isn't the nicest introduction a girl could ever receive. I've already met the very charming Nickolaus Kelley. He's one of my regulars." Grace grinned. "Chief, huh? I'm guessing that to mean you were my son's superior officer." At Frank's slight nod, she reached over the table and gave him a swift peck on his bristly jaw. "Thank you from the bottom of my heart, for keeping my boy safe."

After a round-the-table chorus of throat clearing, she said, "Okay, enough of the sappy stuff, let's get you fed. I know what

Jared likes, so what can I get you, boys? We have on special a Meat lover's Omelet filled with ham, bacon, sausage, and Monterey Jack cheese, or we have an eight-ounce sirloin steak and three eggs, any style. What's it going to be, fellas?"

"A steak sounds just about perfect, thank-you ma'am, and please, call me Frank."

"Well, Frank, I can do that if you'll drop the Ma'am, which makes me feel about a billion years old, and call me Grace." Winking she turned to Nick, "Okay honey, what about you, and where's my Sara Sunshine?"

"She's on the way. The omelet sounds fine to me, Grace, and about a gallon of coffee, please. Have you given any more thought to leaving this place and running away with me to Vegas to get married?" He teased.

"Go on now; you wouldn't know what to do with me if you had me." She chuckled as she called out to Susan, "Sue, look who's here. Grab 'em some coffee, would ya? I have to head back and whip my boy up a welcome home meal." With a swift hug and a lingering kiss on one cheek while she patted the other, Grace bestowed a watery smile on Jared before turning into the kitchen where they could hear her giving orders left and right, as good as any drill sergeant they'd ever had.

"So, I didn't see that one coming, though I probably should have. You look like her."

"Well if you think I'm calling you dad, forget it." Jared replied, "What are you doing hitting on my momma anyway? How many women do you need, Kelley?"

"Hey don't blame me, blame my stomach. That woman can cook." Nick grinned appreciatively.

"Yeah well, since you tried picking her up I think the bill should be yours...Pops."

"I told you it wouldn't be so bad. Family is everything, Jare. I love you like a brother but I was about ready to kick your ass if you hadn't decided to mend your fences." Frank rumbled from the corner as a thin as a rail woman came barreling up to their table, mugs in one hand, coffee pot in the other.

"Well, if it isn't the prodigal son returned, and looking about a million bucks." She slammed the cups and pot on the table and threw herself into Jared's arms, narrowly missing taking out an eye from the pen she had tucked into her salt and pepper beehive hairdo. "Your mom missed you so bad, sugar. Welcome home."

"Sue, I can't believe some handsome guy hasn't swept you off to a land of leisure yet. You look the same."

She hooted, her eyes glued on Jared as she poured out the three coffees, barely watching what she was doing. "I told you a long time ago, honey, you spoiled me for any other man."

Interesting as this was, Nick had been keeping a close eye on the door every time it opened, and then suddenly, there she was. The sun coming through the open doorway behind her created a nimbus over her head as she hesitated for a moment, letting her eyes accustom to the dim setting as she searched the room for him. She had a pair of dark trousers on that highlighted her slim thighs and mile-long legs. Over that, she had put some kind of silvery diaphanous top that flowed around her body from the outside breeze, creating an almost otherworldly look, especially with her golden eyes catching the light.

As she moved toward him, almost seeming to float among

the sun's rays, Nick wanted her with a fierceness he was beyond hiding. There had to be a way to convince her he hadn't withheld from her to purposely deceive her. She arrived at the table, and after glancing for a long moment at the empty spot beside him, chose to instead slide in beside Jared. Ouch.

"Good morning, beautiful, where've you been all my life?" He slung an arm over her shoulders and gave a squeeze, and swear-to-God, Nick was going to punch his nose in if he kept that crap up for long.

"Morning yourself, sounds as if you got plenty of sleep last night. That's good, because after today I think we're all going to be running on nerves. In case I forget to say it, thank-you again for agreeing to come and help me with this, I can never repay you enough."

"Don't even think about it, we're happy to help. I needed to get Jared out of Vegas for a while anyway, before he wrecked the whole damn city." Frank clapped his friend over the shoulder, causing a hard grunt as Jared bore the impact.

Jared raised an eyebrow, "I wouldn't have shut down the entire strip, just the places that pissed me off."

Nick wasn't sure if he was kidding or not, the boy was seriously wacko. But then they say that's the flipside of being a genius.

Sue stopped by to refill cups and get Sara's order. "Just coffee for me thanks, I've had breakfast already."

"Sure honey, no worries. Jared, your momma says to tell you it's coming right up. We got hit with a bit of a rush so she's backed up in there for a few."

"Tell her to leave us for last, Susan. We're good, especially since a sweet server I know is keeping us happy with plenty of strong black coffee."

Sue giggled like a fifteen-year-old as she moved on to the next table, fluffing her hair up with her pen as she gazed adoringly at Jared.

"Another conquest for your little black book?" Nick said, and ducked the creamer missile hurled at his head.

Sara stared at Jared, "Your Mom? Is Grace really your mother, Jared?"

"Well, you don't have to sound quite so shocked about it. Is it so hard to believe she might have raised a hooligan like me?" Jared only half jested.

"Of course not, it just caught me by surprise. Wow, talk about a small world. She's one of the nicest people I've ever met. Her and Tess have done so much to make Jessica and I feel at home here. I count her as a very dear friend." Sara smiled warmly at him and even though Nick knew it was platonic, he still had to clench his hands in his lap, because he wanted those smiles.

He needed to put an end to this whole Sheridan business so maybe Sara and he could finally talk. Right now, with it hanging over their heads reminding her of what she thought he'd done, there was no chance.

"If you two are done with the mutual admiration party, think we can get down to business? I want to make sure we're prepared for anything before we bring Sheridan anywhere near here." he growled.

Sara regarded him as if he had a screw loose before replying to the table in general, "He's expecting Nick to take me back today, so I think the first thing we have to do is call him, let him know there's a change of plans. He thinks Nick's working for him, so why don't we continue to let him think that?"

At his immediate move to object, Sara turned those lasers on him, the hurt and betrayal he could see swimming in their beautiful depths, cutting him to the bone. "You owe me this, you know I'm right. The only way he's going to give us the time we need to get the DEA here is if he believes you'll be watching me."

Turning back to Frank, Sara asked, "How much time do you think it will take them to come? We have to hurry; I'm scared of what he might do to Fiona."

"I agree, time is of the essence. Which is why I phoned Agent Holt as soon as I woke this morning. They're on a plane headed this way even as we speak."

"That's perfect then, we can all coordinate together."

"Their plane is scheduled to land in Seattle at one, so Jared and I will leave from here to go pick them up. You two can head back to the house...Sara's?" At her nod. "We'll meet up there around three, then you can make your call. I need you to make a list and keep to it. Do not let him change anything. You have to be the one in charge. Nick can help you get prepared. If Sheridan senses for one moment that something isn't right we'll lose him, so your preparation for this is critical, you get me?" He gave Nick a hard stare over Sara's down-bent head.

Oh yeah, Nick got the message, loud and clear. Keep the personal issues out until they had this thing wrapped up. He could do that, he didn't have to like it, but he would do it. It was far more crucial right now to keep the focus on the case, he knew that. The most important thing was to keep Jessica and Sara safe, the rest could come later. But it didn't stop him from wanting to take her in his arms so bad it hurt. She had to be freaking out at the thought of both the phone call and then ultimately Sheridan arriving here in a few short days. It must be messing with her head. It sure as hell was messing with his.

Grace came bustling out of the kitchen, big platters of piping hot food held in her capable hands. "There you are, Sara. Have you met my boy? Look at him, isn't he the most handsome man you ever set eyes on? He's single...you are single, aren't you?" Jared looked slightly dazed as he nodded dutifully. "He's a good man, my baby. He would make a great father."

"Mama, settle down, I only just arrived. I'm not looking to hook up...Ouch!" as both Grace and Frank clobbered him. "Sorry, I'm not looking to date right now. Besides, she's with Nick."

Sara seemed entertained by his friend's antics and took no offence, a smile breaking across her gorgeous face as she watched the byplay before catching his gaze, eyes sparkling with mirth. He loved her. He sat back in his seat, the sounds of the busy restaurant, the continued bantering between mother and son, the ring of the till amid John Denver's "Take me Home" blaring from the old jukebox. It all faded, leaving him staring at her and her staring at him, her smile slowly evaporating as she finally...finally acknowledged him.

———

SARA HAD AVOIDED LOOKING at Nick ever since she'd arrived

at the coffee shop. When she'd first walked in her senses had known where to find him almost before her head. They were like opposing magnets, drawn together by the sheer force of their attraction for each other, even over the dictates of her mind. Corny, maybe, but true.

He looked handsome, lounging in the big booth near the kitchen. The busy sounds of the morning breakfast crowd, the sizzle of smoky bacon cooking on the grill, and the splat-dribble-dribble of the nearby coffee machine starting its third pot to try to keep up to the boisterous crowd, all muted the moment she saw him.

He'd been waiting for her to arrive. She could tell because he'd looked up as soon as the door opened and hadn't taken his eyes off her since. Even though she was a hot mess inside, she pulled her shoulders back and slowed her hurried stride to more of a hip-rolling walk, as if she were performing a mating dance. Crazy.

It looked as if he'd had about as much sleep as her last night. His eyelids at half-mast over those deep pools of blue, and his jaw sporting a five-o'clock shadow, drew her right back into her bedroom. Her thighs clenched imagining those bristles against her tender flesh. And his lips—she gulped—the visceral pull of his full sensual lips tugged hard at her belly. She wished things were different. She'd thought they had a chance before...yeah, before everything went to hell in a hand basket.

The timely reminder shadowed her to the table, and though an obvious seat was left open beside him, Sara chose to sit with Jared. She gave a quick hello around the table, ignoring the sardonic look darkening Nick's face. Space, that's all they needed. With time she could probably forget the kindness he exhibited to her daughter. She could even forget his gentleness with Jake. In a while the laughter and warmth would fade. The safety and security she felt in his presence would be replaced by steel and locks once more. But the essence of him...the woodsy scent, the leathery skin, the tenor of his voice whispering in her ear...those would take far longer. Space.

She couldn't believe Grace was Jared's mother, though even when she first met him something had seemed familiar about him. Now it was glaringly obvious, they shared the same Caribbean blue eyes, and the smile was a dead giveaway. No wonder she'd felt at ease around him right from the start—flirting aside.

Frank sat to her right. His solid presence made her a little uncomfortable. He could squash her like a bug if he wanted to and she wouldn't be able to do a thing to stop him. The others seemed sure of him, but Sara sensed a lot of darkness in him.

Nick sat across from her and the occasional brushing of their legs under the table amped her awareness of him up to unbearable. The hostility emanating from his broad form whenever Jared happened to flirt a little, even though it was obviously in jest, gave her perverse pleasure.

After being pulled into a tight hug from Grace and a promise to return Frank and Jared left for Seattle to pick up the DEA agents. Which left Sara with Nick. Awkward didn't begin to cover it.

The last time they'd sat in the restaurant together they had spent the time getting to know each other, laughing and talking. This time in marked contrast, Nick sat silent, a forbidding scowl on his attractive face. Sara fiddled with first her cup and then the place settings, not sure whether she wanted to apologize or not. What good would it do? They were over, so if he wanted to think her capable of moving on with some other man that fast, maybe it was just as well.

"Look Sara..."

"Maybe we..." At the simultaneous sound of each other's voices, they locked eyes, remembering all the times they had done that in the past. Sara's breath hitched in her throat, her chest tightening at the thought of not having times like this with him ever again.

"Look, Sara, I think we should set everything else aside for now. Let's just concentrate on getting your friend free and Sheridan and company behind bars. I'm already not very happy with the part you're going to be playing in this. I could just as easily be the one to phone and say you've changed the stakes. You don't need to be involved at all."

"Don't you get it, I am involved. This whole mess is because I'm involved." Her voice rose, and a couple of pensioners at the next table swiveled like a pair of bobble heads, hoping to catch some juicy gossip for the next senior's bridge game, no doubt.

Sara waited until they gave up trying to turn up their hearing devices and turned back to complaining about so and so's dog peeing in the hydrangea's. Lowering her voice, she said, "I get that you're worried about me, and I appreciate it, really. But here's the thing. My whole life, decisions have been made for me, and I've had no choice but to follow along. Even after I was married—actually it was worse when I was married. I need to choose my own path, Nick. I need to be responsible for my own resolution, my own life. I know what we're attempting to do is dangerous. I admit I'd like nothing better than to take my daughter and run as fast and far as I can go to get away from here, but what's that going to accomplish? Another town, another identity, how many times should I put Jess through that?"

Bridging the gap between them, Sara slid her cool fingers between his, and closed her eyes briefly at the sensation of his skin against hers. Then, scanning his face to try and ascertain whether anything she'd said made any kind of impact on him, she continued, "Nick, please. Trust me. Help me to do this."

He sat for a long while, gazing out the window as he rubbed the back of her hand with his thumb. She'd almost given up hope when he looked back to her, resolution in the strong planes of his face. He gave a light squeeze before turning them over and setting a soft kiss to her palm, closing the fingers gently to seal it "We're going to need to prepare so you're ready for anything he might throw at you."

"So that means you'll help?"

"Yeah, I'll help."

CHAPTER NINETEEN

Frank and Jared stood in the southern satellite terminal of Seattle's SEA-TAC Airport for the agents to clear security. Rain splashed against the glass making wavy grey ribbons of the runways as aircraft of varying dimensions landed and took off like an intricate dance choreography.

Frank turned from his search for Holt—for about the tenth time, not that he was counting—and gazed at the slumped shoulders and blurred face of his friend reflected in the window. He knew it'd been hard for Jared going home. He'd tried to talk to him about it a few times over the years but Jared remained close-mouthed. You could ask the guy almost anything else, from a date he'd been on the night before, to how to hotwire a car, and he was happy to share, but ask about his hometown? Not so much. The fastest way Frank knew to morph the easy-going man they all knew into Mr. Inimical.

Talk of home was a way to keep the ghouls at bay. They'd all been so Goddamn close as a unit, it was hard to imagine any of them holding secrets from the others. That kind of life, it bled out the confidences, a way to pass the long dark hours lying in their tents waiting on the next adrenalin-fueled mission.

Speaking of ghosts. The wavy mirage taking shape in the glass to his right was the spitting image of Adam O'Connor. His curly blond hair and pretty boy looks gaining him adoring looks from passersby, caused Frank to grin in remembrance. The apparition gained substance as it came to a halt a few feet behind him, and Frank wasn't grinning anymore. He rubbed his eyes, half afraid to turn around in case what he'd seen was all a figment of his imagination. Jared's eyes bugged out of his head as he looked at the phantom in the glass before pulling a one eighty and falling back against the cool panes as reality almost knocked him off his feet, and Frank knew. Secrets indeed.

"Hello, Sir, it's been a while."

"Holy, sweet Mary, mother of Christ." Jared whispered.

Slowly revolving around on the broken down heels of his old boots, Frank barely acknowledged the pretty Agent Holt, now standing a step in front of O'Connor as if prepared to protect him, which she just might need to do. His gaze moved to his old teammate and cataloged five years of changes even as he brushed past the vigilant Maggie, grasping Adam in a body-clinching man hug.

Emotions like a volcano set to erupt bubbled inside him. His throat locked and tears sprang to his tightly closed eyes. All these years of anger and pain over the loss of yet another important person in his life. Yet now here he was, holding him in his arms. Alive.

Reluctant to let him go in case he disappeared, he eased

back, adjusting to the reality of seeing his friend. Gone were the laugh lines around his mouth and chocolate brown eyes. Gone were the ropey muscles and lean form. This Adam had broader shoulders and well-defined musculature, his lean face more mature, his eyes seasoned, sure.

"You're looking pretty Goddamned healthy—for a dead man." Frank said, dealing with the problem directly, no use beating around the bush.

"Yeah, about that..."

Jared, still looking a little shell-shocked, came up and punched Adam hard in the jaw, setting him back a step. "You cocksucker, scaring the living shit out of us like that."

"Hey!" Adam grimaced, rubbing his face.

"Step back." From an obviously armed Agent Holt, turning Frank on and pissing him off at the same time.

"Let's all take a breath here. You have to admit this is something of a humdinger. You can't blame us for feeling somewhat flummoxed. Last time we saw your ugly mug the medics were pumping blood in as fast it was flowing out. And then a couple days later we were informed you hadn't made it. Christ man, how do you think we're going to feel to suddenly see you again?"

"I know, Chief, I get it. If there had been any other way I would never have allowed them to pull that on you, I swear."

Raw anger dripped venom from Jared's tongue, "That's fucking bullshit man. Do you have any idea how hard it was to watch them take you away, not knowing if we'd ever see you again? I can't fucking believe you were alive all these years and never said a fucking word." He was hurt, hell they all were. "Did Nick know?"

"No, no one did, not even my family. I had to totally disappear. Look, I realize you're angry, but if you'll let me explain maybe I can shed some light on why."

"I don't mean to interrupt the cozy reunion," Maggie said, aiming a belligerent look Jared's way. "But I think we should carry this out to our ride. We're attracting a crowd."

Sure enough, here came airport security, no doubt alerted to the fact the four of them were standing there creating a sideshow for dismounting passengers. Way to keep on the down low.

"Is there a problem here?" A portly TSA agent asked, hand twitching by his sidearm as he registered the sheer size of Frank.

Flashing her badge, Agent Holt replied, "No, everything is fine. We were just leaving. Thank you, officer."

He kept his eye on them as Maggie grabbed Adam's wrist and began to haul ass out the door. Temper rode every stride she took with those mile long legs, her long braided hair, snapping against her back. She'd dressed more conservatively today, a feminine version of Adam's dark suit and tie, though much more evocative on her lithe form.

"Where to?" She glanced over her shoulder, spearing him with her sooty lashed, cinnamon colored eyes.

Frank nodded towards the Impala resting in the loading zone, a little surprised when she gave him an approving look on his vehicular choice. At least someone got that it was about blending in, hiding in plain sight.

Stowing their overnight bags in the roomy trunk, Adam and Maggie climbed in the back, leaving Jared and Frank the front. As he eased his oversized frame in behind the wheel and turned the ignition with a satisfying rumble, Frank couldn't help himself, he had to take one last peek at the living, breathing ghost in his backseat. Their eyes met, both a little moist. "I'm glad you're alive, so fucking glad. Pardon me, Agent Holt," He apologized yet again for his fabulous fricken vocabulary.

Adam grinned back, "Good to be alive, Chief, more than you know. And don't worry about Mags, she's heard plenty worse." He reached over and gave her thigh a squeeze. Frank turned back to the front, and pealed out of the parking lot with more zeal than warranted.

"So, do you want to explain where you've been for the last five fricken years?" Jared asked, still uncharacteristically acrimonious, slouched in his corner of the car; a pair of dark sunglasses covering his eyes. Something was eating at Jare's insides. It was past time he confided in someone.

One thing at a time though. "Yes, I think you better share with us what happened. And how do you come to be part of the DEA team which happens to be in on the same case that we find ourselves neck deep in?' Frank stopped at a red light and glance over his shoulder.

"You're right, it's not a coincidence. Maggie and I have been working this case for years. We'd catch a break at one end and everything would unravel from the other end. It's been a real clusterfuck, but Sheridan is the key. I'm sure you guys noticed I spent a fair amount of time keeping an eye on that prick. The DEA had already tagged me. Before I decided to try my luck on the Teams, I'd looked into joining the Drug Enforcement Association. When I happened to be on the SEAL team assigned to safeguarding Sheridan, they asked me to keep an eye out for anything suspicious. He was on their watch-list for connections to some, shall we say, unsavory characters."

Other than the whistle of wind through Jared's partially open window and the muted roar of thousands of motorists trying to beat the afternoon rush home, silence reigned. How the hell did someone the Feds already have their eye on manage to get appointed to a hotspot, with a team of SEALs no less, watching his six? Jared was right. It was bullshit.

"Obviously they caught on to what I was doing, hence the attempt to have me killed. If not for you two that night, I probably wouldn't have made it. Believe me, I've wanted nothing more than to catch up and let you know I was alive and to thank you for saving my sorry ass. But the higher-ups decided that I had to stay dead, both for my family's safety and for the case."

"So you're telling us that you getting shot, and *presumably killed*, then subsequently disappearing for the last five fricken years, were all due to Sheridan? Fuck man, why didn't you talk to us about it? You know we would have had your back. Maybe then we wouldn't have had to spend all this time feeling as if we failed you that night." Jared flung the words at Adam, his eyes shooting daggers into the back seat.

"Jare, it's all right. The man was following orders, you need to respect that." Frank knew most of Jared's anger was self-directed. Hell, they'd both had trouble getting over watching their friend shot down right in front of them. He had to live every day with the responsibility. His commands had placed them behind the town well. He'd never forgiven himself. One of many fucked up decisions that had cost the people he cared for.

Shaking off the darkness of his thoughts, Frank glanced into his rear-view mirror, his attention absorbed by the beauticious Ms. Holt seated directly behind him. Her scent, a bouquet of lilac, vanilla, and old-fashioned roses drifted around him, amping his awareness of her. She sat gazing out the side window, her profile full of mystery, the shadows created by the swiftly passing trees flirting with the dips and planes of her body. She and Adam seemed pretty close, sharing the comfort of long time partners. But there was more. He'd caught the meditative looks Adam kept sending her way. Just then as if sensing his regard, Maggie brought her gaze to his in the mirror, and awareness flashed to life. Not good, not good at all. He didn't poach. Especially on newly returned from the dead friends.

"No, I get it, I really do." Adam's voice jerked Frank's attention forward, breaking the connection. "If there were any way I could have done things different, believe me I would have. It's not exactly been a picnic for me either. I hated having to let my family, my friends, believe I'd died. But in order to stop the person at the head of this organization, the DEA needed me to go undercover. Sheridan was—is, our link to this person." At the zero response from Jared, Adam's voice rose, "He's also a human smuggling, drug pushing, gunrunner who we've been doing our Goddamn best to take down. So you can stay annoyed with me for as long as you want, but none of this was my idea. When it first began I figured okay, cool, I'll play spymaster, catch me a bad guy and then get back to doing what SEALs do best, blow shit up." He grinned and slapped Jared's tense shoulder. "Seriously, we all took a vow to defend our country no matter what that entailed. *The Only Easy Day Was Yesterday*, remember?"

Again the hum of tires as the car ate up the miles and they

all acknowledged the motto and their pledge to protect with their lives if needs be.

The smooth, silky contralto of Maggie's voice broke the silence. "Listen, I think we're all forgetting the important thing here. Sheridan. I'm sure by now you must have realized the game we're playing is high stakes—you should like that, Martin." Jared accepted her little dig with a shrug. "I think it's in all our best interests to set aside our differences until we catch this creep."

Frank nodded his agreement. "She's right, boys. We need to team up and take care of business. We can hash the rest out later. With that in mind, how about a sit-rep on what you have compiled so far?"

Chancing a backward glance, Frank caught Adam waving his hand toward Maggie, giving her the floor. "Okay, here is our bullet list so far, 1) Sheridan somehow pulls strings, and joins SEAL Team 5 right after they are deployed to Iraq.

2) He makes contact with a known group of smugglers hidden under the guise of the Peshmerga militia.

3) He uses his ships, magically clearing all security checks, in the conveyance of drugs, arms and humans to Europe and Africa.

4) Sheridan finds out that O'Connor is a little too curious and shoots him.

5) Back in good old U.S.A Sheridan continues his lucrative career as a lawyer and has the suspiciously good luck to fall into a relationship with none other than Ramos Guerra, right hand man of El Chapo, head of the Sinaloa Cartel.

6) Everything is coming up rosy for our boy. The drug trade

is booming, he has a beautiful wife, Sara Wilcox, a daughter, and reaps the rewards of becoming Massachusetts next U.S. Attorney.

7) Rumors abound, is he beating his spouse? He pulls her out for a variety of functions; see perfect couple, no problems. Then a couple of years pass, he's preparing to run for governor and we hear he has a big reward out for his missing wife and daughter.

8) One day I'm out with vice, chasing leads on a bunch of missing hookers that seem to track back to Sheridan, and I hear word on the street about a multimillion-dollar deal in the pipe-line between the Cartel and our man.

9) A week later Martin here, manages to get himself arrested. Adam convinces me, against my better judgment, to make contact. Find out what you know. But I have to say, I figured you to be in on it."

Jared swung around in his seat, a WTF look on his face. "Relax buddy, I told her she was wrong, there was no way." Adam reassured him.

"Why would you even think Jare would be involved in this sort of thing? I don't get it." Frank asked the question bugging him ever since that day in the interrogation room.

Maggie answered, "We knew Sheridan was dirty, but there had to be someone else helping him. Where was he getting his info? How did he keep avoiding our attempts to nab him? Martin fit the bill. He has a gambling problem and has had for years, yet he always has the cash to play. His family is estranged. And most importantly, he is a genius when it comes to electronics and surveillance. It would have been child-play for him to watch our frequencies, warn Sheridan of any nets." She sighed and it curled under Frank's guard like smoke under a closed door. Dangerous, but nearly impossible to resist.

"That brings us to ten. Adam convinced me to break silence and make contact with you two and so now we hopefully, have evidence to lock that asshole away and if it's as good as you say, maybe we can hook the whole organization."

Digesting all the new Intel, Frank was embarrassed by how much had gone down right under his nose. His job was to know everything about his men. It's how you stay alive out there. He'd failed.

Jared, as usual seemed to sense his turmoil and snapped him a quick punch. "Don't. Don't you dare start blaming yourself for shit that had nothing to do with you. I was proud to be under your command. We all were." He shot a step up glance to the back.

Adam agreed. "He's right, Senior Chief, don't blame yourself. Sheridan had us all snowed. We knew he was a jerk, but not how big of a horse's ass he was, that's all."

While Frank appreciated his friends support, it still didn't change the fact he had seriously slipped in his duties as an officer. He thought of how it had been him who told his brother to cut through the field that day, he would catch up. He thought of the day his father died. How he hadn't been there for him. Now this, where he had failed his unit by missing something of such importance it had almost gotten two of his men killed.

It all piled up like a big car wreck in his chest. He was tired of it. Tired of always feeling to blame for things he had no control over. His fingers whitened as he strangled the steering wheel. His foot pressing down on the gas shot the car forward with a satisfying rumble. It was time to correct some of those transgressions, and it was going to begin with Sheridan. The man had made himself a deal with the devil. Now he had to pay.

CHAPTER TWENTY

Sara pulled up in front of her house and turned the key off on Mirabelle to hear the chirp of contented little birds, the joyful barks of playful puppies, and the clinking groan of the old car as it settled down as if for a much needed rest. She and Nick sat for a couple of minutes listening to the breeze play a song with the leaves through their lowered windows, neither one anxious to disrupt the peaceful moment.

"Is Jessica staying with your friend Annie for a couple of days?" Nick's quiet voice blended with the breeze drifting across Sara's cheek.

She sighed, soothed by the harmony between them. "Yes, she insisted. I explained some of what was going on, not all of it, but she figured it out, I think. Anyway, she said Jess would be no problem at all."

"Good, that's good. She'll be safe with her, there's no way he'll trace her to Annie."

Sara rolled her head on the backrest toward Nick, only to

see he'd done the same. They stared at each other, and the poignancy of the moment made her throat clench with suppressed longing.

Nick raised his hand and gently brushed her hair back from her cheek, his calloused fingers against her ear sending little zaps of electricity throughout her body.

"I want you in my life, Sara. I'm not ready to give up what's happening between us, are you?"

Mesmerized by his gentle touch and soft words, she viewed him with sleepy eyes as those sensual lips moved gradually closer. Her breath suspended as everything around them seemed to hush, the animals, the click-clacking motor, her heartbeat, all poised for the connection.

Nick's warm mouth touched hers, and her eyes drifted shut, soaking up the sensation like a starving bird. Her lips parted, inviting him in as he kissed first one side of her mouth and then the other. Soft, gentle, butterfly kisses that soon had her craving more. She brought her hand up and wrapped it around his neck. Her fingers delved into his mink soft hair to pull him closer, little mewling sounds escaping from her throat, but she didn't even care. This man was her other half. It didn't matter anymore that he'd hurt her. She'd hurt him too, she knew that. What they had *was* worth fighting for. Desperation clawed her gut thinking how close they'd come to losing each other.

The kisses became anything but tender as they both surrendered to the passion between them. Nick slid his hand down her neck and around to her jaw, raising her face ever closer to his as his tongue licked into her mouth, and tangled with hers.

Her left hand traced his pectoral muscles through his shirt, their firmness tempting her to trace ever lower, until she could pull the soft cotton of his top out of his jeans and delve beneath. The skin on skin contact drove a ragged groan out of him, filling Sara with feminine satisfaction. She'd brought this strong, proud man pleasure. He needed her.

Soon all she could do was feel. Nick's hand dropped from her jawline and trailed down the line of her neck to the tops of her breasts swelling out of her favorite bra. Her nipples tightened into hard little nubs and as his palm cupped one and squeezed, she broke away from his lips, needing to draw air, and maybe some sanity. They were making out in the front seat of her car like a couple of teenagers, in broad daylight no less.

"Nick." She moaned as his dislodged mouth nibbled and sucked her earlobe, causing comets to fly behind her eyelids. "Nick, we have to stop."

Her eyes fluttered open and Sara gazed into the hot sapphire depths of his. She was so tempted to ask him into her bed—but that wouldn't solve anything between them. In fact, it could only muddy already dirty waters, so she kept silent.

NICK EASED BACK, rubbing a shaky hand across the back of his neck in a bid to calm himself down. He'd only meant to give her a gentle kiss. She looked so beguiling, her golden eyes glowing in the ambient light filtering through the leaves of the Aspen above them.

The citrus of her shampoo and the rose scent that was pure Sara made his muscles tense in response. There were distinct signs of arousal in her flushed cheeks, quickened breathing, and swollen breasts. It took every ounce of control he had to sit back onto his own side of her dinky little car, giving her back her space. His eyes narrowed as she tried to straighten her rumpled shirt and smooth her messed-from-his-hands hair, causing her breasts to thrust forward with the motion, and his heart to want to leap out of his chest.

"I'm not going to apologize because we're combustible together. I for one, am damned happy to keep that fuse lit. I know we have more pressing concerns right now than how bad I want to pull you from your seat and finish what we started, but sooner or later..." His voice came out husky, thinking of passion-filled nights spent slaking their thirst for each other. He hoped this was a sign she was willing to forgive if not forget, otherwise he wasn't sure what he would do.

She gripped the steering wheel and stared out the window for a long moment before turning to him, and what he saw in her face made his heart lurch. "You're right, Nick. What we had was pretty special, which is why you need to understand how hurt I am because you weren't honest with me. I had the right to know you're an old acquaintance of Tom's, apparently close enough that he thinks you're willing to work..."

"Yeah, well he's wrong, and if you honestly believe I would do such a thing, you don't know me at all." He interrupted, pissed off at the whole situation. When was she going to get it through her thick skull he'd never do anything to deliberately hurt her? When he got his hands on Sheridan they were going to have to pull him off the son-of-a-bitch.

"Pardon me, but in all the time you spent getting to know

us, you never thought to say, "Hey, by the way, funny story." Didn't you think I had a right to know, Nick?"

"Of course you had a right to know, but what in the hell did you want me to do? Oh wait, no, we can't have mind-blowing sex right now, I have to tell you something first. Give me a break, Sara, I'm a man and sometimes my little head wins out over my big head, so sue me." Her attitude frustrated him so much his fist slammed down on the dash of the car, causing a rattle, bang and clang as it protested the abuse. And since he'd been staring daggers at her when it happened, he couldn't help but see her flinch away.

I'm a dumb asshole.

He wanted to gain her trust, not scare the shit out of her.

"Sara." He sighed, this wasn't getting them anywhere. "Honey, I'm sorry. I was angry. No not even angry, frustrated. But I would never, ever raise a hand to hurt you, swear to God."

After a moment of tense silence, her shoulders slumped and she stretched her hand to rest on his forearm. "Look, Nick, I know you wouldn't hurt me physically, but there's still a lot more than sex to building a relationship and I'm not sure I can. I would have to be able to fully trust in the other person, and right now I'm just not there."

While he wanted to argue the point, he could see he wouldn't get anywhere with her right now. She felt her marriage had damaged her for a *real* relationship, and even though he knew if she'd only give him half a chance they could overcome it together, he wasn't sure how to make her realize that.

"I suggest we take a step back. We'll go into the house, make some coffee and work on your negotiation skills, and let this rest for now, how does that sound?"

Sara nodded, pushing open Mirabelle's creaky door, and leading the way to her front door. She waved, as Tess called out a hello from where she'd been attending to her front flowerbeds, and then turned a bright pink, right up to the tips of her dainty ears.

She was so cute.

The house was cool and silent as they moved towards the kitchen and Nick was surprised to find himself missing Jessica's noisy chatter.

"Where's Jake?" She asked, searching her handbag for keys.

"I left him at home this morning. He was sure happy to see the guys again though, we both were." He couldn't resist, he reached over and planted a tender kiss on the back of her bared neck.

"I MEANT TO ASK YOU, Jess was worried about him." She smiled over her shoulder. "She's really attached to the great brute. I'm glad you showed up with him that day."

Great, lie number two. "About that, it wasn't quite an accidental meeting." It was true, his Mom always preached it but he'd never appreciated the value until now. It doesn't pay to lie because it will come back and bite you in the ass. Every stinking time.

"Are you kidding me?"

At her darkening look, Nick hastened to add, "It's not what you're thinking. I just want to clean the slate, that's all. I'd actually noticed you a couple of weeks earlier when I first came to town, but didn't know how to approach you, so I used Jake." He shrugged uncomfortably, it seemed so silly now. "I didn't exactly pick Tidal Falls randomly, as I led you to believe, either." He hated rehashing this stuff, but for her... "A couple of years ago Jake and I were injured while I was in the Marines."

"Oh, Nick, why didn't you tell me? That's what happened to your poor back, isn't it? I noticed the scars the other morning but didn't want to mention it." She stretched up and ran a gentle finger over his scarred forehead. "And Jake's hip?"

He grimaced, it was all coming back to him now. The explosion, the percussion as he went flying. The god-awful site of his team annihilated. "I needed to get away from it all for a while. My CO suggested a therapist here. I didn't want anyone knowing the truth because I didn't want to be treated differently. Back where I come from everyone acted as if I were a hero or some shit, instead of which that couldn't be further from the truth. If I'd done my job maybe my teammates wouldn't have been blasted to hell and gone. Even Jake was hurt. That's not a hero, it's a zero."

Sure this was going to be the straw that broke the proverbial camel's back, he sighed. "I know this just adds to all the other crap, but I wanted you to know the truth."

She turned away, and when her shoulders began to shake, he wanted to smack himself for causing her more anguish. Instead, as he swung her around to pull her into his arms he saw tears all right, but they were tears of laughter. She was laughing at him.

"What's so funny? I'm in a cold sweat here, wondering if I should have said anything, and you think it's funny."

———

SARA COULDN'T HELP IT. The whole slapstick comedy routine of their relationship tickled her funny bone. It was the icing on the cake. Their whole relationship, from day one, had been a web of lies, small wonder it crumbled at the first hurdle. "That's just it, it is funny. I'm sorry for what happened to you, I truly am. But if not for the fact I was running from my drug selling, lying, cheating, husband, we never would have met. Then you add a messed up, slightly neurotic woman, a lonely kid, a beat up dog and a guy who carries the weight of the world on his shoulders. We could have ourselves a Broadway classic here." She could see Nick thought she'd gone around the bend, and maybe she had a little. That's okay, laughter was a great stress reliever. She felt better already.

A slow smile lit his face like a ray of sunshine bursting through a cloudy sky. "You're right, our relationship up to this point has been something of a farce. But that doesn't mean my feelings are any less real. I never thought I'd meet someone I would want to wake up beside every morning for the rest of my life, but I have. And I think you feel the same. Don't negate everything between us, Sara, because of a couple of dumb mistakes. We're good together, you can't deny that."

Yes, they were good together. Images of the two of them talking, kissing, making love, flashed before her eyes, heating her from the inside out. More than almost anything else, she wished that they could have met under different circumstances, without all of this background between them.

Gazing up into his rugged face, Sara admitted Nick was worth much more than she could give him. He'd already been through so much, he deserved someone whole. Someone who wasn't so messed up. Someone who would love him for the imperfect, amazing, frustrating man he was. He looked so handsome as the light from the kitchen window streamed over his dark hair picking out the coffee colored highlights and accentuating the thin white battle scar. She traced it with her fingertip, so glad he wasn't one of those who'd lost their lives that day.

She was trying to think of a way to explain all the mixed up feelings tumbling around inside her head when a muffled trill from the depths of her handbag indicated an incoming call from her cellphone. Pulling out of his arms, she hurried to the counter where she'd dropped her bag; worried something was wrong with Jessica.

The number highlighted on the face was one she knew well, Tom.

She locked helpless eyes with Nick, who obviously knew something was amiss because in a couple of long strides he was there, hands on her hips, his big warm body offering silent support. Gulping in a quick breath and praying for strength she pushed send, accepting the call, and placed it on speaker so they both could hear.

"Hello, my dear, shouldn't you be on a plane by now? I've been sitting here keeping your lovely little friend company while we wait, but we were getting a little concerned as we hadn't heard from either Nickolaus or yourself. Fiona desperately wants to see you again. She has so much to tell you, don't you my pet?"

"I'm okay." Fiona's voice reached out in desperate warning, "Stay away, Sara. Stay..." fading as the phone was obviously yanked away. "Ouch! You son of a bitch."

"Tom...Tom, listen to me, don't hurt her. If you want me to cooperate you need to leave Fiona alone. Do you understand me? Leave. Her. Alone." Sara yelled, gritting her teeth against the stream of vitriol she wanted to lash at him.

"Enough. Where's Nick? I know he must be nearby, after all he's a man of his word, right, Nick?"

Nick continued to hold her close, reassuring her as he took control of the conversation, "I'm here, let's quit playing games and get down to business. There's been a change of plan. Your ex-wife tells me she has something you want, quite desperately actually. She's made me a better deal so I'm afraid I am going to have to terminate our agreement. You know how it is, money talks."

Tom swore, "Are you fricken kidding me? I would never have taken you for a gambler, because that's what you are doing, my friend. You're gambling with lives. Are you sure you want to start something with me you have no chance of finishing? Think carefully, Kelley. My offer stands if you want to change your mind. Otherwise I can't guarantee you'll make it out of this alive. Business, you understand."

Nick laughed, a quick, harsh bark of sound. "Yeah, I get it. Fortunately for me, I seem to be the one holding all the aces, don't I. *Your* very pretty wife, your daughter, and, oh yeah, a sweet file loaded with names that would make for some very interesting phone calls. I'm sure your associates would love to know how I managed to find out as much about their little dealings as what you've written in here. They would wonder what you were planning on doing with this information, don't you think? I bet these same men would really appreciate me calling them about this. Be grateful even, if you catch my drift."

Sara's breath suspended as she waited through the static noise of Sheridan as his fury at the situation practically burned through the airwaves. Nick had pushed the bastard too far.

"You still there, Sheridan? Time's a-wasting as you pointed out, what's it to be? Are we doing this my way or am I placing a few long distance phone calls?"

Tom's harsh laugh rang through the room, and her fingers tightened on the phone.

"Well, well, Nick, I see you've grown a set of balls in the last few years. Okay, I'll play along—for now—but know this, my friend, fuck with me and I will be more than happy to feed them down your cock-sucking throat, understand?"

Nick gently squeezed her hips in reassurance before answering, "Yeah, I understand you're as big a prick now as you were five years ago. Some things never change, right, *buddy?* More importantly, I see by your handy dandy notes here that you are kind of in a time crunch. I don't imagine your friends are big in the patience department, and since I'm not anxious to take part in a Mexican stand-off we can save a lot of mileage and time by you bringing Miss Radcliffe here, to us. Then in exchange for her *Healthy* person, I'll return your file to you, intact."

Sara had some requests of her own. "I also want you to bring divorce papers signing full custody of Jessica over to me. It's past time to end our relationship, and you never wanted our daughter so that should be no problem for you, right, Tom?" She was happy her voice came through inflexible and strong, not showing how scared she actually was.

"Demands, my love? I'm impressed. I wouldn't have thought you had it in you. You're correct, I never wanted to bring a child into my world, can you blame me? I'm well aware of my short-comings, Sara, but for a while, with you, I was a different man. We had some good times, didn't we?"

Now it was Nick's turn to tense. She knew he didn't want to hear about her supposed *good times* with her ex. Dropping a hand to her side, she intertwined her fingers with Nick's before replying, "Anything good that happened between us was over-shadowed long ago by your mistrust and cruelty. The only thing I want to remember about you is saying good-bye after you turn over Fiona and those papers. We're done, Tom."

"You're talking a brave story, my pet. What have you done, Sara? You better not be screwing our mutual friend, Nickolaus. That would be a grave error on your part. Adultery is frowned upon in a marriage, you know."

A disbelieving laugh escaped her throat, what temerity. "Well you would know all about that, wouldn't you, Tom?"

"Ah yes, the nanny. I wondered how much you saw the day you stole my files. I had video surveillance in that room, you didn't know that, did you?" Tom's self-satisfied tone rubbed at already raw nerves. "I knew exactly who to blame for the theft, right from the start. As to the bountiful Belinda, she meets my needs. It's not as if sex between us was ever anything more than bland. You aren't exactly sensual, my dear. Have you noticed that already, Nickolaus?"

Sara's head dropped in embarrassment. She'd known he was cruel, but...Nick's anger was a powerful force at her back. He growled his answer, "Enough with the bullshit already. Look, do we have a deal here or not? I don't have time to stand around chitchatting. Make up your mind, Sheridan. What's it to be?"

Staring out the window into the backyard Sara was surprised to see the sun still shining. The neighbor's calico cat stalked through the overgrown grass toward a fat Robin busy looking for juicy worms at the base of the Cherry tree. Just as the cat pounced, the Robin flew away, its bounty dangling from its beak.

Hoping it was a metaphor for their own situation, she turned in Nick's arms and smiled when he dropped a deliberately loud, smacking kiss on her upturned mouth.

There was a sudden hissing over the line, like water hitting a hot pan. "Dangerous, my love, very dangerous. You better let lover boy know what happens when you fuck around on me. You remember that, don't you?"

THE BLANCHING of color from her face was all the proof Nick needed, if he had ever doubted her story, which he hadn't. The fucker was his. "Enough. Make your arrangements and fly to Seattle. Call me, and I do mean me. No more calls to Sara. I'll tell you where from there—and Sheridan—make it fast." He pressed end and taking the cell out of her trembling fingers, set it on the counter behind her, before drawing Sara into the shelter of his arms.

She snuggled into him for a gratifying couple of minutes before pulling back to look into his eyes, her own a melting pot of turmoil and fear. "Why didn't you let me handle him, Nick? He was already mad, but now you've driven him right into crazy. It's bad enough he thinks we're colluding together, but to make him think there's more between us...he won't stand for that. I hope you know what you're doing."

Nick was grateful she was still talking to him after he pulled that foolish stunt of male posturing. Talk about tweaking the tail of the monster—he'd spit in its face. But he couldn't let the comment about Sara being bland go, she was the exact opposite of that. Exciting him with just a touch, he'd had the privilege of watching her fall apart in his arms also, perfection.

She'd put up with Sheridan's maligning for more than enough years. She had him now to protect her and Jessica, to provide a buffer against her prick of an ex. "I know you wanted to handle this on your own, but I couldn't stand back and let him tear you apart like that. I wanted him believing we've collaborated. That way he'll be so busy formulating his revenge he won't clue into the fact it's a trap."

"Well, I think you achieved your goal, he was spitting mad when you hung up. I don't think we'll have many days to pull this off. God, if he hurts Fiona..." She looked up at him, her face almost gaunt with worry.

Nick set his hand to her soft cheek and rubbed away tears, hating to see her upset like this. "He won't, she's his bargaining chip, and he wants what we have too much to screw with that. I don't foresee any problems until after the exchange, which is when we'll have to be prepared. He's livid and he's under pressure, both from me and the Cartel, his brain must be short-circuiting right about now." Nick grinned, he loved it when a plan came together.

Sara came back into his arms, her own wrapping him tightly around the waist as her head burrowed into his chest. Nick laid his cheek along her soft hair. Closing his eyes he absorbed the warmth of her skin as he inhaled her delicate rose scent. The heat of the sun was a benediction to their gently swaying bodies and as he relaxed into the moment, Nick knew he wanted her more than he'd ever wanted anything in his life.

Adam would have loved this. He always said Nick would go down hard, long before he ever did. In fact, they'd had a running bet going. He would have been happy to pay the bastard, too, if he hadn't gone and gotten himself killed. Now Nick's memory had returned, and he knew how, if not quite why, his best friend had died, he was more determined than ever to see Sheridan behind bars.

CHAPTER TWENTY-ONE

Tom stared at the now silent cell phone in his hand, stifling the urge to launch the fucking thing through the nearest window. How dare they try to dictate to him, didn't they know better by now? Had he not shown them repeatedly who was running this show? Did they think this was some stupid game they were all playing? That if they out-maneuvered him they would shake hands and go their separate ways?

He was very disappointed with Nick, he'd thought him to be a man of his word, obviously not. All it had taken was the offer of more money and the lure of a siren and he'd flipped sides, the traitor.

Then there was Sara. She continually surprised him with her ingenuity. He'd always admired her beauty and charm, knew she was special. Since her enterprising foray into his office and subsequent escape, he was reminded of what had drawn him to her in the beginning, her intelligence as much as her beauty. It had taken a lot of grit to steal from him, he admired that. However, the fact remained that she knew too much and now apparently had shared that knowledge with her *boyfriend*. The thought of her in bed with another man had the predictable effect of making him see red, jealousy twisting his gut into tight knots. Even though he hadn't wanted her sexually in a long time, she was still his, God-dammit.

He didn't have time for this shit. Guerra was due to call any day now for delivery and he had his benefactor breathing down his neck to tie things up. There were rumblings in Washington that neither one of them could afford to ignore.

Tom remembered all those years before when the syndicate first approached him. When he became aware of how powerful they were and how many doors they could open for him, he'd had no problem following their dictates. Mother dearest was already in bed with the man in charge—literally—and on her demise they made clear to him how deeply indebted the Sheridan family was.

The leader, 'Phoenix', who Tom hadn't met, placed him in Iraq and set up his first contacts, carefully monitoring the details of the transactions. After a couple such episodes, he was granted more authority and took full advantage, dispensing with O'Connor when he got in the way, even though they warned him to step back. He rubbed the empty space where his pinky finger used to be, a reminder of the cost of disobedience.

Arriving back in the U.S. he took up his position at a leading law practice, and presumed he was out, of no more use to them. He was wrong.

Moving up through the firm, he won himself an appointment to the U.S. Attorney's office. Then, not long after, a key case went to trial involving the son of one of the leaders from the Sinaloa Cartel, a high-ranking lieutenant. Seeing it as an opportunity, and thanks to his ingenuity, Ramos Guerra escaped prosecution. And so their partnership began. Or so he thought. Instead, later he found he'd been nothing more than a marionette, guided along on invisible strings held by the Syndicate. Giving in to the inevitable Tom began to see the benefits of his alliance. His career soared, his dreams of making it to the White House coming ever closer.

Now everything rode on those files being returned intact. He hated to think what might happen if either the organization or the men he had dealt with learned of its existence. They might not see it the same way he did, as an insurance policy. Tom was under no delusions. He either remained useful to the Cartel and the Union or they would remove him, simple. Before that happened though, he was going to do everything in his power to get the damn thing back, and take care of his pain-in-the-ass wife and her lover boy.

Turning, he watched as the she-witch worked at the ropes binding her to the old wooden chair, her wrists and ankles both red and swollen from the hemp.

"You're never going to get those loose. I was a boy scout, I think I know my knots."

Sparing him no more than a glance out of frenzied green eyes, she kept her body twisting back and forth, trying to gain a millimeter of space where there was none.

Interesting. Seems Miss Radcliffe might have an aversion to confined places.

While he'd like nothing better than to delve further into

seeing what it would take to break her, time would not allow it. For now. She really was quite lovely. Maybe he would keep her as a new pet after they were through with this. The corners of his lips curled upward. After all, there would be no Sara around to miss her.

"It seems your friend has decided to leave you hanging in the wind. How do you like that, Fiona?"

Her eyes flashed emerald fire. "Don't you say my name, you dirtbag." She tugged on her restraints. "And Sara should leave me. She has a daughter to care for," contempt dripped from every word.

He traced a finger down her jawline.

Fiona jerked her head away, "Don't touch me, you asshole."

"I'm well aware of who she has with her, she is also my daughter. Don't you think I have the right to know she's safe? Not running around the countryside with a mentally unstable parent." He leaned closer, drawn to her inner strength of will.

"The only parent that Jessica has that's unstable is you, you creep." Muttering some unladylike curses she struggled against her bonds. "If I managed in some small way to help them to evade you and your cruelties, I'm happy."

Tom laughed at her cheek. Even though she was obviously in a full-blown panic at the restriction of the ropes, she still had spunk. He became hard at the thought of taming that out of her with hours spent in his bedroom. Running his hand through the fiery tresses of her hair he grabbed a fistful, forcing her head back, before bringing his mouth down hard against her own. There was a clash of teeth and he tasted blood where he split her lip, exciting him more as he forced her mouth open with his tongue. Just as he entered her, the dark sultry taste causing his heart to leap in his chest, she bit him!

He pulled back, swearing at the pain. A triumphant smile formed on her bloody lips. Enraged, he lifted his hand and slapped her across the face.

Fiona cried out, her chair skidding up on to two legs before settling back down with a wobble, the imprint of his hand a deep red against her pale skin.

Tom wiped his hand across his mouth, coming away with a streak of blood, hers and his. As he pulled a pristine white cloth from his pants pocket and wiped it off, he contemplated the damage his temper had wrought. Her eye was already swelling shut, her full lips were swollen and red from his kisses. And still she stared right back at him, defiance gleaming from every pore. No wonder his vapid little wife found herself so easily persuaded to stray, thanks to this irritating creature.

His body urged him to show her who was superior, but he accepted that now was not the time. There were too many arrangements needing to be made for an anonymous trip across country. Last thing Tom needed was for the Syndicate to get wind that there was a problem amidst their ranks. He knew they would not tolerate even a hint of controversy. He'd been given a front row seat to how they handled opposition and had never forgotten it.

They'd arranged a car to chauffeur him across the city. A guard blindfolded him until they arrived at their destination. The screech of gulls and smell of brine permeating the air told him they were on the waterfront. They shepherded him inside a building before removing the blindfold, revealing a cavernous room filled with large wooden crates in various dimensions.

Tom followed the guard's bald head to a side wall, two eyeballs tattooed on the back of his skull staring back at him. After pressing numbers into a small keypad, a hidden door opened into an opulent chamber filled with men, all in fine suits, wandering the perimeters chatting as they admired various pieces of fine art. A large steel barred enclosure took up space at one end of the room.

Two men, their heavily muscled torsos straining their designer cut suits, brought some poor bugger stark naked into the room and threw him inside the contraption, laughing as he fell to his knees sobbing for a pardon. The men outside the ring ignored him, talking and drinking expensive scotch while the robust scent of cedar and coffee from 'Cuban Classic' cigars hung in the air as bookies made their rounds.

Soon everyone took seats surrounding the penned enclosure. Tom followed suit wondering why he'd been brought there, and what they planned on doing to the man. A loud bell pealing startled him. The steel door on the opposite side of the enclosure slowly began to rise on chained pulleys. All noise, except for the victim's frenzied pleading, seized as everyone's eyes focused on the ring.

There was a feeling of expectancy as everyone leaned forward. A thunderous growl lifted the hairs as a humongous grizzly bear charged into the cage, his huge head swiveling from side to side as deep grunts erupted from his chest. Tom watched in horror as the poor idiot inside screamed and ran cowering to the cage door, trying to climb the thing, his skinny ass waving like a white flag to the beast that had caught his scent.

The men around him clapped in delight, shouting encouragement, knowing the sap didn't stand a chance in hell. The bear, enraged at either the yelling or maybe having that ass waving at him, charged a few feet, bounced a couple of times, then rose on his hind legs, easily topping out at eight feet. He let out an ear-piercing roar before dropping hard to the ground, the vibration rattling Tom's teeth, or maybe that was fright. With another deep chest grunt he charged the man, and lifting one massive clawed paw, swiped him off the gate and sent him flying across the pen. The man, screaming now in pain as his arm lay in bloody tatters, tried to get up and run, but the bear catching the scent of fresh blood pounced. And that was it; he ripped half the guys face off in another swipe before settling down to feast.

Nauseous, Tom searched desperately and settled on a nearby waste can.

Holy Fuck.

He kept his face turned away but could do little to stop the horrific sounds as the bear ripped and tore into its prey, meanwhile around him the others were laughing, slapping each other's backs as if they had witnessed a great sport.

The silent guard appeared at his side and led him stumbling back through the warehouse, blindfolding him again before taking him to the waiting car. Before moving, a low rumble from the front warned him, "Fuck with the boss and that will be you, don't ever forget that." It was months before he could get half-a-nights rest after that. No, he had never forgotten.

Swallowing hard on the queasiness thoughts of that day always conjured, Tom turned away from the knowing eyes of his captive, taking in the plainness of the small room. He'd had this little cottage on the back of his estate built a few years earlier, as it became necessary to hold his meetings with Guerra in a more private location. It had a separate road winding through a couple miles of dense forest before veering onto his land through a well-monitored gate.

He'd purposely kept the interior unimposing. The people he dealt with had no need to know how wealthy his family ties had made him. There was a simply appointed kitchen with old-fashioned olive green appliances, and a solid pine table and chair set, currently used by his *guest*. Then through an arched doorway, there was a small bedroom outfitted with a single bed and a utilitarian washroom.

Striding the few feet to the bathroom sink, Tom wet a cloth with cool water before returning to Fiona and setting it against her swelling cheek, remorse hitting him as she flinched from the pain.

"Look, I'm sorry I hit you but you shouldn't have bit me, you upset me, which obviously had bad consequences for you. I'm a reasonable man; I think we could be friends, we're a lot alike. What do you say?"

The look she speared him with told him what her answer was going to be before a word ever left her mouth. "Are you freakin' kidding me? There is nothing on God's green earth that would ever persuade me to even give you the time of day, much less spend time with you of my own free will, that's ridiculous."

She wasn't going to make it easy for him. That's okay, he

enjoyed a challenge. Lifting the cool cloth away, he trailed his finger down the fading red marks, smiling at the shiver of fear she couldn't quite hide. Good, she should be worried.

"We're going on a little trip, you and I. Your *friend*, Sara, has been busy. While you've been here worrying about her, she's gone out and found herself a fuck-buddy. If I were you, I would be a trifle pissed off about that. She's made a life somewhere else and forgotten all about you. Meanwhile here you are, the pawn who lost her money and her brothers vehicle, all for the sake of someone who doesn't give a sweet shit."

Fiona scowled up at him as she spit out the words, "Screw you. I know what you're doing and it's not going to work. Sara *is* my friend. It's no wonder she left you. She never said exactly what happened, I guessed though, and obviously I was right. You're every bit as big a prick as I thought."

"Whatever my dear, sticks and stones. The facts speak for themselves, she's living the high life, while you on the other hand..." Tom had found it paid to stick as close to the truth as possible when swaying a jury, it was the little manipulations of that truth that swung the vote. Leaving her to mull over what he'd told her, he stepped out onto the small front porch to make his call.

"I've found her. We leave in the morning. Get four of your best men together and meet me at the airport, and Sam...come prepared."

CHAPTER TWENTY-TWO

Frank pulled up in front of Nick's and gazed across the road to Ms. Sheridan's house. He hoped they'd managed to patch over their differences. He liked Sara, and had never seen Nick looking so happy or relaxed, even with all this crap hanging like a dark cloud over their heads.

They'd been blessed with silence from Jared for the last half hour, he was still slouched in the corner brooding. The two in the back were all chummy, leaning close, sharing notes on their mobile devices. He couldn't wait to see the surprise on Nick's face when he found out Adam was still in the land of the living, fully aware his reappearance was going to stir a hornet's nest. There was bound to be some anger mixed in with the joy and relief, much as he himself had gone through. The two men had been the best of mates. He doubted Nick ever fully recovered from watching his friend get shot. It wasn't something a man could forget.

"So this is it? Nick gave up the big city for small town

U.S.A? That doesn't seem like him." Adam slid his cell into his suit pocket as his gaze searched the neighborhood.

"How would you know what he likes? None of us are the same as we were back then. Things change, people change," Jared said, sliding out of the front seat.

Frank shook his head at Jared's attitude and hoisted his own bulk out of the car, pausing to open the back door for Maggie. He appreciated the view of her long, suit clad legs stepping out followed by a quick tantalizing peek down the front of her loosely buttoned shirt when she twisted her frame out of the car to stand eye to chin with him. Gazing into her knowing brown eyes, he acknowledged with a quirk of his lips, that yes, he had been looking.

"You think I don't know that?" Adam told Jared as he exited the car, jolting Frank and Maggie apart.

They circled the car, intent on keeping the combatants apart. "In case you were wondering, I've changed too. I even had a real, grown up relationship, which I screwed up, by the way." The sidelong look he sent to Mags, wasn't missed by any of them. "Look, let's get this over with and then you don't have to see my ugly face for another five years if you want, okay?" Adam started across the street, grabbing onto Maggie's hand. Jared's voice stopped him.

"Fuck, I'm sorry, man. I don't know what the hell's the matter with me. I'm no better, actually, I'm worse. At least you had a solid reason for disappearing, I quit. I couldn't deal, so I walked. If not for Frank dragging my sorry ass back from the edge, who knows, maybe we wouldn't be having this conversation."

Adam turned and looked his old friend straight in the eye. "I'm really fucking glad that's the case. Who else would I get to fix my satellite T.V.?" There was a hushed silence.

"Screw you, dude, get with the times. It's all about Netflix these days." Jared grinned, and then all four broke out in laughter, slapping each other on the back in companionship.

It was then that the door opened. Nick stepped out onto the porch closely followed by a curious Sara.

"Frank, is there a problem?" he asked, obviously not noticing who was standing beside Jared.

"Depends on how you want to look at, bro," Adam answered as he stepped forward. "Do you believe in ghosts?"

IT's a damn good thing Sara's palm supported the small of his back because otherwise Nick would have folded like a wet blanket. He rubbed hard at his eyes, sure they were misleading him. Slowly, almost like an old man, he worked his way down the stairs through the afternoon shadows caused by the stirred up clouds streaking across the sky, until he stood sneaker to Ferragamo loafer with his past.

It looked solid and real but...heart pounding, praying his hand didn't slide right through, Nick stretched out to push the apparition, shocked to meet up with flesh and bone.

"Hey, man, don't mess with the threads. You know how fussy I am about my clothes." The spirit grinned. "It's me, Nick. No one else could look this good, right?"

Holy shit. It's him. Adam's alive!

Foregoing explanations, he grabbed on and squeezed the living shit out of him, so fricken glad to see his friend alive unashamed tears rolled down his face.

"Nick, are you okay? What's going on? Who is this?" Sara's worried voice coming from right behind him finally allowed him to loosen his constrictor hold and take a step back. He swiped his cheeks with the palm of one hand while keeping a tight grip on his friend's elbow, just in case.

Sending her a reassuring look, he wrapped an arm around her shoulders to draw her forward. "You're not going to believe this, I hardly believe it myself, but this sorry looking son-of-a-bitch is someone I used to call my best friend. Mind you that was before he went and got himself shot, and supposedly *killed*, right, buddy?"

Now that he'd had a moment to digest the mind-boggling turn of events, Nick took note of some of the changes the years had wrought. Adam had always been the quieter, more reflective of the two of them, but now Nick could see a new maturity to his face. A hardness which had not been apparent in the young idealistic man who was sure they were going over there to make a difference. Yeah, right. Staring into his brown eyes, Nick could see whatever Adam had been through in the past years, had not been easy on his friend.

"You look great, Nick. I've missed you, pal. I can't tell you how many times I started to call before realizing I couldn't. And before you get all bent out of shape, how about introducing me to your friend?" Adam smiled, and it was the charismatic quirk of the lips Nick remembered so well. He really was alive.

How ironic that Sheridan, of all people, would bring first

Sara, and then all of his team, together. Even though he'd been deployed with other units, including the one he'd lost, these guys were the ones he'd connected with. His *brothers*. A couple of months ago he'd been getting by, day by day. Now he knew exactly what he'd been missing and vowed never to go back to that empty existence again.

Sara stepped forward, holding out her hand in greeting. "I'm Sara Reed. Nick's been a little remiss in telling me about his friends. I know Frank and Jared were his teammates. I assume from this reunion you were also?" He dipped his head in acknowledgement so she continued, "I'm guessing you would be the DEA we are expecting?"

Adam shook her hand. "That would be correct. I'm Adam O'Connor, and this is my partner, Magdalena Holt. We are very familiar with your husband, ma'am. Maggie and I have been actively involved in this case for close to six years now."

"And why is that, Mr. O'Connor? Is my *Ex*-husband that smart, or are you just that inept?"

Jared let out a whoop of laughter. "You go, girl."

"Sara..." Nick couldn't believe that his guarded, inhibited, beautiful love had soundly criticized a Special Forces operative as if he were a naughty child.

"No, it's okay," This from the stunning Ms. Holt as she stepped forward. "We understand your frustration, and you're absolutely right. This case should have been wrapped up long ago, and it would have been, except your ex has some high-powered friends. Every time we'd get anywhere close to an arrest, bad Intel would come through to block us. Believe me, we're every bit as frustrated as you."

Nick noticed the neighbors eyeing their little entourage and decided to move things indoors. "The file Sara has can change all that, let's go in and she can show you what she has."

Nearing the front gate he saw Tess staring out her kitchen window, her brow pinched with worry. He lifted his hand in a reassuring wave and Sara, catching the motion, looked over. "I don't want her upset, I'm just going to run over and let her know what's happening. I'll be right back." She reached up and gave him a too swift peck on the lips before angling off toward Tess's front door.

Nick caught up to Adam who'd stopped to watch her enter the neighbor's home. "Never mind, get your own, she's mine."

Adam turned with a quick smile. "Where have I heard that before? You never could hold onto your women once I showed up."

They both grinned at the blatant falsehood. Nick snapped his arm around Adam's thickened shoulders and placed him in a headlock, before letting go with a light shove. "Whatever you need to think to help you sleep at night, buddy. As I remember it, you took the ones I left behind."

Man, it was good to have him back. He'd talked to Adam after he died. Little day to day things, had he noticed the babe in the mess tent? Or why the hell couldn't they have been deployed to Siberia instead of all this sand and heat? And after they'd told him what Adam had done to die—why did the asshole have to go and be a hero?

His chest tightened, "I can't believe you're here. That was the worst night of my life."

Adam's throat bobbed in response. "Yeah, it wasn't a real

highlight for me either, pal. If I'd known they were going to tell you guys I *died*, I sure as hell wouldn't have let them. By the time I found out what they'd done it was too late, it was a done deal. My family had been informed already. Shit, I even had a funeral service, how weird is that? They already had new identification for me, a new life."

He looked to where Frank and Jared were conversing with Maggie in the shadows of the old tree in Sara's yard. "I only agreed to help the DEA out in the first place because Sheridan was rubbing me the wrong way. They'd already tagged him, but at that time, he was low man on the totem pole. They were after the leader. We still are."

"And what about those caught in the middle? It pisses me off to think both you and the fricken DEA let that fucker get away while you went hunting the big fish. Sara shouldn't have had to pay the price for some asshole's decision to let Sheridan walk." Nick growled.

"Frank mentioned things were bad between Sheridan and his wife. If we'd known we would have stepped in, man, you need to believe that. We want the head of the syndicate but not at the cost of women and children. Never."

While Nick was angry they hadn't done something to protect Jessica and Sara long ago, he did understand. What went on behind closed doors often stayed behind closed doors. "I get it. I wish you had let us know what you were involved in though. Maybe we could have helped catch the S.O.B instead of watching you go down. You should have trusted us to have your back. Instead you had to go and play the super-hero. Worked out well for you, didn't it?"

"Wow, not pulling any punches hey, buddy? I fucked up, I admit it, but I've also paid the price for five long years, so cut me a break."

They stood silent for a couple of moments, each lost in painful reflection, then Adam grinned and changed the subject. "She's feisty." He nodded to where Sara had disappeared.

Nick's chest swelled with pride. "She's getting stronger every day. It's not been an easy road, as you can imagine. I can't conceive what she must have gone through with that prick, all I know is he's not going to get anywhere near her ever again. That's a heads up to you. I know you want him, and the rest of the ring, but Sara is not your pawn, understand?"

Adam stared hard at Nick before breaking into a slow smile. "You're hooked. I never thought to see the day when a woman brought the great Nickolaus Kelley low, damn. Guess you owe me fifty, hey pal?"

Nick's lips twisted at the reminder. Funny, he'd thought that very same thing not so many hours ago. It was the easiest cash he would ever part with. Both because it was true, he was hooked, and because Adam was standing right fricken here asking for it. Who would have thought? Slapping him on the back, he guided his friend into Sara's home.

———

SARA WASN'T sure how to explain the men, and woman, Tess had watched enter her house. After only Jessica and herself for the last eighteen months, it was hard enough for her to reconcile the fact they weren't alone in this anymore, much less trying to explain it to her new friends. She'd hoped when they moved here her previous life would be behind them, that they could shed it like an old skin, instead Tom continued to be an albatross around her neck.

Which was the main reason she'd come over to Tess's house. If Nick knew what she planned, he'd step in, endangering himself and his friends. She couldn't allow that. Tom was her problem. When he'd taken Fiona and hurt her, he had broken the final straw. Years of oppression and manipulation fought to free themselves from her body like live entities.

Nick wasn't aware of it, but she'd made copies of the infamous file. She was going to use that to trap Tom and get Fiona back, without risk to Nick. If she failed, he would still have the original copies and could then turn them over to the authorities. She'd also filled in the necessary paperwork so that if, God forbid, something happened to her, there would be a record of why and her wishes that Jessica stay with Annie. Though she prayed it wouldn't come to that.

"Honey child, I'm getting the feeling you didn't come completely clean with me about what kind of trouble you're in. Now you sit yourself down, Grace is on her way over and we're going to figure this out," Tess said the moment she walked through the door.

Feeling rather like a chastised child, Sara sat.

"Okay then, while we wait you can tell me about those very nice looking young men Nick seemed to know rather well."

"He does know them. They all worked together when he was in the Marines. The one I met today, they all apparently thought had died." Tess sucked in a shocked breath. "I know,

243

right? It's a long story, I don't know all the details yet. Did you notice the tall sandy haired guy standing by the hulk? You'll never guess who that is, it's Grace's son!"

Tess clapped her hands together and brought them to her chest. "Oh my good Lord, Jared is back. I thought he looked familiar but it's been so many years. Has Grace seen him yet? She's going to be over the moon. It broke her heart when that boy left like that. He's not been back in probably eight years or so. Life is too short for those kinds of misunderstandings. I hope the two of them can work things out now."

Sara hoped for Grace's sake they could too. She couldn't imagine anything keeping her away from Jessica. Except maybe death. The reality of what she stood to lose should she fail hit her, firming her resolve to end this. Her years of subjugation were over. She was her own woman, and it was time Tom learned that.

With a quick knock, Grace came breezing into the little kitchen, a pan of freshly baked cinnamon buns in her hands. "I hear we have ourselves a state of emergency, so I brought reserve sustenance. Okay, Sara Sunshine, tell us all about it, and then we'll figure out how we're going to fix it."

Quick tears sprang to her eyes. These two scarcely knew her, but had taken her and Jess under their wings and treated them like family almost since day one. She thanked God every day for bringing her here to Tidal Falls.

"Have I mentioned how much I love you guys? I don't know what I would have done without your friendship these last months."

"Oh honey, you've been every bit as special to us. We hate to see you under all this stress, let us help you, Sara." Both women rushed to hug her and the warmth and love she felt flowing between them gave her the strength to explain everything to them, including the guilt she had carried for so long now.

"As you already know my marriage was a mistake. I think maybe the fact I'd spent my childhood in and out of foster homes made me hope for someone for me, to give me the safe and secure home I'd never had. And I thought for a while Tom was that man. In the beginning everything was perfect, he treated me like a princess, we were happy. Then I became pregnant and he changed. He became possessive, cutting my friends and my art out of my life. Then he began to drink, and turned mean." She picked at the still warm cinnamon bun between her fingers. The crumbs falling to the table were like her dream of a happy marriage.

"One day a call snuck through security. It was one of my old friends. She invited me out for lunch. We spent the day shopping and had so much fun. It was late when I returned home. Tom was angrier than I'd ever seen him. He freaked, and accused me of horrible things. Then he hit me." She shuddered in remembrance. "I thought that was the end of it, but instead he followed us to our room and raped me." There, she'd said it aloud, surprised by how freeing it felt to admit.

After a moment of shocked silence Tess said, "It's a good thing that son-of-a-bitch is nowhere near here, I'd shoot him."

Grace disagreed, "I wish he was here, I always wanted to try a Lorena Bobbitt."

A startled, laugh escaped Sara's throat, "I had no idea you ladies were so blood-thirsty."

"Only when it's necessary, dear," Tess replied as she poured them each a cup of steaming tea into delicate porcelain cups.

"Well I appreciate it, but I'm okay now. It only happened the once, after that he never touched me again." She didn't see the need to upset them further by telling them about all the belittling times until she escaped.

"I found out he'd created liaisons with people from a Mexican Cartel. He's a U.S. attorney, they paid him well to keep them out of the jail system. In addition, he was transporting drugs, guns and who knew what else for them." She smiled half-heartedly at the tsking sounds coming from her friends. "I found out he'd made a file detailing all of his transactions, including dates and names. An opportunity arose and I took the file, grabbed Jessica, and ran.

"Good for you, I hope they slam the book on the SOB." Grace said, rocking forward and bumping the table, sloshing the tea.

Sara reached across and grasped her hand. "My friend Fiona, she helped by giving us a vehicle and cash, we couldn't have made it without her. Now, somehow Tom found out and kidnapped her. He's threatening to hurt her if I don't return to him with the file, and I know he will. I have to help her."

"Of course you do, but not alone. What about Nick? I'm sure he would want to help." Tess insisted.

"Yes, he would, and that's just it, Tess, I can't let him. If he was hurt because of me, I couldn't handle it. Besides, like I said before, this is something I need to do for me. Please tell me you understand?" She used her free, slightly sticky hand, to catch Tess's as she went to walk away in frustration.

"We do understand, but we can't let you do this alone. So if not them, you're going to have to accept our help. Do *you* understand?" Tess's gaze speared her own, willing her to agree.

Overwhelmed at their generosity, she answered in the only way she could. "Yes, ma'am."

Grace heaved a relieved sigh, "Okay then, this is what I propose we do. I just happen to have the perfect venue for this little exchange, Grits and Grace." And at Sara's instant denial, "No really, it's perfect. It's public, downtown, and our own domain; we'll have the upper hand."

"Grace, you've had that restaurant for twenty years, are you sure you want to take that chance?" Tess looked as worried as Sara felt.

"Darn rights. It'll be fun." Grace squeezed out a smile.

"*Fun*, that's it, now I know you've gone and smoked something funny. It's going to be dangerous, that's what it'll be. I think we'd better hedge our bets. I'm going to call Jack. Remember, Sara, I told you about him. He's the Chief of Police, he'll know what to do."

Sara nodded, liking the idea of someone with a badge showing up to save the day. As long as Nick and Jessica were safe, that is. "Tess's right, Tom is clever. He's going to know we're planning something. We need to distract him long enough for the police to make their arrest. That's where I come in, he feels that I've betrayed him, he's going to want revenge. We can use that."

"I hope you know what you're doing, honey child. That daughter of yours needs her Momma."

Which was exactly why this had to work.

The strident ring of the doorbell reverberated down the hall, echoing through the quiet rooms, and causing all three women to jump. Sara hopped out of her seat first, waving Tess back down, it was probably Nick, wondering what was keeping her so long. Whereas with Tom she had felt smothered by his over-bearing watchfulness, with Nick she only felt cherished, loved.

Smiling as she flung open the door, she said, "I know, I'm la..." The blood drained from her face and her knees went week as she latched onto the door for support, too stunned to do more than stare blankly at the surprise visitors.

"Hello, dear. Aren't you going to invite us in?"

CHAPTER TWENTY-THREE

Nick looked towards the back door for the tenth time in so many minutes, where was she? Intellectually he knew that she was perfectly safe next door at Tess's house, but he still fought an almost irresistible need to keep her next to him where he could make sure of her well being.

The mingling of deep voices behind him along with the lighter tones of Ms. Holt as she tried without much success to explain the protocol the DEA had to adhere to, was a welcome reprieve from his thoughts. He hated that they had decided to bring Sheridan to them. Nick would have much rather held ball in the other man's court rather than having him anywhere near Sara and Jessica.

The only spot of relief was that Adam had assured him there was a team watching the Sea-Tac airport and would be following Sheridan and company like white on rice. He knew their investment in the case dealt with Tom's involvement with the Syndicate, but for Nick it was much more personal than that. He hoped to see the bastard fry for what he'd done to Sara, and even to Jess. That little girl had managed to burrow her way into his heart; he would do anything to protect them.

Wonder what they would think if he asked them to settle in Tidal Falls—with him. Just thinking it made his palms sweat a little as his heart leap-frogged in his chest, marriage. He was really contemplating marriage.

Wow.

"What are you looking so serious about? Don't worry buddy, we won't let anything happen to your girlfriend." Deep in thought, Nick hadn't noticed Adam coming to stand next to him.

"You better not, I would be extremely unhappy if that dickwad gets within a mile of either one of them, so you better make fricken sure your guys don't lose him."

"We won't, don't worry we want this case over with every bit as much as you want that guy's nuts on a skewer."

"I doubt that, it's Sara's story to share, but trust me, jail's too good for that asshole. If it was up to me his life would be over, and it would end slowly and painfully."

"I hear you, brother, I hear you. If it's any consolation, when they find out he snitched on the syndicate, which you and I both know he's going to bend over backwards to do, his life on the inside will be a series of unfortunate events. He'll be singing Soprano for the rest of his short existence." Adam grinned.

Nick ached with the need to avenge Sara, but acknowledged Sheridan's last days would not be good ones. It would have to suffice.

"So what's with you and the beauticious Ms. Holt? I sensed

a little history between you two, am I right?" He'd missed so much of his friend's life, it was hard to fathom that he could ask the man about it now, instead of talking to his spirit.

"We have a past, but that's what it is, in the past. I was a real dick for a while, did some things I'm not very proud of and it cost me a smart, gorgeous, incredibly sweet, woman. I'm lucky she forgave me enough to remain my friend and partner. I would've hated like hell to lose her completely due to my own stupidity and who knows, maybe one day she'll see what a great catch I truly am." Adam smiled, but it was empty of humor.

Nick gave his friend a little manly nudge, hard shoulder to hard shoulder. "You'll meet someone one day and things will click, you know? Any woman would be lucky to have you—even if you are a moron."

"Aw, I love you too, you homely son-of-a-bitch." Adam shot him a grin, this one filled with affection.

Laughter rumbled through the room, and they turned to see Frank smiling at something Jared had said, and Nick's chest filled with satisfaction. No matter what else happened, he needed to make sure they all remained this close.

He noted Maggie standing off to one side, her attention riveted on Frank as he replied to Jared, laughter still lighting his grey eyes. He hoped Adam was too busy watching the two men to notice. He sensed whatever had happened between the two of them, Adam still had strong feelings for her. He would hate to see his friends torn apart over a woman, not after they just found each other again.

Seeking a distraction, he cleared his throat loudly, then said, "Maybe we should go ahead and start. I'll open the file, Jared, throw on a pot of coffee. I think we're going to need it before the night is over."

"Always the slave, never the master." He quipped, already opening cupboard doors in search of Sara's stash of cups.

"Whine, whine, whine, I can't imagine why some hot young babe hasn't snatched you up yet." Frank said as he pulled one of Sara's suddenly diminutive looking kitchen chairs towards him and gingerly sank down, letting out a faint grunt as his knees protested.

"Back at ya, big guy. Fine looking man such as yourself, in the prime of life, what's not to love?"

"Whatever, is that coffee done yet, peon?"

"Okay, sheesh, you two should get married." Adam broke in as he joined Frank, gesturing Maggie to come have a seat. Instead, she went to the counter, waiting while Jared filled the mugs with steamy, rich smelling nirvana in a cup, carrying two over to the table for the men, smiling as Jared brought her one.

Nick listened to the banter with half an ear as he dug through the kitchen drawer where they'd stuffed the printed copies, grabbing the cup left sitting on his way to the table.

"Okay, before I hand this over I need a promise from the DEA." He focused first on Agent Holt, then Adam. "Sara is free and clear of any charges of theft for these documents, otherwise we have no deal."

Adam chortled, while Maggie affirmed, "Mrs. Sheridan was married at the time of the, dispersal shall we say, of said file, therefore she has as much claim to ownership as Mr. Sheridan does, unless so noted. Now if he wants to claim sole responsibility for said file, we would certainly have to look into the matter. However, as *said* file is supposedly loaded with crucial information critical to our case, we would consider those issues and act upon them accordingly."

She glared at Frank as he clapped, a sarcastic smile on his full lips that did not extend to his gunmetal eyes. "Nice job, *Special Agent,* how many years of schooling did it take to learn that claptrap?"

Maggie visibly bristled at the condemnation apparent in Frank's tone. "Not that it's any of your business, *Chief,* but I became a lawyer before entering the academy. I know what I'm talking about."

"Well, I'm glad one of us does...ma'am."

Pissed off, Maggie turned to Nick, "Look, you don't have to trust us, and in fact you probably shouldn't. I recommend you call a lawyer as soon as we tag this person. That way you're covered. Now why don't you let us see what you have and then we can determine how much use it's going to be."

"Oh it's useful, all right." He laid the folder on the table and pulled the overflowing file from within. "There are a lot of names here our government's been watching for a long time. Some we were even tasked with keeping an eye on. I think you'll find everything you need, including a few surprises."

As the two heads, one straw colored, the other raven black, bent over the sheets of paper, Nick shot a look at Frank, wondering what had climbed up his ass. The big man's gaze was on the dark head, a look of such hunger in his eyes Nick had to turn away. Fuck, nothing good was going to come of this.

"Holy shit, did you guys notice whose name keeps cropping up? General Baker. He's a friggin' four-star General. What the hell is he doing in here? Look at how far back this goes, there's got to be six years or better. No wonder our boy has stayed under the radar. With this kind of network, it's a wonder we got as close as we did." Adam's face lit up with excitement.

"Adam look, it goes right back to before you were shot. I'm betting that's how they found out about you. No wonder they wanted you out of the way, you were too close. They already knew you were watching Sheridan, so it was only a matter of time before you came up with the fact the General had appointed him there in the first place. I bet if we dig a little deeper we're going to find out it was probably so that they could set up their trafficking ring with the Iraqis."

Suddenly Nick remembered the episode at the bar, his gaze shot to the Chief's to see if he had connected the dots also. Yep, that was affirmative. Crap, they'd been right on top of the ring and hadn't even comprehended it. His stomach churned. No doubt that was how that poor American girl had ended up there. How many more had been sold into slavery?

After all the shit he'd seen in his life, it still amazed him how depraved people could be, mostly for the sake of power. He wished now he'd done more to help that poor girl, and others like her, instead of turning away from their plight as if they'd brought it on themselves.

"Look here, what's this Phoenix name that keeps showing up? And there's several passages mentioning a Guerra. I'd place odds on the fact that's Ramos Guerra, so called Lieutenant to El Capo of the Sinaloa Cartel. We've had dealings with him in the past, remember, Chief?" Jared stabbed his finger on the name, loathing oozing out of his expressive eyes.

"Yeah I remember. He's as slippery as a snake, into everything from guns to methamphetamine. This is pointing to a very large network. We know the Cartel has affiliates in Africa, France and England. I guess it's not much of a stretch to assume they would want a piece of the Middle Eastern pie."

"Our pal Sheridan has been a busy man the last few years. No wonder he was fast-tracked into the U.S. Attorney's office. It's not who you know, it's who you..." Jared brought himself up short, glancing sideways at Agent Holt.

"I believe I've heard the term a time or two, Mr. Martin," she said absently without even looking up, her attention on all the beautiful Intel laid out before them like a banquet. "And you're right, we always wondered how Sheridan managed to climb the ropes so fast. With friends like this, it's no wonder."

It pissed Nick off that Sheridan had gotten away with this shit for so long, even though he'd been under surveillance by Uncle Sam's supposed elite. Why had no one stopped him before now? Sara shouldn't have had to endure all that she had if only these guys had stepped up to the plate. Shit, give him a rifle and he'd be more than happy to handle it for them.

"Hey Nick, can you catch the lights? It's getting a little too dark to read by." Adam asked, glancing out at the evening sky.

It was getting gloomy out. Checking his watch on the way over to the wall switch, he noted that it was a little after nine. Funny, he'd already spent four months in the tiny town and still felt no urge to head back to the bright lights. He liked the slower pace here, the friendly faces that were no longer strangers, the general feeling of safety, so different from city life.

Crossing the room he stopped at the kitchen sink, ostensibly to grab some H2O, but in actuality he was becoming concerned with Sara's continued absence. He understood her need to assure her friend she was fine, but still, it shouldn't take three hours to do that.

He could see lights on over there, and an occasional shadow moving beyond the curtained windows, but that was about it. Maybe he should call her. And that was the crux of the problem right there, after what she'd told him about Sheridan needing to know her every move, he was loath to have her thinking he was the same way.

Maybe he'd wait for another hour or so, and then if she still hadn't come home, he'd go over and ask for a cup of sugar.

"How did you find me?" Sara fell back as Tom pushed his way inside, followed closely by Sam, and then she caught sight of Fiona being led in by two other men. Her friend was cuffed, her arms pulled taut behind her back. Her mouth, covered by a bright red handkerchief tied so tight it cut into her whitened cheeks, highlighted an obscene bruise. Her eyes, one of them black and blue, filled with tears, begging Sara to forgive her.

"GPS, my dear, you've heard of that I presume? I traced you from your own phone, that wasn't very smart of you. So, this is where you've been hiding." He waved the others into the room, locking the door behind them. "What, no kiss for your Husband? You do recall you have one of those, don't you?"

He looked the same, so tall and handsome standing there in his perfectly pressed suit and tie, not a hair out of place. A wolf in sheep's clothing. It was so obvious to her now. The narrow, cold eyes, the supercilious attitude, the rigid stance, the not-so-well-hidden-anger, had he always been that way? She didn't like to think so. How could she have been so wrong about him? He'd pulled the wool over her eyes from the beginning. A shiver skated over her chilled flesh, it hadn't taken long for his true form to seep through.

"Let her go, Tom. Are you afraid your goons can't handle two little women?" She spoke loudly, hoping that Tess and Grace would hear her and escape out the back door.

Tom nodded towards his man, his hard stare focused solely on her. "Your *little* friend has a bit of a problem minding her manners. We had to have a tiny chat. I think she understands much better now, don't you, my sweet?"

Hatred flared in Fiona's bright green eyes as she rubbed the circulation back into her wrists and arms, her cheeks a fiery red after their release from bondage. Sara knew her friend well and gave a slight shake of her head, warning her not to stir the pot. She knew from previous, painful, experience Tom was looking for a reason to explode; it was there in every hard line of his face, in his clenched fists. She moved closer, trying to center his attention on her, hoping she could intervene if Fiona didn't heed her warning.

Placing her hand pleadingly on his linen sleeve, she tried to strike a subservient pose. "Look, Tom, why don't we sit down and talk this out. We're all adults here; surely we can come to a mutually beneficial arrangement that works for both of us?"

His gaze dropped to where her hand rested against his arm, a softness entering them for a fleeting moment, then he looked up and around Tess's small cozy living room filled with knick-knacks, handmade doilies and warm, comfortable furniture, and something about the homey atmosphere caused his anger to return. He picked her hand up, carefully inspected the faint smears of blue paint that had not quite faded yet, then squeezed hard enough to bring tears to her eyes before dropping it and turning to Sam. "We'll be staying here tonight," causing Sara's stomach to drop sickeningly, "take a man and check the area. We don't want any surprises."

Sam nodded to one of the men holding Fiona, the other dragged her further into the living room and forced her down onto a wooden rocking chair that occupied a coveted spot in front of the red brick fireplace. Sara hoped Tom wouldn't notice the family pictures on the mantel. In one Tess sat on her flowered sofa flanked by two other women, obviously her sisters, while Ty, two young women and a handsome man in a police uniform stood tall behind them.

But it was the picture on the other end of the mantel that worried her most. A candid shot of Nick, Jessica and herself taken outside in their backyard. Jess was trying to teach Jake to roll over while Nick coached her, laughter shining out of those gorgeous blue eyes. The Sara in the picture stared up at him as if he held the secrets to the universe. Not good.

There was no sound from the back of the house. She hoped Tess and Grace had heard her and run for help. She wasn't sure how long she could keep Tom occupied. Moving past Fiona, she brushed her hand over her shoulder in comfort before seating herself on the edge of the couch, her back up against the wooden arm.

Tom did as she'd hoped and followed her into the room, facing away from the mantle. "Search the house. Make sure that there is no one else. Where is *our* good friend Nickolaus? I would have expected him to be here, protecting his interests."

Sara gripped the back of the couch, "He stepped out for milk. Look, it doesn't matter where Nick is. This is between you and me. Let's cut the chit chat and get down to business. You have my friend and I have your precious file. We trade and you can go back to that mausoleum you call a house and live happily ever after, without us."

Anger flared in his eyes, changing swiftly to laughter. He joined her on the sofa, settling excessively close. She almost fell into him as the cushions sagged beneath his weight, before regaining her balance and leaning back hard, the wood digging into her back.

"You've developed some attitude while you've been away, I like that. It's so much more enjoyable than sparring with the dishrag you were back home." He ran his finger down her cheek and goose-bumps broke out over her skin.

She jerked away. "If I was subservient to you then, it was because you left me no choice. My God, Tom, you threatened to harm our daughter. It was bad enough how you treated me, but that was unforgivable. Surely, you can understand why we had to leave. You changed from the man I married; the man I cared about would never have hurt me the way you did." Emotion rose up choking her. She thought she'd managed to put all of those feelings behind her, but now they bubbled and boiled inside, an angry brew that threatened to erupt.

Regret showed briefly in his eyes before sliding away. "I

wasn't the only one in that relationship to change. You knew how I felt about children, yet you went about your merry way and got yourself pregnant anyway. I asked that you show decorum as befitting your new lifestyle and forget about your bohemian friends." He shot a cold look at Fiona and she glared right back, "instead you went out and flaunted your relationship all over town, making me look like I couldn't even control my own wife. *That*, my love, was unforgivable."

Misunderstandings, their whole marriage had been nothing but a series of ever-growing misunderstandings. She wished now she'd paid more attention to the signs that were now obvious to her. Sara remembered trying to talk to him about getting pregnant but he'd always turned the conversation to something else, or said he had to get to work, they could talk later. And she'd wanted a baby to love so badly, she'd gone blithely ahead, without waiting for him to be ready.

Guilt filled her. That had been wrong. Her own culpability in the breakdown of her marriage was a hard pill to swallow. She should not have presumed such an important decision without him. But she would never be able to forgive him for everything that went wrong afterward.

"Look, this is getting us nowhere. Why don't you agree to give me custody of Jessica, leave Fiona here, and you can have that file with my blessing. We can finish this now and you can be back in Boston by tomorrow. Come on, Tom, let's end our relationship amicably."

In the background she listened as Tom's man did a sweep of the house. He was in one of the bedrooms at the moment. She needed to give Nick time to come up with a plan. It was only a matter of time before he brought something of Tess's to Tom's attention. She didn't want him realizing this wasn't her house. All thoughts of handling this on her own had gone by the wayside the moment Tom arrived with Sam and the others. Sara had a feeling she and Fiona were on borrowed time, she'd noticed the distinct outline of a shoulder holster on the man searching the house, which meant the others were probably carrying also. That file was a flimsy shield, especially against potential bullets.

Tom had risen and was pacing the room, agitation in every step. He moved to the side of the curtained window. Giving them a hard stare that dared them to rise from their seats, he pushed the linen aside to scan the dark yard before letting it fall back in place.

The hit man as she called him, due to his flat black eyes and expressionless face, re-entered the room carrying what she could only describe as a granny dress over one thick forearm, the blue floral material looking rather incongruous against his muscled chest. He held it aloft for his boss to see and it was more than apparent it wasn't hers. While not exactly frumpy, it was definitely old fashioned, with a big crocheted collar and trim.

"I can explain..."

The front door slammed open, causing both women to jump, and Sam came in at a run dragging Grace behind him like a sack of potatoes.

"Grace!" Sara leapt from the sofa and raced over to the older woman, catching her as Sam pushed her away.

"Who the Hell is that? What's going on, where's Brad?" Tom barked over the sound of the slamming door and Sara's cry.

"We found her and another old hag trying to slip through the back fence. The other one set up such a racket when we grabbed them that some asshole came along and clipped Brad against the side of the head, he went down like a ton of bricks and I got the fuck out of there."

"Cut the lights." Sam reached out and hit the switch casting them all into dark shadows. "Did you get a look at the guy?"

"Not really, just an impression of height and agility, the fucker was fast on his feet. We never even saw him coming until it was too Goddamn late."

"Grace, are you okay? God, I'm so sorry," Sara whispered, "was it Nick?" She carefully checked the older woman by touch, all but blinded in the sudden darkness.

"Sara, where are you? I can't see a blessed thing." Fiona's voice rose when she tripped over the two of them crouched on the floor near the fireplace, "Ouch!"

"Ssh, we're right here." She grabbed Fiona's hand where it had landed on top her head, pulling her down with them. "It's okay, Nick's out there. We need to stay calm and be ready."

Grace's voice trembled in the gloom, "Tess and I couldn't believe it when we heard you warning us. I wanted to stay, but Tess convinced me our best bet to help you was to get ourselves next door. We almost made it too, you'd be so proud of Tess, she put up such a fuss when those beastly men grabbed us I'm surprised the whole neighborhood didn't show up." Her body shook and her arms quivered in Sara's hands.

She squinted through the darkness, trying to discern where

the other three were. They'd gone silent, which worried her. She was scared Nick would make some grand entry to save them and get himself shot.

Suddenly, from much closer than she expected, "Spread out, we have company out there." Tom's harsh whisper came from about three feet to her right. She gently pressed her friends' arms, warning them to be silent.

Stretching out her hand, she touched the poker she'd remembered seeing earlier and lifted it towards them, cringing as it scraped slightly against the brick hearth.

"What was that?" From hit-man, his voice sounding queer as it echoed down the hall giving away his position, the kitchen.

"I didn't hear anything." Sam's voice, coming from the back bedroom.

"Would you two idiots like to send out party invitations? KEEP IT DOWN!" Tom's harsh whisper reverberated through the old house, causing a frightened gasp from Grace. Sara squeezed her arm again in comfort, at the same time she lifted the poker and set it down in Grace's lap, showing her by touch what she was holding. At least she would have some kind of protection if things went sideways, it was the best she could come up with, for now.

"Look, Tom, let's keep things simple. I'll give you the file, and you can take your *friends* and leave, okay?" She tried to sound firm but a tremor made her words come out with a distinct tremble instead.

"What's wrong, my dear, are you afraid I might hurt your lover?" Sarcasm dripped from the words, and she knew this was not about the file anymore, she had tweaked his male pride.

"It's no wonder Sara left you, you arrogant jerk. If she's managed to find herself someone good and decent then hooray for her. Why don't you move on, go and scare some other poor chumps and leave us the hell alone." Fiona had contained herself for as long as she could; now her very redheaded temper came spewing forth in a venomous cloud of loathing.

"Fiona, you're not helping matters, please." She pleaded with her friend to not escalate an already volatile situation.

"I see something." Hit-man's calm voice again, as if this were a day at the park.

"Yeah, me to. I've got at least three bogey's out here." Sam, much more excited, a day at the park with fairgrounds.

Then, out of the darkness, a voice Sara feared hearing, but had desperately hoped for at the same time. "Let them go, Sheridan. I have what you've come for. If you want it, let them out."

Her heart leapt into her throat, as if it could break the bonds that held it to fly straight into his safe arms. Nick. She was so relieved he was out there, but at the same time so very frightened. She had to warn him. "They have guns. There's three and they have..." She screeched as a rough hand grabbed her by the hair and wrenched her to her feet.

"You fucking little bitch. You couldn't just sit there and keep your dumb trap shut, could you." She felt like a rag doll as he shook her before pulling her around in front of him. The other hand, the one holding a FREAKING GUN, went around her neck in a chokehold that threatened to cut off all her air supply.

Grace and Fiona screamed at him to let her go, beginning to rise up after them. Tom changed gun hands and fired, once, twice, hitting the wall behind them, plaster and glass flying everywhere as one of the pictures crashed to the floor. "Hold. Still. Just fucking hold still. The next time I won't miss."

Outside they could hear Nick's desperate shout, "Sara, Sara honey, talk to me. Sara!"

CHAPTER TWENTY-FOUR

Nick was going through seven kinds of Hell, as he stood behind the Aspen in Tess's postage stamp sized front lawn. He couldn't believe how dumb he'd been. Tom must have laughed his ass off after their phone call. It would have been a simple matter for him to find out where it had originated from. What a fuck-up. He couldn't believe he'd missed something so obvious, and now Sara was paying the price. If Sheridan hurt one hair on her beautiful head, he would die.

Checking the illuminated dial of his watch, he was surprised only half an hour had passed since he'd walked out of the house next door to check on Sara, only to come up short when he heard thumps and cries coming from the break between the two yard's fences. Racing silently over, heart pounding, he came upon Tess and Grace, both women fighting off attackers three times their size, Tess screaming like a banshee.

Gliding through the moonless shadows, Nick crept up on

asshole number one and with a swift upper cut to the jaw; he was down and out for the count, yanking poor Tess to the ground as he fell. Dropping down to her, he made sure she was unharmed, losing precious seconds, before turning on dick number two, only to see him pulling a resisting Grace through the front hedges and up the steps into Tess's house, slamming the door behind him.

Hurrying back to Tess's side he quickly stripped off his shirt, tying numb-nut's hands behind his back, and then used his belt to tie his feet tightly together before leading the shaken woman into the kitchen and setting her down amidst his friend's concerned eyes.

"There's a tango outside by the back fence. Someone drag his sorry ass in here, we need to have a little chat."

Crouching beside the dazed female, he took one of her frail hands in his own, sharing his warmth as quakes shook her lean frame. "Can you tell me what happened, Tess? Is Sara still there? How many men did you see?"

"Let her catch her breath, you can see how upset she is, just give her a minute. Would you like a cup of tea, ma'am? My momma swears tea is a cure all." The scent of honey and bergamot drifted from Frank's hands as he brought her over a delicate cup, all but lost in his giant mitts.

"Here, I found this in the living room," Maggie said as she draped a soft multi-colored afghan over her hunched back.

Jared came back into the room with a swarthy looking man with dark shaggy hair draped over his shoulder. He gave a heave and dropped the dead weight in a corner of the room, the solid thunk proving the guy was still dead to the world.

"I'm sorry for rushing you, Tess, but I'm worried about Sara. Is there anything you can share with me?" Nick asked, his chest tight with fear.

Taking a fortifying sip of the hot brew and a sharing a shaky smile aimed at Maggie for her kindness, Tess looked to Nick. "I know, honey. I'm every bit as scared as you are. I'm not quite sure what happened. We were sitting in the kitchen talking about that scoundrel ex-husband of hers when the doorbell rang and Sara jumped up to get it, no doubt thinking it was you. Only it wasn't."

She shook her head in bewilderment. "We heard her hollering at someone named Tom, her ex I'm sure. She warned us he wasn't alone, and we could tell from her tone she didn't want him knowing we were there. Grace wanted to stay, to help her, but then I remembered you were over here with your friends." She glanced at each of them before turning back to him, "so we tried to sneak out the back door and across the yard. We almost made it to, if not for those creeps that came out of nowhere and snatched us."

Jared slammed a fist into the wall above the lump on the floor, leaving a nice crack in the plaster. "Fuck." He swung away, stomping into the living room. Nick knew how he felt, both their loved ones were in that house.

He turned his gaze back to Tess who shrugged helplessly. "You have to help her, Nick, she's in terrible danger. I looked down the hall as we were leaving and saw a young woman with those men. They had her hands tied behind her and her mouth was covered, but worse than that, her face was all bruised like she'd taken a bad fall but I don't think she did. I think they hurt her, and now they have our Sara."

Nick stood paced the room. He wanted to rush out and force his way in, he needed to be there. Anger fought with the fear that was building inside his chest, crushing his lungs and making his heartbeat slow and sluggish, his worst nightmare and there wasn't a fucking thing he could do about it, or was there? He still had the all-important file. It wasn't much, but he hoped it'd buy him a little time, at least until they could figure a way into the house that wouldn't get the women killed.

"I assume you came prepared for a little action?" He looked at Adam standing by the kitchen sink staring out across the dark lawn at the shadowed forms moving beyond the closed curtains next door.

"Of course, Maggie and I both have Glocks. What about you guys?"

"I still have a license for my Sig Blackwater, and practice regularly, if things go to shit over there and he hurts her, I'm going to kill that bastard."

"I know you're upset but you have to remain calm, going off the handle isn't going to help you or your girlfriend." Special Agent Holt warned him.

Whatever. He had more than enough on his plate already; he didn't care if he censored his words in front of federal agents, as long as Sara was returned safely they could toss him behind bars and throw away the keys, if that's what they wanted.

"Relax, Maggie, he's blowing smoke, right buddy?" Adam stepped between them, ever the peacemaker.

"You want to explain to me how the hell he managed to get

by your team who supposedly had the airport covered. Want to explain that, *buddy*?" He was spiraling out of control and knew he had to reel it in. He was no help to Sara this way, but fuck, he had promised her that son-of-a-bitch would never have the opportunity to hurt her again. He'd failed.

"We all need to calm down and figure out a course of action. If we go in there half-cocked someone is going to get hurt." Adam said as Maggie moved closer as if to protect him, probably a good idea right now.

"I know that, but my gut is telling me we don't have much time. We need get pro-active and take the power out of his hands. I want to offer him the file. We all know how important it is to him. I think it's our only chance." Nick looked to Frank, hoping he'd at least agree, "After he makes the exchange and Sara is safe, you guys can go in and do your thing, I don't give a shit; all I want is to have her out of there."

"I agree with Nick, time is of the essence, hashing over who screwed up where is not going to accomplish anything. Jared and I can go around back, find a way in. You, Adam, and Agent Holt can flank Nick and make sure he doesn't get his sorry ass shot." Frank pushed himself away from the old wooden table, the chair legs groaning their relief. "Nick, you can be our voice. Give him the ultimatum, and with any luck he'll accept and the rest of the mission will go like clockwork. If not, we'll be there, and he'll wish that he accepted."

For a too brief moment, the thrill of the chase brought an answering smile to each of their faces, before the gravity of the situation reasserted itself, wiping the grins away and replacing them with intent. Hooyah.

Nick went to gather up the scattered file pages on the table, pleased to see Tess's color looking better, her nerves settling. Now they were moving forward his were also, he centered himself on a successful outcome. Nothing else was acceptable.

He handed the elder woman a heavy cast iron frying pan they had used to make pancakes for Jessica just a couple of days ago. "I need you to do me a big favor. Watch that guy," He pointed at the still unconscious bulk in the corner. "If he wakes up make sure he stays put, can you do that?"

"You bet your britches I can; it'll be my pleasure to teach that toad some manners," she answered, sitting up straight, her myopic eyes squinting at the lump.

"Thanks, Tess, I knew I could count on you. Okay, are we ready?"

"Already gone," From Jared and Frank as they ducked out the door, both armed with an assortment of kitchen utensils.

"Waiting for you, my friend." Adam and Maggie moved to stand by the front door, both checking their guns and ammunition.

He grabbed his own weapon from where he had stashed it in the cupboard above Sara's fridge, just in case. File in hand he stepped past his buddy, glad to once again have him at his back.

Gliding through the thick shadows the three of them made it to Tess's front yard without incident, the other two peeling off into the gloom.

Holding his breath, he counted to ten, and then let it out, praying like he'd never prayed before. "Let them go, Sheridan. I have what you've come for; if you want it, let them out." He stood inside the gate, belly up to the giant Aspen that dominated the small yard, his heart pounding uncontrollably. Fuck, he'd not been this scared on any of the missions he'd been on before. He knew every day was a crapshoot. They trained for that, prepared for it, but he was not prepared this time, when the stakes mattered so very much.

Suddenly he heard Sara's voice shouting, followed by a horrifying screech and then something that made his heart stop. Gunshots.

"Sara, Sara honey, talk to me. Sara!" As he leapt for the front stairs, ignoring Adam's whistle to remain in place, his sole focus was getting inside that door. Using his foot, he nailed it close to the handle causing it to crack wide open, thankful that his eyes had adjusted to the darkness as the lights inside were extinguished. He stuck close to one wall and slid through the entry, his gun leading the way.

Assessing the situation, a feeling of hopelessness threatened to overcome him. Sheridan had Sara held tightly in front of him, an arm around her throat pulled her head back against his shoulder exposing her fragile neck. The other hand had a tight grip on a gun, an M&P 9mm by the looks of it.

Off to the side Grace and another young woman, probably Sara's friend Fiona, sat huddled together on the floor, bits of plaster and glass all around them explaining the gunshots.

In his peripheral vision the fast moving shadow of a man as he dodged from one bedroom forward to the next, and a slight scrape from the kitchen let him know of at least one more. Okay three, he could handle three, if only one of them were not holding the love of his life in his hands. Shit.

"Has no one every taught you how to knock? We're kind of

busy right now. Why don't you toddle off, and no one," Tom grunted as he tightened his grip and Sara's feet came off the floor, harsh choking noises emitting from her throat, "will get hurt."

Though there was nothing he wanted more than to look into Sara's beautiful eyes, to reassure her that it was going to be okay and they would find a way out of this, he kept his attention trained on his nemesis, searching for any weaknesses. Unfortunately for now Sheridan held the winning hand. He'd placed himself in a corner of the room with an inside wall at his back, and no blind spots. He also made sure he kept Sara firmly centered in front of him, her head blocking his own, even though it forced her up onto her toes, the prick.

"Look, you want your file back, so take it." Keeping his gun trained on the inch of Sheridan's forehead he could see, Nick pulled the file out from where he had tucked it into the back of his jeans, waving it back and forth like a white flag before throwing it to the floor where they heard it land with a soft slap. "Let the women go, Tom, all they'll do is slow you down, you don't need them. Your little girl needs her mother."

He knew instantly he'd said the exact wrong thing, Sheridan's already constricting hold on Sara turned malevolent, her neck squeezed so tight he could see the whites of her eyes as they rolled back in her head, the cock-sucking, fucking, prick.

"Look man, do what you want, I don't give a shit, but she promised me some big dough so why don't you relax there before you do irreparable damage and we're both out, cause no cash, no file." His finger tightened on the trigger, desperate for a shot.

"You must think I'm an idiot. First, you fuck with my contacts in Iraq," he said coldly as he moved the gun from his aim of Nick's chest down to his crotch, causing his balls to practically climb up his ass in reaction. "Now you want me to calmly turn over my *wife* so that you two can go riding off into the freaking sunset together? I don't think so."

The simultaneous sounds of grunts and the slap of fist against skin coming from both the kitchen and the bedroom as Frank and Jared made their entrance gave Nick the break he'd been looking for. As he leapt towards Sara he sensed Adam and Maggie as they burst through the door right on his six, but then as he set his right foot down his leg buckled beneath him at the same time he registered a fiery pain.

Adam and Maggie caught him under his armpits stopping his downward momentum.

"Drop your weapons," Tom snarled, "drop them now—or she's dead." He placed the barrel of his gun into her temple, causing a whimper of pain to escape.

The three of them crouched there helpless, Nick's leg laying awkwardly in front. Tom kicked their weapons out of reach before sidestepping them to reach the now empty doorway, which would have been covered if he had used his brains and waited the asshole out.

Jared and Frank, having taken care of business slid into the room, and gauging the situation, froze.

"Well, much as this has the makings of a great reunion, I think we'll have to pass on our regrets and leave. After all, my *wife* and I have a lot of catching up to do, don't we dear?" He leaned around far enough to grind his lips into the side of her exposed neck, laughing as hatred consumed Nick and he lunged forward, only to fall back into Adam's arms as shots of fire rose up his body. A cold sweat broke out across his forehead and his vision tunneled until all he could see was Sara.

Staring into her beautiful face, twisted now into one of loathing and fear, he could feel her desperation, and prayed she wouldn't do anything to trigger the beast. A kaleidoscope of their time together raced through his mind even as he was working feverishly to find a way to stop Sheridan from getting out that door. Their first encounter, she'd looked so adorable standing up to him over that silly dog. Their first kiss where he had learned there were kisses, and then there was connecting on a level that he hadn't even known existed. Holding her as she trusted him enough to confess her pain and confusion and cry out her absolution. The first time they made love, when he learned there was a very big difference between having sexual intercourse and becoming intimate with the right woman. The woman meant for him, the woman that meant everything to him.

Their eyes met, hers backlit by the streetlight outside, glowing with love and a thousand unsaid things, and he couldn't let her go out the door that way, without him ever saying those three all important words, "I love you."

Her eyes widened and filled with tears, a look of such joy coming over her that his own throat closed and his eyes became so misty he had to blink rapidly to keep her in focus. "I love you, Sara, forever and ever. We're going to get out of this okay, be strong, baby, for Jessica and for me, we need you."

"How touching," Sarcasm dripped from the words. "Too

bad she's mine. Come on, *baby,* it's time to move, we have a plane to catch." He laughed at the surprise on the DEA agents faces, "did you really think you would catch me that easily? They need to teach you to think outside of the box. I had a feeling there would be a welcoming party at Sea-Tac, not to mention it might have raised a few eyebrows to see the lovely Ms. Radcliffe bound and gagged, even though it was for her own safety." He glanced over his shoulder at Fiona, grinning mock-ingly. "I had my pilot land us at a nice and quiet, rustic little airfield, no questions asked. It's called ingenuity, agents. I'd recommend it."

"You won't get away with this. Our team is on the way, you have nowhere to go." Maggie spoke quietly, evenly. "Why don't you let her go and turn yourself in? It'll go better for you. We can make a deal."

Nick's harsh denial, "You're freakin' kidding me, right?" was almost drowned out by Tom's bitter laughter.

"Of course she is, Nickolaus. It's her job to say things she doesn't mean. As long as she gets her man, isn't that right, O'Connor. Yes, I see you there, so the rumors were true. I thought I got rid of you ages ago. You've been a thorn in my side for more years than I can count, my boy."

"Yeah, good to see you again too, you bastard. Watch your back, 'cause paybacks a bitch. I'm not stopping until you go down, one way or the other." Adam growled from over Nick's shoulder.

"Threats? I expected higher of you. I should of known better. A man's roots always shine through in the end, wouldn't you agree, Nick?"

"Fucking rights, they do. That's how we always knew you were pond scum."

"Tut, tut, you're sounding a little bitter there, my friend. Well, as much fun as this has been, we really need to be on our way. See you gentlemen on the other side."

He gave Sara a rough shove through the doorway as sirens sounded down the block. The strobing of the blue and red lights lit the interior of the house and showed Grace as she rose from her spot on the floor, some kind of pipe in her hands lifted high over her head. Growls from outside coincided with Jared's alarmed cry, "Mom!" and then pandemonium erupted as Sara took her chance, lifting her foot up and slamming it down on Sheridan's instep, causing him to howl in pain, again jerking her off her feet by the neck. At the same moment, Grace's rotund frame rushed forward and brought the pipe down hard on Tom's back and shoulder, missing his head which surely would have killed him, but causing him to loosen his grip on Sara and fall hard on his right side.

Then Jake burst through the door, all fangs and slathering jowls, and locked his teeth around Sheridan's leg, shaking the bejesus out of it. Tom cowered away, face covered, crying and pleading for help. Frank and Maggie were on him, Frank pinning his legs with a flying tackle that caused the old floorboards to groan in protest. Maggie had his arms up and pulled tight behind his back as she used plasticuffs to restrain him and began to read him his rights.

Jared ran to his mother's side where she had fallen to her knees from the force of the blow, gently prying the poker out of her hands before wrapping his arms tightly around her. "That was the stupidest, craziest, bravest, fucking thing I've ever seen, don't ever do that again. You scared ten fricken years off my life."

"Don't swear," She wept from the vicinity of his armpit, the tension of the last hour catching up to her. "Nobody hurts my Sara Sunshine and gets away with it. I love you, son of mine."

"It's alright now, Momma, it's over. You rock by the way, and I love you too. After things settle down we need to talk."

"Okay, son."

Sara ran to where Nick had fallen, still cradled in his best friend's arms and crumbled to the floor beside him. Her hands were shaking as she searched his body in the gloomy light, and he bit down on a groan when her fingers encountered a warm stickiness along his outer thigh. "Nick, oh my God, Nick, he shot you."

He grunted from the pain as she neared the wound, then was shocked when she whipped her shirt up over her head and bundled it up to press it where she thought the injury was, cringing as he flinched away.

"It's going to be okay. Help is on the way, hold on, baby, hold on," she crooned, trying but not quite succeeding to control the quiver in her voice. Her free hand reaching brushed the hair back on his clammy forehead. Jake had curled up beside him, whining a little, sensing his pain.

He rubbed his dog's head and tried to reassure Sara, but his tongue was thick in his mouth, "Don't worry, honey, it's just a knick. I've had worse. I can't believe you and Grace nailed him like that, you could have been hurt. I'm so effin proud of you,

you did it. You'll never have to worry about that jackass again, it's over."

He caught her hand in his, lowering it to his lips. "I was so freaking scared when I heard those gunshots, and then to see what he was doing to you..." He couldn't control the shudder that swept over his body, "I felt so helpless."

His moist gaze sought hers out, "Promise me you'll never take a crazy chance like that again. I can't live without you, Sara. I love you more than I ever thought possible. I need you in my life or it wouldn't be worth living. I never believed in love, never thought I would find someone that I couldn't live without, until you. I can't believe how much I love you."

"Ah, man, I love you too," Adam's deep voice coming from over Nick's shoulder caused them both to start. They'd forgotten he was there. "Does this mean we're getting married?" He grinned.

"Shut up, Adam," Nick said, his focus never wavering. "Well, you heard the man. Are we?"

There was only one answer she could give, "Hooyah."

EPILOGUE

The next morning after everything quietened down and everyone had a chance to recoup, they all met up in the back booth at *Grace and Grits* to catch each other up.

Adam and Maggie had spent the rest of the night at the Sheriff's catching up on paperwork, making sure Sheridan and company had an uncomfortable night in lockup. They were both bleary-eyed but cautiously happy. "Sheridan isn't talking— yet—but his two goons are spilling what they know. We hope to get enough from them to put the pressure on Sheridan. Either way with the papers in that file and what happened last night; he's in a world of hurt."

"Two? There were three others with Tom. Sam, Hit-man, and another guy, right, Fiona?" Sara looked over at her friend, nestled in the corner between Frank and Jared, happy as a girl sporting a shiner could look with two hunks vying for her attention.

"Hmm? Yeah, there was, two dark haired creeps, Tom, and

his shadow." The glance she shared with Sara was filled with remembered terror.

Maggie and Adam looked at each other, "One got away then. We're going to follow up. According to the last entry there's a large shipment of methamphetamines expected soon along the Texas/Mexico border. We'll be there, waiting." Maggie was as determined as ever, arms crossed over her ample chest. Both Adam and Frank wore lovesick looks on their ugly mugs, and Nick hoped their friendship would not be tested because of a woman, no matter how beautiful.

He couldn't believe Jake had managed to escape the house and show up just in time to help save the day. And Grace, he shook his head in bemusement, Jared came by it honestly. He tightened his hand engulfing Sara's where it rested on the seat between them, his casted leg settled onto the chair across the way. He'd been lucky, the bullet had passed through the fleshy part of his thigh above the knee, a little lower and it would have shattered his kneecap. Sara had stayed with him the entire night, from the ambulance ride to the hospital, right up to the casting of his leg, and the overnight stay. He'd tried to talk her into going home, getting some rest, and she'd replied they had the rest of their life to rest. He liked that. The connection to her felt right. When she'd said yes last night to his lame-assed proposal all he could think was, thank God.

As soon as possible, he was going to talk to her about divorcing Sheridan, she had more than enough grounds, and then he was going to ask her properly to take a chance on him. Surprisingly, rather than getting freaked out by the thought, he felt a calmness settle over him, a sense of completeness.

The bell above the door jingled, and he looked up in time to see a little human tornado flying down the aisle towards them. He leaned back to let her at her mother, but instead she flew into his arms, her tiny ones wrapping tightly around his neck. "Nick. Oh, Nick. Annie told me you got hurt, are you gonna be ok? I'll take care of you, don't worry."

Now he knew how the Grinch felt, he could swear his heart grew two sizes as he carefully hugged her back, tears springing unashamedly as he looked into Sara's misty eyes.

He was home.

TO MY READERS:

I HOPE you enjoyed **Tidal Falls**. I love second chance romances, don't you?

If you'd like to leave a review and share your thoughts with other readers, click here.

I'M INCLUDING an excerpt from The Rebel's Redemption, book #2 in the Wounded Hearts series.

If you'd like to know when I have a new book out, contest news, and more sign up for my newsletter here!

Happy reading,

Jacquie Biggar

AFTERWORD

Reviews are the lifeblood of any successful author. Without you, we can't be heard.

If you enjoy the story, please consider sharing on your favorite social media sites, as well as GoodReads and from wherever you've bought the book.

Thank you,

Jacquie Biggar

Jacqbiggar.com

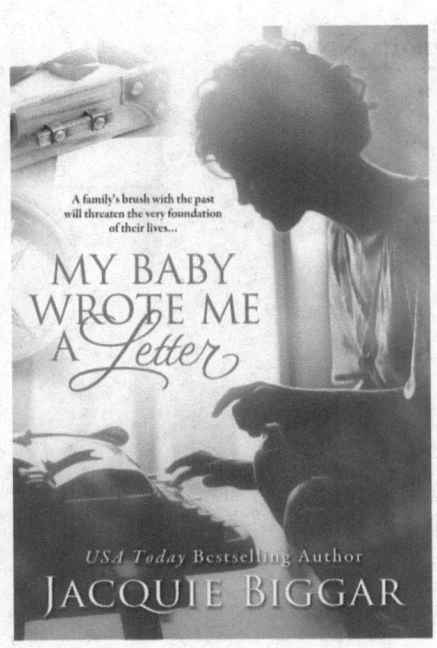

A family's brush with the past will threaten the fabric of their lives.

Eight months pregnant and her Navy husband away on a mission, Grace Freeman craves the security of her childhood home in Canada.

When a letter written by her long-lost mother is found in an old writing desk it creates a tear in the fabric of her family.

Can Grace find a way to bring peace to those she loves, or will a message from the past destroy their future?

Newsletter subscribers also get bonus content and insider information every month. I love giveaways and there is lots of interesting stuff for me to share with you!

Newsletter- Sign up Now!

BONUS RECIPE

Grace's Pumpkin Bread Pudding with Caramel Sauce

Fill Dutch oven with mixed bread cubes. I save my crusts of white, brown and cinnamon raison and then rip them into bite size pieces.

Add a couple handfuls of raisins for flavor.

In a separate large bowl, mix **6-8 large eggs** and approx. **4 cups of sugar**, **cinnamon** and shake of **salt**. Add can of **pumpkin puree** (not pie fill), mix. Slowly add **milk** until mixture is loose, approx. 1 litre.

Pour mix over bread and stir, should be soupy (not too loose though) Just so you see the liquid through the bread. If not, add a couple more eggs and milk blended together to the mix.

When you have a nice consistency: sprinkle **brown sugar**, **cinnamon** and small dollops of **margarine** over the top.

Cook in pre-heated 350 oven for 1- 1.5 hours. Top will gain a nice crunchy golden look. Take a knife and spread the center apart to tell if done.

Drizzle some of your favorite caramel sundae sauce over the top and enjoy.

PREVIEW THE REBEL'S REDEMPTION

by Jacquie Biggar

Is it too late for second chances?

Jared Martin left Tidal Falls a hotheaded youth. Eight years in the military has turned him into a cynical, disillusioned man.

Then he returns home to find out he's a father.

When an old enemy follows and causes mayhem in the small town, can Jared overcome the odds to protect the woman he's always loved and the child he never knew?

Or is it too late for them to have a second chance?

Chapter One

Sergei Barnikov's lips twisted with derision as he followed the manservant who led him through his client's expansive home. This type of grandeur seemed ridiculous to him. The servant, dressed in a flowing white tunic and loose pants, bowed him into a large den where Chenglei sat like a plump sultan amid piles of velvet and satin cushions spread upon the parquet floor.

"Sergei, what is it that brings you to my humble abode?"

The *poor* home his favored patron spoke of was comprised of five thousand feet of opulent Chinese décor, filled with price-less silks and antiques. There were enough riches here to keep his family back in Russia in splendor for the rest of their lives.

Soon.

Soon he could quit playing these stupid games with this

durak. A lifetime of effort to reach the status he'd achieved within the organization, only to lose it all, thanks to the American.

"I come to you with a request. A favor for a favor, if you will." He first toed off his shoes, as was customary, before entering the silk-lined room to sink down onto one of the cushions scattered around a low table set on the tiled floor. He had to stifle the groan crawling up his throat, a legacy of the beatings he'd sustained because of Jared Martin. His bosses were not forgiving of mistakes.

"I have a small problem and am in need of your vast resources. In return, I agree to *hold* your money at my casino. We deal?" He strove to keep his expression impassive. One hint of how important this was to him, and the snake sitting across the table would strike.

"Hold on. Not so fast. What is it you ask in return for this most generous offer?" The Mexican-Chinese tone grated on Sergei's nerves.

Before he could answer a young woman entered the room; eyes cast downward, a tray of fragrant tea and sweets balanced in her delicate hands. She glided silently over to Chenglei's side of the table, bowed respectfully, and at a signal from him, melted to her knees before setting the china on the round tabletop between them.

"Don't worry, she does not speak the English. She pretty, no? My newest little courtesan. You like?"

Sergei eyed her carefully but could detect no sign she understood them. With her eyes downcast and her head bowed, she appeared like an innocent child. A cherry red dress emphasized her smooth and unblemished skin. It wasn't hard to imagine her in his bed. Her raven's wing hair twisted in a bun behind her left ear, she bent forward to pass him his tea, and his nostrils flared, inhaling the delicate scent of her perfume. He'd almost dismissed her as one of Chenglei's toys when she sliced him with an upward glance. Topaz, her eyes were that of a tiger. This was no Chinese girl. Upon closer inspection he could see she was tall, too tall for the average Asian woman. He'd heard rumors that Chenglei dealt in human trafficking—here it seemed, was the proof. Something to keep in mind for future business endeavors.

Sergei respected the man; their histories were much the same. Despite his name and ancestry, Chenglei was Mexican by birth. Brought up penniless, he'd joined the Sinaloa Cartel at age ten. A ruthless Sicario, he'd worked his way up to one of the top lieutenants. A man who gave the orders, and reaped the benefits. He'd never looked back. Disassociated himself from his blood kin. The Sinaloa were his new family, and they took care of their own.

These days Chenglei was the head of El León's money laundering enterprise. In charge of millions of dollars made in drug trafficking. His job was to filter those sums through legal companies so it became untraceable. Which was how Sergei came to know him. There was nothing like a little gambling to hide a pile of cash.

"Da, she will do. Have her brought to me later, I sample." Other than a slight tensing of her shoulders, which could simply have been from his rough voice, there was no sign she heard.

She finished setting out the pastries, and after a deep bow to Chenglei, rose and withdrew as silently as she'd entered.

Shrugging off his suspicions, he looked to the older man and made him an offer he couldn't refuse. "I have heard of your little problem. I have good answer. You help me, I pat your back, no?"

"You have still to tell me what it is you need from me."

"I wish to find a man. He...owes me. I have searched. He is not in Vegas. I need him found. You help?"

Sergei clenched his fist where it sat on his lap, below the table. He had no wish to let Chenglei know how much this meant to him. The old man was crafty, he hadn't gotten to where he was by being stupid. Sergei would just have to play his cards close to out-fox him.

The Chinese-Mexican sat with fingers steepled, elbows resting on crossed legs and attempted to stare him down, but he would not be cowed by some dirty gang banger, no matter how notorious. His was a greater power—Bratva.

Finally Chenglei leaned back on his pillow and laughed, cutting the thick tension that had pervaded the room. "You are a strong man, my friend. We have deal. So tell me, who is this, oh so important person, you cannot find?"

Satisfaction leapt through Sergei's body. Soon he would have his revenge and it would be sweet. He'd been angry and frustrated when he'd found out the man had escaped town, but no more. It had been a gamble to include the cartel in this, but now his path was illuminated. Soon he would return to Russia

"His name is Martin. Jared Martin."

Jared settled for the night with a heavy sigh of relief. Coming home to face his past bothered him more than he cared to admit. He'd only agreed as a favor to his friend, Nick, who'd wanted to surprise his new fiancé with a vacation. After a harrowing ordeal last spring, Sara's ex-husband was safely behind bars. The two of them needed the time away. They'd managed to find someone to watch her cute kid, Jessica, but the dog had proven to be an issue. Although normally gentle, the retired German Shepherd military K-9 could be a handful.

A sorrowful whine woke him from a light doze right before a cold nose jabbed his chest under the blanket. "Are you kidding me? I just put you out an hour ago, mutt." Nick owed him, big time. He cast the downy comforter back and cursed as his feet hit the icy floor. "Come on, pooch, let's get this over with."

He pulled on an old pair of jeans, grabbed his T-shirt, and followed Jake to the door. He could only shake his head over his own stupidity. This is what life had come to, babysitting a diuretic mutt.

He sighed and shoved bare feet into a worn pair of sneakers before following the animal out. Jared propped a shoulder against a column on the back porch and let the midnight sky grab his attention. In all the years away, he'd never seen a moon as big and beautiful as it was here in Tidal Falls. If he was honest, the bright lights and excitement of Las Vegas had paled long before the little mishap with the Golden Key Casino a few months ago. Although, when the money poured out of those machines and the sprinklers opened up all over the customers— pure poetry. He only wished he could've been a fly on the wall that day. Some of his best work, and it was their own damn fault. If the Russian and his security henchmen hadn't seen fit to rough him up over a little simple card counting, they could have parted ways amicably.

He wanted nothing more than to put it all behind him, so he'd been happy to help Nick and get out of the city for a while. It was time he came home anyway, eight years was a long time to stay away.

Jared stepped off the back deck and crunched through the newly fallen leaves, whistling for Jake. All that answered him was the rasping hiss of an old barn owl disturbed from his perch. Where the hell? He shook his head and started down the side-walk, hoping he hadn't gotten too far. He'd already learned Jake had a mind of his own earlier in the day when they'd gone for a walk. They'd started out with Jake practically dancing with excitement, stopping to sniff out every other bush. But when Jared turned north at the end of the block intending to stop by his old friend, Ty Garrett's place, Jake balked and headed off in the opposite direction.

"When Nick gets back, I'm having a little chat with him. Puppy obedience school mean anything to you?"

As they'd neared the end of the next block he suddenly got an idea of where Jake might be heading in such an all-fired hurry. Sure enough, the dog detoured into the next alley and headed straight for the back door of the Grits and Grace Café. *Damn.* Jared had planned to let his mother know he was back in town. He just hadn't had a chance yet. He could just imagine her surprise. He'd stayed away for years, now here he was back for the second time after only a few months.

The smell of fried onions and bacon had his stomach

rumbling. Jake stood at attention, eyes trained on the screen door where they could hear the sizzle and hiss of frying and the faint sounds of the morning crowd waiting to chow down. His tail began wagging a second before the back door slammed back on its hinges and out came his mom's best friend and long-time employee, Susan. She held a large ham bone in one hand while the other reached for a pack of smokes from inside her shirt.

"Good morning, Jake. I thought I heard you out here. Look what Grace saved for you, lucky boy." She held it out and the contrary mutt wrapped gentle teeth around the hank and sank to the ground to feast.

Susan caught sight of Jared and let out a squeal he was pretty sure could be heard three states over, before rushing to throw herself into his arms. The remembered scents of coffee, fryer, and smoke from her graying hair made his arms clench her tight.

"Jared Matthew Martin, what in the world are you doing hiding out in back alleys? Does your momma know you're here? She never made a single peep about it. I can't believe you're back in town. You look good, a little thin, but good. Your mom's cooking will fix that soon enough. Well come on, what do you have to say for yourself, cat got your tongue?"

He laughed and tightened his arms around her skinny ribs once more before setting her back to get a good look at her. "How can I get a word in edgewise with you blathering on like that?"

He ducked, grinning when she gave him a cuff on the shoulder. She looked just the same, a few more lines at the edges of her eyes, maybe a couple of age spots he didn't recall, but otherwise just the same.

"When are you going to let me take you out on the town, Sue. We'd show 'em how to have a good ol' time."

"You haven't changed a bit, you rascal. Still the handsomest devil I know. Biggest charmer too," she smirked. Her eyes shone with mirth, obviously not buying his blarney. "So really, what are you doing back in our neck of the woods? And why do you have Nick Kelley's dog, Jake?"

Hearing his name, Jake's ears perked and he looked from one to the other of them as if to say, "See, aren't you glad I brought you here?"

Jared explained he was dog-sitting, and gazed enviously as Sue lit one up before offering him the pack.

He shook his head regretfully. "Those things are going to kill you."

She rolled her eyes in reply.

"I just arrived yesterday, and haven't had time yet to call Ma. So no, she wasn't keeping any secrets from you." He leaned a little closer and inhaled as her smoke billowed into the air.

"Well, you'd better go in and see her now. It won't be long before she knows you're here. You know this town." She winked and gave him a little nudge.

Yeah, he did. That was one of the reasons he'd left.

Suddenly Jake stood, his focus back on the screen door of the diner. With a joyful yelp he took off running just as two young children came tumbling out the back door.

"Susan," a little tow-headed girl called, "Grace says you

better get back in there before she blows a gasket. A big crowd of high school kids just came in."

It was Jessica Sheridan, Sara's daughter. A young boy followed close behind. Jared remembered her from his trip with Frank to Tidal Falls last spring. When they caught sight of Jake, both kids started chattering like a couple of magpies. "Jake, what are you doing here, boy? Look, Chris, it's Jake." Jessica threw her arms around her beloved pet as the boy, Chris, looked on with a wistful smile.

"Hi, Jake. Hi, boy. How you doing, Jake?" He tentatively held out his hand. Jake gave him a big sloppy lick, and a spontaneous giggle erupted from the kid.

Jared squinted, and took a closer look at the child. That laugh, it sounded familiar, but he couldn't quite place it. He stood a little shorter than Sara's daughter, sturdy with reddish-brown hair and a splatter of freckles across his cheeks and nose. When the kid realized there was someone on the other end of Jake's leash and looked up at him, Jared sucked in a harsh breath. Those eyes. He knew someone with that exact shade of fern green eyes. That giggle...suddenly all the dots connected and his gut tightened up like he'd been sucker-punched.

Annie.

ABOUT THE AUTHOR

 JACQUIE BIGGAR is a USA Today bestselling author of Romantic Suspense who loves to write about tough, alpha males and strong, contemporary women willing to show their men that true power comes from love.

She is the author of the popular Wounded Hearts series and has just started a new series in paranormal suspense, Mended Souls.

She has been blessed with a long, happy marriage and enjoys writing romance novels that end with happily-ever-afters.

Jacquie lives in paradise along the west coast of Canada with her family and loves reading, writing, and flower gardening. She swears she can't function without coffee, preferably at the beach with her sweetheart. :)

Follow Jacquie's website below - if you check out her giveaways page you'll find tons of great prizes every month!

Newsletter- Sign up Now!

For more information:
jacqbiggar.com
jbiggar@jacqbiggar.com

f facebook.com/jacqbiggar

t twitter.com/jacqbiggar

O instagram.com/jacqbiggar

a amazon.com/author/jacquiebiggar

BB bookbub.com/authors/jacquie-biggar

g goodreads.com/JacquieBiggar

ALSO BY JACQUIE BIGGAR

WOUNDED HEARTS SERIES

Tidal Falls

The Rebel's Redemption

Twilight's Encore

The Sheriff Meets His Match

Summer Lovin'

Wounded Hearts Box Set

Maggie's Revenge

With This Heart

MENDED SOULS SERIES

The Guardian

The Beast Within

GAMBLING HEARTS

Hold 'Em

Crazy Little Thing Called Love

SINGLE TITLES

Silver Bells

Missing: The Lady Said No

My Baby Wrote Me A Letter

Tempted by Mr. Wrong

Valentine: A Hearts and Kisses Romance